The Goblin

Forest

Copyright © 2023 Mark Stary
Editing by An Avid Reader Editing Services
www.anavidreader.com

Cover design by Dianna Blanchard
blanchard.dianna@gmail.com

The moral right of the author has been asserted
ISBN-13: 978-0-6482963-5-5
Published by:

RUSHCUTTER
PRESS

For my children. I learned my lesson. No more pranks —
honest!

Dad xx.

Chapter One

Uninvited Guests

Cook Strait, New Zealand — 1841

'All hands on deck! Reef in the sails before this cursed storm sends us all to Davy Jones' locker!' Bosun Seamus O'Reilly cursed as another wave crashed over the ship.

Spitting out seawater, he yelled, 'Come on, come on, look lively now ye bilge-rats — get a move on!' Sailors skidded down the heaving deck, trying to get to the cleats to haul down the sails. O'Reilly latched an arm through the rigging, frantically cataloguing the damage. This was the worst storm the bosun had seen in all his years.

'BOSUN!' cried Second Mate Timbs.

O'Reilly spun around and paled at the cliff of solid water coming for them.

'God have mercy. Watch it now, lads — grab on to something, at the rush!'

The bow rose sharply as the monster wave struck. Up and up the ship surged, her bowsprit reaching for the thundery sky. She reached the crest of the wave and then tumbled down to slam into a trough. The angry seas surged inboard, knocking over even the strongest men and slamming others against the ship's gunnels. From below decks came the sound of the ships' cargo breaking loose.

'God almighty,' muttered the bosun, picking himself up off the deck. 'We won't survive much more of this ...'

The voyage from England had been one disaster after another for the sailing ship *Springwood*, carrying a cargo of metal goods and liquor, plus a few passengers. She had been chased by storms all the way down the Horn. Sails tore when they shouldn't have. The grog had leaked out of the barrels and the meat spoiled early. Evil seemed to reside in the very timbers of the ship.

Now, as they neared the end of their journey, an epic storm had risen out of nowhere and threatened to kill them all. The bosun had never seen the like before.

For the first time in his life, he was afraid.

From below deck, a man scrambled out of a hatch and lurched towards the bosun. 'We're taking on water,' he shouted into O'Reilly's ear. 'That last wave has stove in the hull.'

'Right, rig the hand pumps,' he ordered. 'I'll see to the capt'n.'

'I ain't going back down there!'

O'Reilly gripped the man by his tunic. He pressed his face up to the panicked mate's and yelled over the howling gale, 'Get down there and do yer blasted job. If ye don't, I'll toss ye in the sea myself!'

He flung the deckhand towards the hatch and staggered aft towards the quarterdeck. He reached the swaying steps, but before he could put a foot on the first rung, another tremendous wave launched the bow skywards and the bosun was flung onto the quarterdeck with a painful thump. O'Reilly looked up and found himself looking into the red salt encrusted eyes of the ship's captain.

'We're taking on water, sir. We need to be getting out of this storm.'

Captain Jonathan Winifred gripped the railing, trying to see through the driving rain. 'I came to that conclusion also, Mr. O'Reilly,' bellowed Winfred. 'Port Nicholson lies not far ahead, but this devil wind howls through the strait. It would be too perilous to alter course now.'

'Sir, we either turn-about and risk broaching or end up on the seabed as shark bait.'

'It is too——,' but Winifred's words cut out as he disappeared in a wall of white water. The battered *Springwood* slammed sideways as a colossal wave engulfed the ship. Over she leaned as the seas surged inboard. Winifred lost his footing and slid down the tilting deck towards the gunwale. Over he went and only by grabbing a stay was he able to stop himself from falling into the boiling cauldron below.

'Give me yer hand, John!'

A terrified Winifred looked up at the rain-soaked face of the bosun. He felt the seas swirling around his legs like clawing hands, intent on ripping him free and pulling him under to die a most horrible death. He felt himself detach from what was happening, as if it was too horrible to be real.

'REACH!' screamed O'Reilly.

That brought him back to reality with a snap. He gripped hard with his right hand, gave a silent prayer, and then thrust his left towards the bosun. Strong hands grabbed another. O'Reilly was a big man and easily lifted the captain up over the gunwale and back on deck in one swift movement.

Winifred sat on the deck, hunched over, breathing hard. 'Th-thank you, Seamus,' he croaked. 'That … that was too close.' After a minute or two of gaining his composure, he yelled to the helmsman, 'Come about to port two points!'

The helmsman spun the spokes and the twisting bow eased away from the pounding Cook Strait to head north.

Winifred turned to O'Reilly. 'We'll hide under the lee of the land until the storm breaks. Ride it out at anchor if we can.'

'Aye, capt'n. That will give me time to sort out the damage below and plug the leaks … maybe.'

'Good man,' said Winifred, his voice back to normal. 'Carry on, bosun and prepare to anchor.'

O'Reilly swayed down the steps to the main deck and crawled forward, yelling orders as went. Those still able to do so responded and prepared the anchor, whilst others continued to reef in the sails one by one. Below was pure mayhem as water sloshed around the splintered lower decks, mixing with the groans of the injured.

Winifred let the ship continue north through the storm and soon the peak of Mount Egmont became visible through the storm-lit skies. The hurricane-force winds met this impenetrable stone fortress and the horrid conditions on the *Springwood* eased somewhat. He decided it would not get any better and made the call.

'Let go anchor!'

A sailor cut the lashings and the heavy anchor disappearing into the swirling water. After a while, the first mate yelled, 'Ship has her anchor!'

'Mr O'Reilly, carry on below.'

'Aye, capt'n.'

The bosun ordered those on deck to follow him down to the lower deck and left sailor on deck to watch that the anchor didn't drag along the seabed.

Winifred took the opportunity to head to his cabin. Battling the storm had exhausted him and he needed to rest before taking on the strait in these conditions, especially with nightfall quickly approaching. With the moon sure to be hidden from view, he would need to be fully alert to navigate the ship safely to port.

As Winifred entered his quarters, his cabin boy handed him a freshwater-soaked towel.

'Thank you, Baxter. You're alright then? No bumps or bruises?'

'No, sir,' said Baxter. 'I stayed here and kept the cabin battened down for you, sir.'

'Good lad. Now prepare a pot of tea, if you will. I am most sorely in need of one.'

Winfred sat down as the cabin boy left and wiped the salt from his stinging eyes. He leaned back in his chair and closed his eyes as fatigue washed over him, the worry over the damage to his ship foremost in his mind. The *Springwood* would need careening at high tide to assess the hull damage. This would not please the ship's owners, but he knew it could not be helped. It was a miracle she was still afloat. He closed his eyes for just a spell …

In the small captain's pantry outside the cabin, Baxter lifted a pot off the hook near the stove and reached for the tea. A faint flurry of muffled voices outside the pantry made him turn his head, causing him to spill the tea leaves. Then another sound, like that of scraping bare nails on wood. He poked his head outside the pantry door.

'Is someone there?' he asked timidly, peering down the dimly lit passageway.

Silence.

Baxter shrugged and returned to clean up the small mess he'd made before setting the tea to boil.

In the captain's cabin, Winifred jerked awake. 'Good God, John, you can ill afford sleep now,' he muttered to himself. He remembered the tea and frowned. Baxter was late. **He thought this was most unusual, as the lad was usually quite reliable.** He rose from his chair and made his way to his galley. But when he arrived, the stove was unlit and tea leaves lay scattered over the deck.

'What the devil? Baxter! Where are you, boy? Baxter?'

No response.

The sounds of repair work echoed from below, but not a soul stirred in this part of the ship. Winifred climbed the stairs to the main deck and looked around. Alarm registered on his face when he found the deckhand in charge of the anchor watch passed out on deck, asleep.

'BOSUN!' he yelled. 'On deck please!'

O'Reilly appeared in quick time.

'Mr. O'Reilly,' said a slightly affronted Winifred. 'Perhaps you should have chosen someone more reliable than Jenkins to watch the anchor? You know the man is a known malingerer.'

The bosun leant over Jenkins. His rough hands were surprisingly delicate as he lifted his head. He looked up at the captain, his eyes wide in surprise.

'E's been knocked out, sir. Some wretched sod clobbered him one.' O'Reilly lowered Jenkins to the deck and stood up. He opened his mouth to speak but stopped cold, zeroing in on the ship's boats.

'Capt'n, the whaler!'

Winifred wheeled around towards the boat stowage. The whaler was gone. He hurried to the ship's starboard side and saw nothing. He then made a dash for the port side.

'*There!*' he pointed.

A little way off, the ship's whaler drifted alone on the dirty seas. O'Reilly ran back to the hatch and bellowed below, 'On deck, lads! Stand by to launch the cutter — *move!*'

Men streamed out from below as the bosun joined his captain at the bow.

'My cabin boy is missing, bosun ... could he have taken the boat?'

O'Reilly frowned. 'Young Baxter, sir? No, 'e couldn't have launched the boat himself. And Baxter isn't like that anyhow, sir. 'E's a likeable enough lad with good potential. 'E wouldn't do anything so daft.'

Winifred nodded. 'A count of the crew after the cutter is away, if you please, bosun. It didn't just launch itself. Find out who has taken my boat.'

'Aye, capt'n.'

Winifred turned to stare at the whaler as the bosun moved off to supervise the launching of the cutter. It was darkening rapidly and the driving rain didn't help the visibility much, either. The occasional lightning flash lit up the boat. No oars cut through the water though, nor was the tiller manned.

But there was something ...

'You there,' said Winifred, pointing to a passing deckhand. 'Fetch my telescope from my cabin; look lively now.'

'Yes, captain!'

The deckhand rushed off, past the sailors straining on the

tackles to lift the heavy boat out of its cradle. He returned in good time with the captain's telescope and handed it to him. Winifred snapped it open and observed the boat. Now he could make out the boat detail more clearly and saw movement — but his senses couldn't quite make out what he was seeing.

Then a spectacular flash of lightning lit up the whaler and Captain Jonathan Winifred got his first clear look at what was in the boat. His hands shook, causing him to lose his grip on the telescope which clanged to the deck.

He bent down to pick it up, but it took a few attempts for his shaking hands to grip the telescope firmly.

From behind him came the words, '*Heave … heave … heave.*' He got his hands under control and pointed the telescope at the boat again.

There was no mistake.

'Avast launching! Secure the boat for sea. Stand by to raise anchor and hoist all sails.'

Shock registered on the bosun's face as he came hurrying over.

'But … but, capt'n? We ain't even got a good start on the repairs yet … and the boat …young Baxter … and the storm …'

'Do as I say, damn it, man! Prepare to get underway this instant. That is an order!'

O'Reilly paled. He had never heard his captain speak to anyone like that before, let alone himself.

'Aye, capt'n,' he muttered. 'Right, you heard the capt'n. Get the boat stowed and man your stations … *at the rush!*'

Sailors grunted in exertion as they lowered the cutter back into its cradle. Other sailors rushed forward and coiled the anchor rope around the capstan before commencing heaving the anchor in. Winifred strode aft toward the quarterdeck without another word. O'Reilly supervised the unfurling of the sails before moving aft to join his captain.

Winifred had his telescope out again, looking at the drifting boat. O'Reilly stood next to him, noticing the slight shaking of his captain's hands. Never had he seen that before, either.

In a low voice, he spoke. 'We've sailed together for a long time now. Seen things no sailor should ever see. Survived encounters where others would have perished. I trust ye with my life — ye know that. Now I'm asking ye to return that trust.'

Winifred lowered his telescope and faced his bosun.

'What is it, John? What's wrong?'

Winifred's eyes bored into O'Reilly's for a few seconds before he handed over his telescope.

The bosun raised the telescope towards the drifting boat. He continued to watch for a moment, saying,' I don't see what I'm —'

Then another flash of lightning revealed Winifred's secret.

'OH, DEAR GOD IN HEAVEN!' cried O'Reilly.

Winifred hissed, 'Not a word to the crew, Seamus ... not a word, you hear?'

O'Reilly could only nod as he handed back the telescope to Winifred, his own hands now shaking.

'Anchor's home!' came a cry from forward.

'Helmsman, come about to starboard, steer due south.'

The *Springwood* gathered speed as the storm wind filled her sails. The bosun took a last glance at the boat as it faded from sight. On his deathbed many years later, he would swear he saw the boat surge forward towards the shore on its own. For now, all he wanted to do was get as far away from the whaler as possible.

The Helmsman exclaimed, 'Captain, the storm, it … it's vanishing!'

This snapped O'Reilly back with a round turn. The rain eased, and the wind died down in moments. Even the rolling dark masses of cloud faded before their very eyes. All along the decks, the crew looked around uneasily. Winifred looked up to see stars now poking out of the clouds in ever-increasing numbers. Shortly, the ship was sailing on calm waters with only the creaking of her timbers breaking the silence. It was as if the storm had never existed.

'Keep the crew occupied, bosun,' whispered Winifred. 'Put their minds to better use or we'll have a panic on our hands.'

'Aye, capt'n.' He turned and almost ran down the steps to the main deck. 'Alright, ye ain't never seen a storm die out before? Get to work below on the leaks and check the womenfolk as well. I want this ship looking neat 'n tiddly before we enter Nicolson, ye hear? Move yer backsides!'

***

At the 2300 hour, the *Springwood* lay tied up fast alongside Port Nicholson. The crew had left the ship long ago to get blind rolling drunk at the first inn they could find open.

Winfred sat in his cabin by lantern light, finishing up writing the details of the last leg of the voyage in to the ship's log. The storm was mentioned, as was the loss of a boat to a rogue wave. He put down the quill and rubbed his eyes before fastening the log in twine and securing it in his drawer.

His eyes turned to his cot. His body craved sleep, but Winifred knew his mind would not allow it until he wrote what needed to be written. He opened another drawer and pulled out his personal journal. The quill was picked up and dipped in ink. The images in his mind he had buried deep for the last few hours flooded back in all their horror.

He began writing:

May 28th 1841, Day forty-two at sea. 1830 hours. Position: 39°26S, 172°16E.

Subject — the creatures.

— Chapter Two —

A Father's Folly

Present day

Darkness had fallen as people exited Faulconbridge neighbourhood aquatic centre and moved towards their cars. The last two people leaving happily bypassed the mad scramble of reversing cars and honking horns. Instead, they crossed the road and began walking home.

Alan Dwyer glanced uneasily up at the night sky.

'I think we need to get a move on.'

'Why, Dad?'

Alan looked down at his 11-year-old daughter walking beside him and said, 'I dunno, kiddo, just a bad feeling ...'

Leigh Dwyer scowled at her father. He'd pranked her once already this week, and she didn't want to fall for another. But she couldn't help the slight tingle of fear as goose-bumps broke out on her arms. They made their way along the familiar roadside path, their home now only a few blocks away. The full moon and autumn breeze caused shadows from the trees to dance menacingly along the footpath.

As they passed the small woodland that they had done so

countless times before, a high-pitched screech shattered the quiet evening. In his mind, the father grinned.

'*What was that?*' cried Leigh.

Alan stared into the woods; his eyes wide. 'Oh no, we may be too late.'

'What do you mean, Dad? What's too late?' whispered Leigh, moving closer to his side.

'That woodland is where a colony of giant bats live.'

Leigh's eyes widened in fright.

'A few kids who used to live around this area have been missing for years,' he said. 'They think the bats may have — no, forget I said that. Just stay close, okay? We're nearly past now.'

Leigh moved so close to her dad's side that he had trouble walking straight.

Suddenly, Alan ducked. 'Did you feel that? It felt like … like something rushing overhead.'

Leigh let out a small sob. He put his arm around his daughter and kept walking. The woodland disappeared from view and a few minutes later they entered their street.

'Phew! Okay, Leigh, I think we're safe now. We're too far away to —'

Before he could finish, she took off for the house in a burst of speed.

Alan watched his daughter race into their yard, up to the door and fling it open before scampering inside. His hands went into his pockets and he began whistling as he walked.

'*Gotcha again!*' he chuckled.

Grinning widely now, Alan waltzed into the open front door.

WHAM!

He recoiled as a smallish fist cannoned into his shoulder.

'*YOU SILLY JERK! YOU WENT TOO FAR THIS TIME!*'

Alan's grin vanished. The fury in his wife's face would easily put an erupting volcano to shame. Leigh hugged her mum's waist tightly, her eyes wet with tears.

His son, Matt, also had tears in his eyes as he lay on the floor in fits of laughter. 'Nice one, Dad. Really got her good this time!'

'Oh yes ... *Very funny,*' hissed his wife. 'Scaring your daughter to death must be *soooo* much fun, you immature sod.'

'It was just a —'

Julie Dwyer cut him off with, 'Oh, zip it! I've heard it all before, Alan. Tonight, Leigh is sleeping in our bed. *You* get the couch. Leigh and I are downloading some movies tonight with takeaway of her choice in our room, you two brave heroes are on your own.'

The girls turned away and stormed from the room, leaving them alone.

Alan sighed. 'Oh well, looks like I'm cooking for us tonight, son.'

Matt's guffawing quickly gave way to a groan. His dad's cooking was a joke all on its own, and not a funny one at that.

***

It took a few days for Julie and Leigh's anger to fade, but Alan was used to that. He was also used to making it up to his daughter soon afterwards. So, on a sunny Friday afternoon, he was pondering over a cup of coffee on how to do that when the phone rang. He picked up the receiver.

'Alan speaking. Oh hi, Laney, how are you? Yeah, she's probably got her phone on silent, you know what she's like when she's writing.' As the woman on the phone spoke, Alan's face clouded. 'Okay, hold on a sec — *Jules!* Your sister's on the landline. It's urgent.'

From the study came a shout. 'Be there in a minute!'

Julie saved the word file she was working on and closed her laptop. A hidden folder in her study bulged with rejection slips from publishing houses over the years. She hoped this latest story might be the one to get her foot in the door. She left her desk to join Alan, wondering if this was yet another urgent Laney call about what to wear on a date.

But when she walked into the kitchen, her husband's worried look signalled that this was much more serious as he passed the phone over.

'Hey, Laney, what's up?' Julie paled as she listened. 'Yes, okay. Look, I can try to get a flight tomorrow. No ... I can take care of her. Leave it with me and I'll get back to you on the details.'

'How bad?' said Alan as Julie hung up the phone.

'The doctor says Mum's hip is badly bruised only, not broken, thank god. She fell coming out of the laundry. That damned linoleum floor gets wet and over you go. I'm going to fly up and take her home when she's released from the hospital. Then spend a week with her to make sure she can get around on her own.'

'I'll get the suitcase out of the garage and help you pack. You know, maybe this will convince your Mother to sell up and move in with us?'

'Not a chance. You know how stubborn Mum is. You'd have a better chance of domesticating a Tassie Devil than have her give up her independence.'

'Yeah, she's stubborn alright,' smiled Alan. 'Not a bit like you, eh?'

'You cheeky bugger! I'm not at all stubborn, just single-minded.'

'Yes, of course, dear.'

'Hmmph!' replied Julie as she left for the bedroom. Alan went to the garage and returned with a wheeled travelling suitcase. As he helped his wife pack, a thought came to him.

'You know, Jules, school holidays start next week. I could take the kids on a trip, just the three of us?'

'But what about your work?'

'Well, I'm pretty much up to date with everything. I can put in for a week off work without being missed.'

Julie stopped packing and turned to her husband. After a minute of thinking, she said, 'I'm not against the idea. You should spend more time with the kids. Put the kettle on for a cuppa and we'll have a chat first, though.'

'A chat?'

'Yes, a chat. I've wanted to talk to you about something for a while now. If you're going to take the kids on a holiday without me, we need to have a serious talk.'

***

On their back deck overlooking a neat garden, Julie sipped her tea, a distant look on her face. After a few minutes, her eyes turned to her husband.

'Alan ... about this pranking.'

Alan groaned.

'Hear me out,' said Julie in a worried tone. 'I've turned a blind eye to it for a long time now, but I can't do that anymore, you understand? I'm worried about how it's affecting the kids, especially Leigh. Okay, I admit Matt can take it and dish it out as well, but Leigh's different. You know how sensitive she is. Your last prank went too far and you know it.'

'Aww come on now, Jules … it was just a —'

'Joke? The jokes have been going on for years now, Alan. It was funny when they were little. Even I laughed about the one on how thunder was the sound of giants playing hopscotch in the backyard. But you've made them scarier and scarier as they've gotten older. The last one really frightened Leigh.'

Alan recalled the last prank and had to admit Leigh's reaction unnerved him a bit after the dust had settled.

'Do you understand me? The pranks have to stop. I want this holiday idea of yours to be the start of turning over a new leaf for you. Do you want your daughter to be afraid of being alone with you? Because that's where I think you're heading, Alan.'

Alan Dwyer thought it over. He loved the part of him that never took anything seriously. Joking and pranking his kids was a natural extension of that. But deliberately upsetting them was not something he'd ever set out to do on purpose. Privately, even he had to admit seeing the mistrust in his daughter's eyes during the last few days had surfaced some regret for the last prank.

'Okay, honey, maybe it is time to turn over a new leaf. I'll tell you what, I'll use this holiday as a stepping stone to a prank free future. Heck … I'll even talk to the kids about it to get their feedback — fair deal?'

Julie nodded in relief. 'Fair deal then.' She drained the last of her tea and stood up. Alan stood as well and wrapped an arm around Julie's waist as they returned to the house to continue packing.

***

At 3:15pm, the sound of a heavy diesel engine rumbling past the house signalled the school bus had dropped off its last load of kids for the day. Barely a minute later, the front door banged open.

'Alright, no school for two whole weeks!' Matt raced to the kitchen and began making himself a ham and cheese sandwich.

'A customary hello would be nice before you gorge yourself, Matt.'

'Sorry, Mum, but I'm starved!'

'Hey, Mum.' Julie turned and smiled as her daughter walked through the door. Leigh was destined to be a stunningly beautiful woman one day, something that gave her dad nightmares. Her fine features, dark long hair and shy smile had many a boy infatuated with her. The normally carefree Alan could turn into a grumpy old man in a heartbeat when spying boys snatching a quick glance her way. Compared to Matt, who could make an excellent rugby forward, Leigh was grace beyond compare.

'Hey, sweetie, how was the last day of school?'

'Oh, so-so, Mum,' sighed Leigh. 'A bit miffed about my grade in the last math test before holidays.'

'Yeah, simply devastating,' said Matt sarcastically. 'Only an A minus. How are you ever gonna show your face at the geek club again after they find out?'

'Oh, go stuff your face, Matt!' huffed Leigh.

'Doing so,' grinned Matt as he shoved the whole sandwich into his mouth.

'Ewww … Gross!'

'Where's Dad?' mumbled Matt, spraying crumbs on the

floor as he spoke.

Julie's smile faded. 'He's out back. Go and fetch him, Matt, and then come back into the living room. We need to talk to you both.'

'Okay, Mum.'

As Matt left, Leigh said, 'What's wrong, Mum?'

'Wait till your father and brother come in, please, Leigh.'

Leigh frowned, but said no more. After a minute, Alan and Matt came inside and the family settled into the living room chairs.

'Your Grandma has had a fall and is in hospital,' said Julie.

Alan added quickly, 'But she's going to be okay,' after noticing the alarmed look on the kids' face. 'Just a bruised hip.'

'But she's going to need at least a week of looking after when she gets out of hospital,' said Julie. 'Just to make sure she can manage on her own. So, I'm going to fly up to take care of her.'

'Can't Aunty Laney go?' moaned Matt. 'It's school holidays and all.'

'Your Aunty Laney went to a party last week with her blouse on back to front. You really want to trust her with Grandma? And besides, you two are not going. You're staying with your dad — and he has an idea.'

'Uh-oh,' muttered Leigh.

'No,' said Alan, 'it's actually a good idea this time. While your mum is looking after Grandma Margaret, the three of us are going on a holiday. I've already booked a flight for us.'

Julie turned to her husband with a surprised look. 'Really? You told me you booked mine to Brisbane, but you didn't mention booking one for this holiday. Where to?'

'We're going to New Zealand.'

'NEW ZEALAND?' chorused all three.

'Yep,' chuckled Alan. 'My work colleague, Graham Betts, is always bragging about how nice New Plymouth is. He goes there all the time. There's hiking and bushwalking, beaches, cafes and everything.' Alan turned to Leigh and added, 'And lots of museums and art galleries to visit as well.'

'Well … okay. Sounds fine to me,' said Julie. 'What do you think, kids?'

Matt said, 'I'm in, sounds like fun. My first time in a plane too … that's gonna be awesome! What do you reckon, Leigh?'

Leigh smiled timidly. 'New Zealand culture is fascinating. And they have some of the most beautiful scenery in the world. But can't we wait till after Mum gets back? School holidays go for two weeks…'

Julie caught her husband's eye, her expression plainly conveying, *see what I mean?*

Alan coughed. 'Well, Leigh, your mum will be … err … quite exhausted after a week with Grandma. Let's give her a week off to herself, eh? Your mum doesn't get much time to herself these days — fair deal?'

Leigh said cautiously, 'Well…okay.'

'It's settled then. New Zealand here we come!'

***

The Qantas Airbus cruised at 38,000 feet over the Tasman Sea, still an hour from landing at Auckland. Leigh turned from the book she was reading to stare down at the sea. Even at this height, it looked pretty rough. Leigh disliked the ocean and absolutely hated boats. Her first trip on a wildly bucking ferry to Manly in stormy conditions had left her battered, bruised and badly seasick. Since then, she refused to step on-board so much as a dingy in the local creek. Her first flight, however, was a different story. When the wheels left the runway and the big Airbus took to the sky, Leigh felt exhilaration like she had never felt before. The sense of freedom while tearing through the skies at over 700 kilometres per hour was one she instantly fell in love with.

Matt, however, was a different story. Leigh smiled inwardly at the sight of her brother's hands still gripping the hand-rests. At ease jumping off the bridge into the waters of Ithaca Creek or tearing down the steep incline of Brindle Street on his bike, Matt was the daredevil of the two. But this was not his cup of tea, to put it lightly. Leigh realised this trip was worth it just to discover Matt had a phobia. Leigh returned to her book, a mischievous smile on her face.

One row up, Alan was going through maps and brochures in the seat pocket in front of him. His notebook already had all the information downloaded from Tourism New Zealand. The coastal walkway was on his list of things to do, as was visiting the Govett-Brewster Art Gallery. He didn't really think the brochures would add anything new to his list when he spied one still in the seat pocket. As he drew it out slowly, the title, *"Explore the Goblin Forest,"* revealed itself. Alan's eyebrows rose in appreciation. He opened the brochure and began to read.

***

After landing at Auckland, Alan and the children boarded a connecting Air New Zealand flight to New Plymouth. It was a fifty-minute flight and with few passengers on-board the small turbo-prop airliner, they all got seating next to each other. Matt didn't like the flight to Auckland much, but in his mind, it was bliss compared to this propeller driven death-trap.

'Hey, Dad,' he groaned. 'When it's time to go home, do you think I could take a cruise ship instead of a plane?'

'Sure, Matt.'

'Wow — really?'

'Of course not, dunderhead. That would cost around two grand. You think I'm made of money?'

Leigh laughed and said, 'It'll be over soon, fraidy-cat. Wait 'til I tell your friends you don't like flying.'

Matt turned his pale face to Leigh. 'Going to be hard to speak to any of my mates after you've eaten a few knuckle sandwiches.'

'DAD!'

'Don't threaten your sister, Matt,' chuckled Alan, as he pulled the same brochure from the previous flight out of his coat pocket to read again.

'What's the brochure, Dad?' asked Matt.

Alan handed it over.

'The Goblin Forest?'

'Borrowed it off the other plane,' said Alan. 'Have a read and see what you think.'

Matt opened the brochure with Leigh leaning over to read as well.

"A short distance from the town of Stratford lies the fabled Goblin Forest, otherwise known as the Kamahi Walk. This forest looks like something from another world. A gnarled, twisted forest, full of mystery and magic. If you were ever to come across a real goblin, this would be the place for it to happen. In fact, local legend talks of the four G's that roam the forest at night. Goblins, Gremlins, Gnomes and Ghosts. Hanging mosses, liverworts and ferns have added to the strange effect. For

an unforgettable trekking adventure, you simply cannot miss the Goblin Forest. Cabins available on request."

Alan said, 'I think we should stay in New Plymouth for the first few days and then head over to Stratford. I'll see if I can book a cabin at ... Matt, hand me the brochure back please,' who did so.

'Hmm, a few to choose from. Dawson Falls Lodge, Konini Lodge, couple of smaller huts as well. It's not school holidays over here, so it shouldn't be busy. We should be able to book something without much fuss.'

'I ... I don't really like the sound of it, Dad,' mumbled Leigh.

Matt smirked. 'Who's the fraidy-cat now, Leigh? What, you think goblins are going to kidnap you and take you away? I couldn't be so lucky.'

'Oh, ha, ha! You're a real riot, Matt.'

Alan's eyes glazed over as Matt and Leigh squabbled.

Real Goblins ... now that would be a sight. Imagine real Goblins charging out of the forest! Alan chuckled at the thought of Matt and Leigh screaming at the sight of —

'Dad, this isn't funny!' huffed Leigh.

'Eh?'

'I said I'd rather stay at New Plymouth and do the walking tracks around there.'

Alan said, 'But the ones at New Plymouth won't come close to the Goblin Forest, Leigh. There's also a place called the Wilkies Pools we can visit. The pools were formed by old lava flows. We could even go for a swim?'

'No thanks, Dad, I'd rather not.'

Matt held his hand out for the brochure again and stared at

the picture of the forest. 'Well, I'm in, Dad. That's a wicked looking forest.'

Turning to Leigh, Alan asked, 'Come on, how about it, Leigh? The Goblin Forest is one of the natural wonders of New Zealand. You'll regret it if you miss it.'

Leigh looked out the small window of the plane, thinking it over. 'Well … okay,' she relented.

'Excellent, sweetie.'

Leigh gave her dad a small smile and put on her headphones to listen to her iPod. As Alan leaned back in his chair, Matt's words echoed in his mind.

What, you think Goblins are going to kidnap you and take you away?

He closed his eyes and imagined goblins bursting into their cabin, demanding the kids. What a fantastic prank that would make.

Then Julie's warning pierced his thoughts.

No more pranks, Alan!

Alan hadn't spoken to his kids yet about ending the pranks. He was waiting for them to be settled into their hotel rooms before having that conversation. But maybe … just maybe, he thought, one last big one to end it all with. Go out with a bang as it were. *Then* have the talk, saying that was the last one, pinky-promise and all that. Although the kids were older now, they still held firm on the old pinky-promise.

Alan wrestled briefly with his conscience, which never really had much of a chance, anyway. Eyes closed, a small smile formed on his face as he planned what would be his final and most epic prank ever. And what better place for it to happen than a place called the Goblin Forest?

Alan Dwyer, husband and father of two, would forever

look back at this moment as the greatest regret of his life.

— Chapter Three —

Storm Warning

The hire car pulled out of the motel parking lot and headed south. After a few minutes, it turned onto Opunake road.

'Okay, keep a lookout for Manaia Road … should be on the right.'

'Okay, Dad,' said Matt. 'I'm glad we only stayed in Stratford one night. What a dump!'

Leigh rolled her eyes. 'Only because the internet was flaky, Matt. It looked like a beautiful town to me. And what an incredible view to Mount Taranaki. '

'Yeah, whatever. At least New Plymouth was good.'

It was true. They had a wonderful time in New Plymouth. The family spent many hours in Pukekura Park and at Back Beach. It seemed a shame to leave. Alan had briefly pondered cancelling his booking at Konini Lodge and staying put. Leigh adored the art galleries, and she had to be dragged away from the Puke Ariki modern science and history museum. But the prank beckoned, so Alan stuck to heading to the Goblin Forest. As they drove down Opunake road, with the towering Mount Taranaki on their right, Leigh gave some serious thought to moving to New Plymouth for a while when she entered adulthood. No visa was required to travel between Australia and New Zealand.

They drove past Palmer Road, and Matt had another look at the map. 'Next right should be it, Dad.'

'Roger that.'

Alan slowed down as the next right turn appeared and swung onto Manaia Road. But it was like no other road they had ever travelled on before.

'Whoa,' whispered Matt.

Alan didn't reply. So far, driving in New Zealand had been a very pleasant affair. Not anymore. He concentrated on the narrow, winding road ahead of him. Leigh sank deeper into her seat, her face resembling her brother's on the flight to New Zealand. Massive trees and ferns lay on the very edges of the bitumen road, like the forest was just waiting for a chance to devour the road completely. Alan slowed right down. Should another car approach from the other way, there was almost no room for a safe passing.

'Umm … Dad. Is it like this way the whole way up?' asked Leigh.

'Not sure, honey, but it's a short drive now to the lodge. We'll be there soon enough.'

Leigh bit her lip and stared out at the forest. Occasionally, a fern would brush along the side of the car, causing her to flinch. Matt leaned over and gently punched his sister's arm, which was his usual charming way of reassuring her.

They continued on until they reached a sharp left before the road took a winding, blind loop to the right.

'Damn!' Alan hit the brakes as a large campervan approached from around the bend. He manoeuvred the car onto what road edge there was and the campervan squeezed past. The ferns on the side of the road pressed eagerly against the car sides.

Leigh peered through the window, trying to see through the dense foliage of the forest.

Suddenly, the ferns swayed back and forth, scraping along her car window, followed by what sounded like subdued growling.

Leigh yelped in fright.

Alan turned around. 'What the heck is wrong, Leigh?' he said, frowning at his daughter.

'There … there's something out there, Dad! In the bushes!'

'Well, of course there is. It's a forest, after all. Probably wild goats, I reckon. This area is renowned for them according to the guide.'

'Y … you sure?' said Leigh.

'The forest is so dense here. It could have been a dinosaur and you wouldn't have known it. Relax, kiddo, we're nearly there.'

The campervan had moved clear now, and Alan returned the car to the road. As they drove, eyes watched the car disappear around the bend. Eyes no goat ever possessed.

***

Konini Lodge could easily sleep three or four families in comfort, but Alan and the kids had it to themselves. The next lot of guests weren't due for another week and by then, they would be back home in Australia. After unpacking her gear, Leigh went out and stood on the deck, taking in the view of Mount Taranaki. It was so close; you felt like you could reach forward and touch it.

'Not bad, eh?' said Alan as he moved alongside her with a

cup of coffee in hand.

'All I can say is — wow! I'm glad we came. This is stunning, Dad.'

'Yeah, knew it would be good, but not *this* good. We'll have a bite to eat, and then head over to the visitor's centre. They should have some good maps of —'

'Hey, Dad, that's the last of the stuff from the hire car,' said Matt as he joined them on the deck. 'There's some heavy cardboard left, though. And markers and fishing wire. Why'd you get that stuff for?'

'Oh, for an idea I had for work. A cheap mock up design for a promotion we're doing. I was going to work on it tomorrow for an hour, but probably won't bother now. This place is too beautiful to worry about work.'

'I wish Mum were here,' said Leigh. 'She's missing out big time.'

'Well, don't forget to take lots of pictures for her. Show her what to expect when she comes with us next time.'

'Yeah, pictures … not one of your fancy drawings, sis — Mum's not a Picasso fan.'

Leigh wheeled fiercely on her grinning brother. 'I do not draw like Picasso! And you're one to talk; *your* drawings usually look like stick figures drawn by a one-armed sloth.'

Alan tilted his head back and roared with laughter.

Matt open and closed his mouth a few times but came up with nothing. He knew when he'd been bested.

***

After a typical Alan lunch, which had the kids wishing their mum was here, the trio wandered over to the centre. It was quite a large building with a tall carved Māori post outside. As they entered inside, the park ranger moved forward to greet

33

them.

'Welcome everyone, name's Bill Gardiner. And before we begin … any puns or references between my name and parks or forests gets you chucked out of here pronto.'

Alan chuckled and held out his hand. 'Alan … and these two are Matt and Leigh.' Bill grinned to show the kids he was only joking and shook Alan's hand.

'Nice to meet you three.' He waved a hand around and said, 'As you can see, you have the place to yourself. Must be the weather forecast for tonight that's kept the usual day visitors away.'

'Oh?' said Alan. 'What weather? Must admit I didn't check that this morning.'

'Storm front coming through. Should be quite a blow tonight. But the Lodge is pretty sturdy and the fireplace will keep you warm enough.'

'Hey, I have a pretty decent signal!' said Matt, as he held up his phone.

'Yep,' smiled Bill. 'The centre is higher up than your lodge, so you can get better reception here. Lots of kids who stay here tend to spend a fair bit of time at the centre.'

Matt excused himself and took off back to the lodge to collect his iPad. Leigh spotted a long, low bookshelf along the wall and wandered over.

'Mr. Gardiner, is it okay if have a look at some of your books, please?' she asked.

Bill waved his hand at the bookshelf and said, 'Feel free. There are many books on the park to choose from. Also, the armchairs here are quite comfy and there's tea and coffee available just over by the sink near the window there.'

Alan watched Leigh move over to the shelf and pick out a

few books before settling into one of the old green armchairs. 'Well, that's her gone for the next hour or two,' he smirked.

'So, what brings you here, Alan? The pools, the falls, or the walking tracks?'

'Last minute decision, actually. On the plane over here from Australia, I picked up a brochure on the Goblin Forest — it looked amazing, so here we are.'

Bill nodded as Matt walked back in with his iPad and grabbed a spare armchair. 'There's nothing like it anywhere else in New Zealand, mate. Folks go nuts over the Goblin Forest, pretending they're in some sort of enchanted fairy-tale. Making up stories an' such.' Bill looked away. 'Sometimes I wish they wouldn't, though. Just enjoy the scenery with none of that mumbo jumbo.'

Alan grinned, 'Why not? Nothing wrong with a bit of make believe in my book.'

Bill shrugged but didn't elaborate.

Alan didn't press him. Instead, his thoughts turned to the forecasted storm, and his eyes lit up. 'Talk to you later, Bill,' he muttered, and moved over to the kids. 'I'm heading back to the lodge to clean up. You guys happy to stay here?'

'Yeah, Dad,' said Matt, as he scrolled through his online comic book. Leigh barely nodded; her eyes glued to a book on Māori culture.

Alan left the visitor's centre and headed back to the lodge. As he did, he noticed dark clouds forming to the distant west and grinned.

Perfect!

***

That afternoon, Alan, Matt and Leigh explored the walking tracks. The 1.4km long Kapuni Loop track took them through the Goblin Forest to Dawson Falls. The brochure did not do it justice.

'Oh man, this place is scary … and brilliant!' Matt walked up to the moss-covered trees and felt the stale dampness. 'I can see why it's called the Goblin Forest. I wouldn't be surprised if a few jumped out behind the trees right now and tried to eat us.'

'Not funny, Matt,' said Leigh. 'Dad, tell him to grow up!'

'Oh, I dunno. This forest is pretty ancient. Who knows what lives here? Not goblins, of course, that's silly. But certain to be some unusual animals in these parts, though. In fact, Bill Gardiner tried to tell me something secret about this forest before I left to clean up.'

'Did he hint what it was, Dad?' asked Matt.

'No, but I'll ask him if he's still at the centre when we get back. Let's continue on … shouldn't be far to go now.'

The trio moved on, Leigh sticking close to her dad. Soon a sign appeared on the trail stating they had arrived at the Wilkies Pools. They approached the rocky edges past the trees and peered down.

'Wow, the water is so clear,' said Leigh breathlessly. 'You can see every single stone on the bottom.' The skies had clouded over, allowing every detail to be observed. They moved around the pools for a while, Matt eventually sticking a hand into the water.

'Brrrr,' he said, yanking his hand back, 'Bugger swimming in that.'

'Well, the water flows from the top of the mountain, Matt, so of course it's going to be cold,' said Leigh.

'Thanks, sis … *whatever* would we do without your insight?'

Leigh gave Matt a time-honoured middle finger salute that

sisters often give their brothers — hidden from her dad's view, of course.

Alan looked up at the greying clouds and said, 'We'd better head back. It's a long walk back to the lodge and those clouds are coming over fast. We don't want to be caught outside if that storm hits early.'

Leigh didn't like storms at all and moved to the start of the trail at once. 'Come on then, let's go,' she said with a hint of impatience. Alan and Matt grinned at each other.

'Okay, okay — relax, we're going.'

They entered the trail, and Wilkies Pools faded from view. Suddenly, the sound of an enormous splash came from the direction of the pools. Like something had fallen in.

'What was that?' cried Leigh.

Matt answered, 'Hang on, I'll check,' and doubled back. Leigh moved up really close to Alan as they waited. Matt arrived back at the pools. He didn't see anyone around, but the once calm waters still rippled from some unknown disturbance, lapping back and forward between the pool edges. He shrugged before turning back to join up with his dad and sister.

As he approached, Alan asked, 'See anything, son?'

'No … must have been a big rock falling into the pools.'

'Fair enough. Let us tarry not, fruits of my loins, for evening supper awaits. Cooked by the hands of one who could hold his own against the finest chefs in the world!'

'Oh great,' muttered Matt, 'Chef ala baked beans again.' He looked over at Leigh, expecting a giggle, but saw only concern.

As they walked along the trail, Matt moved next to Leigh and whispered, 'What's up?'

Leigh bowed her head and said, 'You said that splash must

have been a big rock falling in to the pools?'

'Yeah?'

'Lava flows formed the pools, Matt. The rock formations are all smooth. There aren't any large, loose rocks around the edge, only ones already in the pools. I certainly don't remember seeing any.'

Matt frowned. 'Well, maybe …' Matt's voice trailed off, and he shrugged. 'Come on, sis, it's no big deal,' and gave her a friendly nudge.

The light was fading as they emerged from the trail and made their way onto the grounds. From the visitor's centre, Bill gave them a relieved wave.

Alan said, 'Head back to the lodge, guys. I want to have a quick chat with Bill.'

'Okay, Dad,' said Matt, and he and Leigh departed for the lodge, Leigh glancing up at the sound of distant thunder. Alan walked up to Bill, who was also staring skyward.

'Going to be a nasty one tonight,' said Bill. His grey eyes held a hint of concern. 'Nastier than I first thought. Think I'll stay the night at the centre, make sure you folks are okay.'

Alan smiled. 'We'll be fine, Bill. We've faced worse storms when camping. No need to hang about.'

Bill hesitated before saying, 'Fair enough. Just stay indoors, okay? This place isn't safe at night, especially during a storm.'

Alan smirked. 'Why? The bogey-man live around here?'

Bill's eyes bored into Alan's, causing his smirk to retract somewhat. 'No … but there are worse things than the Bogey -man …'

Alan frowned, waiting for Bill to enlarge on that extra- ordinary statement. With nothing forthcoming, Alan said, 'Oh? Like what, for instance?'

'I … err —'

Rumble!

The sound of thunder was much louder this time, signalling the storm was nearing. Whatever Bill was going to say, the thunder changed his mind.

'Forget it.' He handed Alan a slip of paper. 'Here's my home number. I live in Stratford, so if you have any problems, call me on your mobile. I can be here pretty quick if need be. You can just get a signal on the second floor of the lodge.'

Alan took the note and slipped it in his pocket. 'Will do, Bill. You'd better get going before it gets dark.'

Bill nodded. But before he left, he said, 'Alan … do me a favour. No ghost or goblin stories tonight, eh? It's considered bad manners to local Māori culture.'

Before Alan could reply, Bill turned and left. He got into his 4x4 and drove out of the park; his headlights disappearing down Manaia Road.

Alan looked up at the roof of the lodge. Why the warning, he wondered? Had Bill seen his handiwork? he wondered. Surely, he was pulling his leg about the Māoris? A flash of lightning lit up the area and a sudden gust of wind had Alan moving quickly to get indoors. He shrugged off Bill's warning as he walked, taking one last look around before entering the lodge. The wind was increasing and the thunder and lightning kept building. The kids were tired and would be sleepy after a meal. Alan rubbed his hands together and walked through the lodge door.

— Chapter Four —

The Creatures

Alan did slightly better than baked beans. His bacon, lettuce and tomato burgers ended up being really tasty, surprising Matt and Leigh. *Who knew dad could cook* they joked between themselves. The wood burned merrily in the fireplace as they bunkered down in the living room. Outside, the wind howled through the trees, causing quite a racket as branches clashed together. Leigh no longer jumped at the sound of thunder, but still flinched when the deep booms reverberated through the thin walls of Konini Lodge.

It was almost pitch black outside now; the lightning revealing the looming peak of Mount Taranaki like a giant standing watch over the campgrounds. Alan was chuffed the rain hadn't started. But if the wind worsened, it might damage his surprise.

No time to waste …

'Okay, kids, time for a story. Bill gave me a ripper of a yarn for tonight.'

'Oh, come on, Dad, we're getting too old for stories,' said Matt, not bothering to look up from his iPad.

'Ahh,' said Alan, 'but this one is a little closer to home,

Matt. It's about the origins of the Goblin Forest. Bill learnt it from the local Māori.'

Leigh put down her book and said rather guardedly, 'We know the origins, Dad. The forest is named for the state of the trees and vegetation. I read it online.'

Alan shook his head. 'That's only half the story. The truth is far more interesting ...'

Matt sat up from the lounge, interest showing on his face. 'Oh, really? Like what?'

Alan grabbed a chair and sat down. Gravely, his eyes flicked between Matt and Leigh. 'As you know, Bill and I had a chat. I wasn't happy to hear what Bill had to say; especially his warning about staying indoors tonight, but here goes. This place is called the Goblin Forest because locals believe goblins really do reside in the woods.'

Lightning flashed in the windows as Leigh sank deeper in to her chair. 'Not funny, Dad,' she muttered. 'It wasn't funny when Matt talked about it, either.'

'I'm not trying to be funny, Leigh. You ever wonder why there are no large animals in these forests apart from wild goats? And even then, the goat population is a fraction of what it once was. Something is hunting them. Bill thinks he has seen goblins on nights he has stayed here. He's not a 100% sure but the local legends are fairly detailed. And he's found weird tracks on the forest trails during the day. Tracks he can't explain.'

'Goblins?' smirked a clearly sceptical Matt.

'Yes, goblins. They live on Mount Taranaki inside hollow dead trees or small caves. They mostly come out when it's dark, Bill reckons ... mostly. I think he was dead serious.'

Alan played his ace card. 'Bill told me a goblin's favourite pastime is playing in the Wilkies Pools.'

Leigh's eyes widened. 'The Wilkies Pools,' she whispered, and then jumped a little as a rumble of thunder shook the lodge. 'That splash we heard …'

'Look, honestly I think Bill was having a bit of a lend of us, anyway. I mean goblins … come on! Even I wouldn't come up with something as ridiculous as that.'

Alan chuckled and stood up. 'Here endeth the story. So who's up for some hot chocolate?'

Two hands shot up in record time.

As Alan moved to the kitchen, he stopped to stare outside the lounge window. 'Hey, I think I see someone outside. I think it's Bill. Wonder why he came back?'

'Maybe he forgot something, Dad?' said Matt.

Alan moved over to the window. 'Hmm, that doesn't look like Bill. Come up and have a look.'

Matt rose from his chair and came over. 'Can't see anything,' he said, staring hard through the pane glass.

'I'll grab the torch. Leigh, stay next to your brother, please.'

Alan headed to the kitchen to grab the torch as Leigh reluctantly moved over to her brother. He waited until Matt and Leigh were peering out the lounge window before creeping over to the sink. The window there was open just a fraction, enough for a strong bit of fishing line to poke through tied to a spoon. He yanked the line and, outside, two goblin cardboard cut-outs fell from the roof, landing in front of the window. Alan couldn't believe his luck as a gigantic bolt of lightning lit up the cut-outs.

Leigh screamed in terror and fell, scrambling backwards across the floor.

Matt's eyes bulged as he let out a garbled cry. He then

looked closer at the cardboard goblins banging against the window and began laughing.

'Oh, bloody brilliant, Dad, you got us there — even I fell for it that time.'

Alan roared with laughter as Leigh turned on him fiercely. 'It was another dumb trick? I should have known better! Wait till I tell Mum what you did!'

Alan danced around in glee, saying between fits of laughter, 'Oh my oh my oh my ... goblins got Leigh, goblins got Leigh!' Alan continued to chant those same three words. On the sixth chant, a massive lightning bolt lit up the sky, illuminating the inside of the lodge like it was daylight. This lightning was so strong the hairs on everyone's necks stood up. Thunder followed, but it was a different kind of thunder. It was so deep and guttural that it caused their bones to vibrate. The lodge shook violently, and a few small bits of plaster fell from the ceiling. Then the power went out, only the glow of the fire remained.

'Damn,' muttered Alan, 'that was bloody nasty,' as the rain finally arrived to lash the lodge. The lightning increased in intensity ...

***

In Stratford, Bill had finished his tea early and was engaged in some light reading before bed. He loved reading, but tonight, he could not concentrate on the book. Deep down, Bill knew why, but kept denying the reason. He put the book down and removed his glasses, listening to the storm. It had been fairly intense but was fading, he thought, just as the forecast had predicted. Tomorrow morning, he concluded, a quick assessment of Manaia Road would be needed to ensure no damage had occurred. Bill was not worried about the centre or the lodge, they were sturdily built. He closed his eyes to give them a rub, wondering on whether to have a nightcap and head to bed when the sound hit him.

Bill's eyes snapped open.

The sound of the thunder was strong … much too strong. It should not even be possible … unless … He got up quickly and strode to the front door, flinging it open. Staring towards Mount Taranaki, his eyes widened at the sight of the entire top of the mountain, covered in huge bolts of arcing lightning.

Bill paled at the fierce display.

'Oh no! What have you done, Alan?'

***

'Maybe a tree has fallen on the power lines?' said Alan. 'If that's the case, no power tonight. Good thing we've already had dinner.'

Matt thumped down in a chair. 'Oh that's just great. How will I charge my iPad? There's nothing else to do here.'

Alan laughed and said, 'I could always tell some more stories?'

Leigh said nothing, still furious at her dad's prank. Her arms were folded so tight, they were turning red.

Matt shook his head. 'Dad, when Mum finds out what you did, she'll put you in traction for a month.'

Alan chuckled. 'True … true. Which is why that was the last prank ever. I promised your Mum to end the pranks after the trip. So that's it. End, finito, over and out, and etcetera. Your dad has officially retired from the prank business.'

Leigh looked at her dad. 'I don't believe you!' she hissed.

Alan walked over to Leigh's chair, bent down and offered his hand — and then a finger.

'Pinky-promise.'

Matt whistled. 'Now that's a sure fired guarantee, sis. Dad never breaks those.'

Leigh stared at the extended pinky finger. She reached out with hers, hooked it with his, and smiled timidly.

Alan said, 'Okay, it's getting late. Since there is no power, do you two want to bunk here tonight?'

Matt arched his back. 'No way *I'm* taking that couch. The springs are ready to punch through and skewer some poor bugger. I'll take a loft bed.'

'I'll bunk in the loft as well,' said Leigh.

More thunder rumbled in the background as Alan said, 'Suit yourself. I'll take the lounge then so I can keep an eye on the fire. Hopefully, when Bill arrives in the morning, he can get the power sorted. At least the storm is abating, anyway.'

Matt yawned and rose from the couch. 'Sack time I reckon.'

Grabbing the torch, he added, 'Come on, sis, I'll tuck you in.'

Leigh threw a cushion at Matt. 'Oh ha-ha, Matt, *I'm* not the one who used to have a teddy bear called Mr. Snuggles!'

Matt's faced soured as Alan roared with laughter. 'You'll keep,' Matt muttered menacingly to his sister.

The children headed for the loft whilst Alan went to the kitchen to make a cuppa. The little gas burner ignited, and he put the kettle on. 'Might as well get the blankets,' he murmured and moved to the linen cupboard by the foot of the stairs. As he went to pull a pile of blankets and a pillow out, he overheard Matt talking in a subdued voice from the landing above.

'I reckon the best way to get dad back is to prank him ourselves. Let's give it an hour, then I'll sneak out and see if those cardboard cut-outs are still intact. Make some loud noises to get him up here and have them drop in front of the door. I saw a ladder outside I can use. Beat him at his own game, sis?'

Leigh responded softly and Alan couldn't hear her words. The kettle gave a wail as steam blew out of the sprout. Alan tip-toed back to the kitchen.

So, going to try to prank me back, eh? He mused. As Alan made his coffee, he smiled, vowing to ignore any ruckus from above.

***

Tyres screeched in protest as the Toyota Hilux lurched onto Manaia Road. Bill threw all caution to the wind, driving faster than he knew was wise. He cursed his complacency. Five years had lulled him in to a false sense of security. Gunning the engine, he hoped he was wrong in his assessment of the lightning. And if he was right, he hoped he was not too late.

Around the last bend before entering the forest road, he cringed as flashing blue and red lights appeared through the trees. He slowed and emerged around the turn to see two police cars and a local fire truck blocking the road. Bill pulled off the road and got out. Bracing himself before the wind and rain, he stumbled towards the police car.

'Hey, Bill, what the heck are you doing here?'

Bill smiled grimly as he strode towards his old friend, Sergeant Michael Simonka.

'What's happening, Mike?'

Mike turned and pointed toward the up-rooted tree sprawled across the road.

'We got a call about a lightning strike causing an explosion of some sort out this way. It's like that all the way up, I think.

Wind's too bad to start clearing operations, so I'm closing the road till conditions improve.'

Bill's arm shot forward and his hand gripped Mike's shoulder. 'I need to get to the grounds. There's a family up there. I think they could be in trouble, Mike.'

Simonka's eyes narrowed. 'Way too dangerous, mate. No one's going up there for a few hours at least.'

'But —'

'No buts. It ain't happening. Look, you and I know there are only a few trees near the lodge and that lodge is solid as heck. So long as they stay put, they'll be okay.'

'Chopper?' said Bill hopefully.

Mike shook his head. 'Not a chance in these conditions. Jeez, Bill, what's got into you? Never seen you so edgy before.'

'Mike … there is—' but Bill halted, knowing he couldn't reveal his worry, even to his good friend.

'Ok if I stay here? I won't get in the way.'

'Suit yourself, mate, but you could be in for a long night.'

Bill looked up at the unfriendly sky, raindrops splattering on his face.

'I know …'

***

Alan's eyes opened a fraction to the sound of the back door opening. He was a light sleeper, having served in the military before getting married. He smiled vaguely, thinking the kids should have remembered that. The door clicked shut and Alan rolled over and went back to sleep.

Upstairs, Leigh waited for Matt to appear on the sloping roof outside the window. He had the torch, which meant she had to wait in the dark. She peered out the rain-streaked window. The roof would be slippery and Leigh started to think this whole thing was a bad idea. She went to open the window, when …

GROWL!

She jumped in fright as a goblin slid in front of the window. Matt roared with laughter as he poked his head around from behind the cardboard cut-out, the torch held under his chin to light up his face.

'That's for the "Mr Snuggles" jibe, sis.'

'Oh, you stinker!' she said as she opened the window.

Matt grinned as he passed the cardboard cut-out through. 'It's damaged, but still usable. Dad must have used varnish on them or something. I'll be right back with the other one. And see if you can find a towel. I'm soaked!'

Matt faded back into the darkness. Leigh put the cardboard goblin down and rummaged around in the dark for a towel. After a few minutes, another growl came from the window. Leigh sighed and moved back to the window.

'Wasn't funny the first time, Matt. Doing it a second time is just lame.' She reached out to take the cut-out but froze as a green matted arm shot forward and a clawed hand gripped her forearm. Leigh's jaw dropped as the cardboard goblin came to life and leaped into the room. And then a terrible voice spoke.

'Fun you want, is it? Well, you and I are going to have lots of fun! Oh yes indeed, human … lots of fun!' The clawed hand tightened its vice like grip on her forearm.

Leigh could not comprehend what she was seeing. The voice of reason in her looked for comprehension and saw none. Her mind refused to acknowledge that this was no piece of cardboard, despite the pain shooting up her arm.

Outside the window, a voice that sounded like dead leaves being walked on said, 'The boy-child is now subdued, Lord

Harbin.'

Leigh's eyes darted to the window. There stood two other goblins, one holding her unconscious brother.

And then her screams began.

Downstairs, Alan woke with a start. He leapt off the couch, looking around wildly at what had woken him, his eyes trying to focus. The screams from upstairs bombarded his senses. Alan lurched towards the stairs when he remembered. He halted and smiled, calming down quickly. Scratching his belly, he yawned and headed to the dying fire to place a few logs inside.

Moving back to the couch, Alan mumbled, 'Nice screams, Leigh … almost believable, oh daughter of mine,' and flopped back on to the cushions. As he drifted off back to sleep, Alan figured he had about ten minutes before the kids came down to jump on him, miffed he hadn't taken the bait.

Leigh's screams were cut off abruptly as the goblin called Harbin covered her mouth.

'Shut it, human! Arcmedan, take this one as well. Wait at the path for me.'

Another goblin jumped into the room and grabbed Leigh. 'Two boy-child's, Lord Harbin … a double celebration! Perhaps there are more?'

'Why do you think I stay behind? A further search for needs doing. Do as I say and wait on the path … go!'

The goblin jerked Leigh forward and dragged her towards the window. The other goblin holding Matt leered at her, his hot breath washing over her.

'You — you're not real!' she whimpered.

Both goblins screeched with laughter.

'It has been many years since a taking. A feast will occur

tonight to celebrate such a fortunate event. And you humans will be guests of honour.'

The goblin called Arcmedan picked up Leigh and leapt off the roof, causing her to scream as they sailed through the rainy night to thump on to the slippery grass.

'You scream high for a boy-child,' muttered the goblin. He thrusted his ugly face right up to Leigh's eyes, peering intently. He grabbed her hair and sniffed. His yellow eyes bulged in excitement as he realised what he had in his hands.

In the lodge, Harbin searched the upper floor and found no one. The stairs came into his view and he descended to the lower floor, his eyes easily seeing through the darkness. At the foot of the stairs, he glanced around. The glow from the fire lit up the room to reveal a human adult asleep. Harbin's pointed teeth gleamed in the fire's glow. He moved into the kitchen and bathrooms to check for more children. Finding nothing, he re-entered the living room.

Alan stirred, one eye partially opening. He rolled over yawning, 'Ooh, a goblin … I'm so scared. Satisfied now, kids? Big day tomorrow … so back to bed, eh?'

Harbin raised a hand and a sharp nail sprung out from a gnarled finger. He raised it over Alan, ready to slash downwards, but hesitated as Alan broke into a snore. He backed away, grinning at the thought of what this human would find in the morning. Back up to the loft he went and leapt out of the window. An idea formed as he readied to jump to the ground. He turned back to the wooden shutters of the window. The nail extended again and dug deep into the rain-soaked wood.

***

'Uhhh … what happened?'

Matt shook his head and immediately regretted it as pain erupted from his temples.

'Must have fallen off the roof,' he muttered. When he went to rub his throbbing head, he found he couldn't move his arms. In fact, he couldn't stand up either.

'What the heck?'

'QUIET!'

Matt turned to the voice. In the darkness, he could not make out who had said it, but that was quickly remedied as Crawfin jerked Matt up off the ground.

The colour drained from Matt's face. His normally loud voice failed him as he stared wide eyed at the goblin.

'W-what the ...'

A sobbing Leigh said, 'Matt ... they're g ... goblins — OH MY GOD ... *real goblins!*

Matt's heart raced as he saw his sister tied up with goblins surrounding her. He felt sick.

'Oh, this is utter bull-dust! Y-you can't be real ... you just can't be!'

One goblin moved up to Matt and unleashed a withering blow that knocked him back to the ground.

'I warned you to be quiet, boy-child.'

'Leave him alone!' cried Leigh.

The goblin cackled, 'Or what?' He moved over and raised a matted foot over Matt's head.

'OR WHAT!'

'That will do, Derrein. We do not want our prizes spoiled. Not after such a long time between takings.'

All wheeled around as Harbin appeared.

Arcmedan made his way to him and said excitedly, 'Lord Harbin, we have news.' He yelled over his shoulder, 'Bring her forward!'

Harbin frowned. 'Her?'

Crawfin grabbed Leigh and thrust her forward. The slippery ground made her fall in front of Harbin.

'My lord … *a girl-child!*

The goblin king's eyes widened. He bent down immediately and stared at Leigh, his yellow eyes taking in all of her appearance. He then stood up and gave an ear-splitting roar of triumph. A roar that seemed to cause the very mountain itself to shudder in despair.

'*At last — at long last!'*

— Chapter Five —

The Maori Guild

The first rays of the daylight crept through the wooden blinds. Alan's eyes squinted open. He yawned and rose from the couch.

'Ugh, Matt was right, those damn springs pack a punch,' he grumbled, stretching his back. He gingerly made his way to the kitchen.

'Who wants bacon and eggs?' yelled Alan. 'Come on sleepy heads, rise and shine.' He flicked the light switch, but no electricity flowed. 'Power's still out. Looks like the gas burner again. And no cracks about me burning water!'

Silence.

'If I have to come up there, two certain children are going to be carried downstairs fireman style!'

Alan grinned and took a step towards the stairwell when he heard cars pull up outside. Frowning, he made his way to the door. He walked outside to see a police officer approaching, with Bill following close behind. The police car had its warning blue lights flashing and Bill looked pale as a ghost.

'Morning, Officer … hey, Bill. Bit early for a social call, fellas?'

'Just checking up on you, mate — everything okay?' said the sergeant. 'That was quite a storm last night. Crews have been busy clearing the road up here. Bill here thought you might be in a spot of bother.'

Alan looked around and whistled. Branches lay scattered on the road, and park signs lay torn off their poles. 'Yeah, was quite a blow all right, but the kids and I are fine. Just going to make some breakfast. Power's out though, Bill.'

'The breakers probably tripped last night,' muttered Bill. 'The switch box is around the back of the visitors centre — be right back.' He strode towards the centre, his eyes darting everywhere as he walked.

'So, the road is clear now, officer?'

'Yep, good to go now, mate.'

'No worries,' said Alan. 'Come on in for a cuppa. I can tell the kids the cops are here and if they don't wake up soon, they're —'

'OH, CHRIST ALMIGHTY!'

Mike and Alan wheeled around to see Bill rooted to a spot on the road, mouth hanging slack.

'Bill?' Simonka walked up to him. 'Bill … what's wrong?' But he didn't answer; he just continued to stare at the lodge roof.

The sergeant gripped his shoulder. 'BILL!'

Bill shook his head clear and looked away from a sight he'd prayed he would not find this morning.

'Sorry, Mike, I … I was, err, just working out the damage costs. Bit of a shock, you know? Anyway, you'd better head off and check all is okay in town. I'll stay here with Alan and get things sorted here.'

Sergeant Simonka hesitated a moment as his police training

kicked in. Something was not right here . .

'Mike, trust me.'

Simonka looked into his friend's almost pleading eyes. He had not seen that look before. But Bill was one of his few friends worthy of complete trust.

'Okay, Bill, but call if you need anything, okay?'

With that, he put on his cap and walked over to his patrol car. Alan walked up to Bill, hands in pockets. As Simonka started the engine and pulled out of the car park, Alan said, 'What was all that about?'

Bill's eyes returned to the lodge roof. 'Come with me,' he said and strode towards the lodge.

'Wait ... what the —'

'Right now, Alan!'

Bill increased his stride and marched into the lodge, with Alan breaking into a jog to catch up. Bill's eyes searched the room. 'Where are your kids?'

'Upstairs. Jesus, Bill, what the hell is your problem?'

Bill ignored him and made for the steps. Alan felt the first stirrings of unease. This wasn't the mild-mannered ranger he met yesterday. Bill's face now wore a mask of worry that ill-suited him. He ran up the stairs to see Bill reaching for the doorknob to the loft room. Alan pushed Bill's hand away. He stared at Alan for a moment before taking a step back.

'Kids, wake up. Bill's here to fix the power. Kids ...?'

Alan turned the handle and pushed the door open. The beds lay empty, sheets still tightly bound over the mattresses. The curtains gently blew inwards as a morning breeze drifted through the open window.

'What the hell?'

Bill walked in and moved towards the window, glancing

down as his boots made squishing sounds. 'Floor's damp. Window's been open all night.' He squatted down and surveyed the floor. 'Muddy tracks … and lots of them,' he muttered.

'What's going on? Where are my kids?' said Alan. He was then astonished to watch Bill climb out the window onto the roof.

He turned and gestured for Alan to follow him, pointing to something outside. Bewildered by Bill's actions, he eased himself out onto the sloping roof. And there he saw carved in the wood of the window shutter were the words:

'WE'RE BACK BILLY!'

'Goblins have your kids, Alan.'

Alan snorted angrily as he turned from the carved words to Bill. 'Oh, you're just too frigging funny this morning, mate! I'm not in the damn mood for games. Now stop this rubbish and tell me —'

Bill suddenly shoved Alan, causing him to fall back through the window. He leapt in, grabbed Alan by his shirt, and hauled him from the floor. His eyes blazed as he got right up into Alan's face.

'You told a story last night … didn't you? About goblins. DIDN'T YOU! I warned you not to tell ghost stories, but you did anyway, you damned fool! Now you've unleashed a god-damn nightmare. You as good as invited them in, and they accepted. Now your kids are in mortal danger.'

Alan stared back in shock. The rage in Bill's eyes burned for a few seconds more before they softened. He released his grip and backed away. Bill closed his eyes as he massaged his temples for a minute.

'Okay then ... time to get to work.' He pulled a mobile phone out of his pocket and held it up. Seeing a faint signal, he punched in a number and held it to his ear. After a few seconds, he said, 'It's Bill, I need to talk to Amiria and quickly, please.'

Alan went to speak, but Bill raised a silencing hand. 'Amiria, it's Bill. It's happened again. Yes, of course I'm sure, no doubt at all. Two kids, last night. We're at the lodge now. No, just the father.'

Bill's face drained of colour as urgent words flowed from the phone.

'OH CRAP! DAMN, DAMN, DAMN! How could I have forgotten that? Yes, one is a girl. Okay .. I'll be waiting.' Bill snapped the phone shut and grimaced. 'My god ...' he muttered '... a girl. How did I forget that?' He turned to Alan. 'They'll be here in 30 minutes, quicker if they can.'

'Who will be here?' demanded Alan.

'Help. Now you need to tell me everything you did last night ... everything you understand? Then I'll fill you in what I know, okay?'

'Okay ... and it had better be good if you know what's good for you. Goblins ... what utter garbage!'

Alan strode out of the room. Bill watched him disappear as he thumped down the stairs. He turned back to the window and stared out at the forest.

'Okay Harbin,' muttered Bill. 'You finally got your prize. We'll meet again, you bastard. And this time I won't fail ...'

***

Alan sat in silence. The cup he held shook slightly now and then, spilling coffee on his hands, yet he didn't feel the hot liquid on his skin.

'It was just a prank, Bill, a silly prank using cardboard. I can't believe it — no, I refuse to believe it. It's not possible. My kids are missing, dammit! I want to call the police!'

'You slept on the couch last night,' said Bill

'Well … yes. How did you know that?'

Bill nodded towards the couch. 'Have a look on the floor.'

It startled Alan to see muddy tracks on the floorboards, the same type as in the loft room.

'You're lucky to be alive. The goblins checked you out. Not sure why they didn't kill you, though. Maybe even his royal high-bastardness himself spared you, although I'm buggered if I know why.'

'Who?'

'Harbin — the goblin leader. We've crossed swords once before,' said Bill coolly. 'He's the one who left the message …no doubt about that.'

Alan wondered if this was all some great revenge prank the kids had thought up and last night was a diversion to put him off guard. He looked at Bill, trying to gauge his part in it. Alan latched onto this train of thought like a drowning man does to a floating branch.

'Alan, stop it!' snapped Bill.

'Eh?'

'I've seen that damned stupid look before. Five years ago, I had a similar conversation with a man called David after his kids disappeared. On a night very much like last night.' Bill lowered his eyes to hide his grief. 'They were never found, Alan. You've heard of the Hellier kids before, right?'

Alan paled. The entire world had heard of the two Hellier kids who disappeared on holiday in New Zealand many years ago.

'That happened around here?' whispered Alan.

'Not just around here, but *right from here,*' said Bill. 'All sorts of vile crap was spouted on how the parents were involved. Other media knuckleheads reported the kids had run away. All wrong. They even brought a psychic here like some damned circus. Dave and I knew the truth, of course, but what could you say? That goblins took his children? We'd both have been thrown into the loony bin.'

Bill began pacing, eying the window now and then.

'Okay, Alan, once again before the guild arrives. Go over everything that happened here last night. Don't leave anything out; even if you think it's trivial, it could be vital.'

'Guild?'

'I'll explain later. Start talking.'

Alan nodded and recounted the previous evening, starting from where Bill left. The ranger bit his tongue as Alan told of setting up the cardboard goblins. But he couldn't stop himself when Alan mentioned the victory dance taunt and what he taunted Leigh with.

'And that's when the lightning struck and the power went out — right?'

Alan nodded.

'That's it then,' said Bill. 'That's what allowed Harbin inside the lodge.'

'How so?'

*'SIX TIMES UTTERED OF NAME AND KIN
SHALL OPEN THE PATH FOR THE GOBLIN'*

Alan jumped up from his chair. Standing at the door stood

five people. The woman who spoke moved clear of the others.

'The word "goblin" and your children's names were uttered together … six times or more. Do you deny this?'

Alan stammered, 'H - how on earth did you —'

The woman raised her hand. Her eyes were a shade of deep blue that held a hint of power. Alan looked into those eyes and his thoughts of a revenge prank by the kids faded. Those were not the eyes to carry any amusement.

'Amiria, you made quick time,' said Bill.

She made her way to Bill and, to Alan's astonishment, gave a traditional Maori greeting of pressing their noses together.

'If we are to stop Harbin, we must act quickly. Time is not on our side. We must retrieve them before the 4th moon ends or face ruination.'

Amiria eyed the pale-looking man in the chair. 'The ones taken — what are their names?'

'Matt and Leigh,' offered Alan.

'And you?'

'Alan.'

'I am Amiria, Kaumātua … or elder if you like. And these,' she gestured to the others, 'are my guild. We answer the call we hoped Bill would never make in our lifetime. If we do not retrieve your kids from the goblins in time, the world ends …'

Alan could not contain himself any longer. 'Now wait just a god-damn minute here! Look, I'm a reasonable sort of guy, but come on, goblins? End of the world? Seriously? Do I look like some sort of fool?'

Bill said in a matter-of-fact tone, 'Yes, actually, you do.'

Alan wheeled around to face Bill, who jabbed a finger at him and said, 'You'd better listen up, mate, or Matt and Leigh are good as dead.' His hands reached down and slowly he lifted the shirt up.

Alan's eyes bulged as a large, angry scar stretching from Bill's hip to his chest was revealed.

'The goblin king did that to me, Alan, five years ago. I nearly died from his attack. If it were not for the guild, I would not be here. Do you understand? This is no sick joke, prank, wind-up or anything of the sort. This is as real as it gets.'

The anger faded from Bill as his shoulders sagged.

'You'd best start believing in goblins, Alan, or you'll end up being a father to —'

'Bill!'

'Amiria,' said Bill, staring at her with determination, 'he needs to know ...'

Amiria thought for a minute before replying, 'You are right, of course he does. But I need to explain everything first so he has a fully understanding of what we face ... agreed?'

'Agreed,' said Bill.

Alan lowered himself back into his chair. He looked up at Bill and then to Amiria. In a husky voice, he pleaded, 'What is going on? Please ... tell me, where are my kids?'

***

Bill made tea and coffee for the group. They sat around in a semi-circle in the living room with Alan's eyes flicking to each person, noting they were quite a diverse group of people. In turn, each of them stared back at Alan with grave faces.

After Bill handed everyone a cup, Amiria nodded at the eldest man in the group. The man searched Alan's face, wondering if he had any idea of the enormous task facing him.

'Alan, I am Ari, Tohunga Ahurewa, high priest of the guild.

'Tohunga what?'

Amiria interjected. 'Tohunga is a Māori term for an expert practitioner of their chosen craft. Each of my Tohunga will call upon their skills to aid you, Alan. Ari is gifted with communicating with the gods. And you will need their wisdom to guide you. You must heed all that is spoken here today. Accept, understand, and prepare for what will come. For if you do not, you will fail and your children will be lost … understand?'

Alan stammered, 'Yes.'

Amiria's stoic mask slipped for the first time. 'Why couldn't it have been two boys?' she muttered.

Ari continued on. 'We, the Guild of Taranaki, have studied the goblin lore for many generations. What we know is their presence here is an abomination. The Land of the Long White Cloud is not their land of origin. That lies in the Northern Hemisphere.'

'They stowed away on a ship from England, Alan,' said Bill.

'Correct,' said Ari. 'The creatures were first identified during an unusually fierce storm not far from here. We narrowed it down to three possible vessels that carried the creatures. It took us years to track down each ship's logs, but they revealed nothing. By chance, an old journal of one of the captains surfaced in a junk shop in England. He detailed the goblins killing his cabin boy, stealing one of his ship's boats, and coming ashore.'

'When was this?' asked Alan.

'1841.'

'1841! Are you frigging serious? But … but was nearly —'

'One hundred and eighty years ago,' said Ari.

Alan looked stunned. He turned to Bill and whispered, 'Why didn't you tell me?'

Bill grunted, 'As if you would have believed me …'

'Harbin will begin the ritual as fast as he can,' said Amiria, 'if he has not already done so.'

'Ritual?' said a now utterly bewildered Alan.

Amiria took a deep breath. The very air around the cabin seemed to chill as she said, 'Goblins breed through one female, a queen if you like. The queen can birth a dozen goblins a week, enough to raise an army within a month. But she can only produce male warriors, less she breed a challenger to her throne. A queen will live for many centuries. They are the most protected of all goblins and are nearly impossible to get close to and kill. They are also quite powerful.'

'If I may?' said a young woman standing next to Amiria, who nodded her approval.

'I am Beccia. I am the warrior arm of the guild, along with my brother Makoa.' A man standing next to her nodded at Alan. 'We are Tohunga Tumatauenga — war party and weapons bearers. I have studied the strengths and weaknesses of the goblins. Knowledge handed down through countless clashes with Harbin and his beasts. The biggest clash between man and goblin occurred in 1907. We call it *The Day of Red Tears,* because afterwards, the night skies turned red from the fires on the mountain … not to mention the blood on the soil.

'We lost many warriors that day … the day the goblins left their underground lair to attempt to enslave humanity. All Māori tribes fought as one and we drove the green hordes back. One fabled warrior, called Tomas, managed to slip into the goblin lair and spear the queen. Her minders tore him apart soon afterwards, but he earned eternal status in Māori legend for his sacrifice. They have been without a queen since.'

Amiria rose from her chair. She kneeled down before Alan and took his hand. The look on her face chilled his bones.

'Harbin can increase his clan's numbers by what they call *A Taking* — the hunting of human children. Once captured, the children undergo a ritual … The Ritual of Zulear. The ritual will turn human children into goblins over a period of four days. So far as we know, the change is irreversible. Harbin has only done this less than a dozen times in the past century. And they have all been male children.'

Amiria squeezed Alan's hand. 'Your daughter is the first female taken since their queen was killed. Once transformed … your daughter will become the new goblin queen. And then the breeding will begin once again.'

The colour drained from Alan's face. He lurched out of the chair and staggered to the kitchen, arriving just in time to retch loudly into the sink.

Bill moved quickly to him and placed a hand on Alan's heaving back, saying, 'Take it easy, mate … easy now.'

A low moan of, 'No, no, no …' came repeatedly from Alan as he continued retching. Bill turned on the tap to clean the mess and eased him away from the sink to his chair. Breccia put the kettle back to boil and prepare more coffee. After a few minutes, a steaming mug was placed in Alan's hand.

Amiria's voice took a most gentle tone as she said, 'Calm your heart, Alan, you stand not alone against the green hordes. We will do everything in our power to save your children. Five years ago, we faced Harbin and failed.' Grief flickered on the faces of the guild, but Bill's face was particularly ashen.

She turned to her guild, locking eyes with all. 'If we do not defeat him this time, there will be no second chance. A new queen means the end of the world as we know it — and the rise of the goblin world.'

— Chapter Six —

The Queen

Plunk!

Leigh stirred.

Plunk!

Her eyes creaked open.

Plunk!

She sat up bolt straight, looking around with fearful eyes.

'Easy, sis,' said Matt, and he shuffled over to his sister and placed an arm around her.

'W- Where are we?'

Matt whispered, 'Keep your voice down. Those things are in earshot. As far as I can tell, we're in a cave of some sort. Only one way in or out and that's barred by a pretty thick wooden gate or something.'

Leigh glanced around. A small flaming torch on the wall outside gave just enough light to illuminate the cave. Not that there was much to see. The cave held them and nothing else.

'Watch your footing when you get up. The ground is slippery. Water keeps dripping from the ceiling. We might be near Wilkies Pools, I think.'

'How long have I been asleep?'

Matt shrugged. 'I'm not sure. I only came to a little while ago myself.'

'Oh god, Matt, what is going on? How can goblins exist with no one knowing?'

'I don't know. I don't have any —'

'Idea?' queried a loud snickering voice.

Leigh gave a small yelp. The heavy gate swung outwards and two flaming torches approached from outside. Arcmedan and Derrein grinned as Matt and Leigh leapt up and retreated to the end of the cave.

'Where are you going?' chuckled the goblins. 'Don't you remember? You're guests of honour for dinner. But seeing as we're too late for that, breakfast will have to do. Out of the cave … now!'

Matt tensed as he gauged the distance between him and the goblins. Never one for being subtle, he didn't realise he had already given himself away. Each goblin pulled a sword out from their scabbards.

'Go on — try it, boy-child. Your blood won't be the first my sword has tasted.' Derrein grinned, showing off every one of his razor-sharp teeth. He threw his sword at Matt's feet. 'If you fancy yourself with the blade, pick it up. Arcmedan here will be more than willing to test your skills …'

Matt bent down, eager to pick up the sword, but Leigh grabbed his arm.

'Matt, no! They're looking for a reason to hurt you. Please, don't give them one — I need you!'

He looked into his sister's pleading eyes, took a deep breath and muttered, 'Okay.' Matt left the sword on the ground and held his sister's hand instead, naked anger showing on his face. Arcmedan's face soured as Derrein came forward and picked up his sword. In a flash, a clawed hand shot out and Matt flew backwards, crashing painfully against the cave wall.

'A wise choice, *Matt*,' grunted Derrein. 'Arcmedan is our finest warrior with the sword. We really only need the girl-child. You are, how should I put this ... a novelty item now. Stop being a source of amusement and —'

Darrein leapt forward and slashed the cave wall above Matt with his sword, causing sparks to fly.

'Understand?'

Matt tried to get to his feet, but slipped on a wet patch. Leigh scrambled forward to stand in front of her brother.

'Okay, he understands. Now leave him alone!' she cried.

Darrein smirked. 'Oh, so brave. A fine quality to have for our future —'

'Quiet, Derrein. You know what Harbin has ordered.'

The goblin's face screwed up. 'Ah yes, I ... I forgot.' He pointed his sword at Leigh. 'Harbin wishes to see you. Follow Arcmedan and stay on the path.' Derrein turned to Matt and growled, 'Try anything, and I kill you.' Glancing to Leigh, he said, 'Try anything, and I kill him. Now MOVE!'

Matt and Leigh followed Arcmedan out of the cave, with Derrein following behind. The small procession moved through a tunnel, a faint sound of running water echoing above them. The tunnel gave way to a large chamber with many tunnels running off in different directions. Some were dark, others were lit by torches. Goblins came in and out of the tunnels, many stopping to stare at the children, whispering, *The girl-child!*

'This way,' hissed Arcmedan as he moved towards another large tunnel. Leigh looked behind to see other goblins falling in behind Derrein. The look of joy on their faces caused her to shudder. The tunnel went on for some time, Matt noticing the sound of running water getting fainter. Then a flickering light appeared before Arcmedan, gaining in intensity at every moment. Matt and Leigh shielded their eyes from the glare.

Arcmedan halted and turned. 'Go forth, humans,' he said.

Matt and Leigh edged forward, past the goblin and out of the tunnel.

'Oh my god ...' Leigh trembled, blocking her ears as loud screeching started.

Matt suddenly felt the urge to urinate, because what lay in front of them was a scene taken straight from the depths of a nightmarish hell.

They stood in an enormous chamber, easily the size of a football field. The ceiling seemed to go on forever, disappearing into blackness. Many flaming torches created shadows along the walls, shadows of nearly a hundred goblins — leering, jabbering, screeching in joy as Matt and Leigh stood before them. In the centre of the chamber stood two massive thrones, carved from rock. One was occupied.

'SILENCE!'

The screeching stopped but excited whispering could still be heard.

'Greetings to our honoured guests,' said Harbin. 'Do not be shy now, come forward ... come forward,' he waved.

Matt and Leigh didn't budge. A rough shove from Arcmedan remedied that, and they staggered forward towards the centre of the chamber. Harbin looked down at his prizes as they halted before him.

Matt stared back defiantly. 'What do you want with us?'

'Speak only when spoken to,' snarled Derrein as he threw a

backhand towards Matt's head. Shock registered on his face as Matt ducked and his hand sailed through empty space.

'Oomph!'

Matt's foot cannoned into Derrein's midriff, sending him flying backwards. He wheeled around to face Arcmedan.

'I'm tired of being a punching bag. You wanna have a go frog guts? Bring it on!'

Darrein rose from the ground. With Arcmedan, he moved in with a snarl in his throat. They both halted, though, as Harbin raised a hand.

'Such courage! This one will be a fine addition to our clan.' Harbin leapt off his throne and landed in front of both kids. His yellow eyes glowed at the sight of Leigh. 'You are indeed a prize beyond compare, girl-child.' He reached forward to touch her hair, causing Leigh to flinch. 'You do not know of your true importance … yet. Let us tarry not. We have waited a century more for this, we will wait no longer. Begin the ritual.'

A roar of approval rang out. Swords clanged and boots stomped as they moved in closer. Matt edged over to his sister, his eyes darting everywhere. But there was no escape. Leigh screamed as Derrein picked her up. Matt tried to protect her, but was picked up by Arcmedan. They were carried a short distance before being thrown into the air.

But instead of thumping onto the hard ground, both landed in a large pool of dirty black water. They surfaced, retching out the foul-tasting liquid.

'What the hell?' spluttered Matt. Leigh hugged herself to stop from shaking.

Harbin clapped his hands. 'Come forth, Meido and Reido,' he commanded.

The baying horde parted and two robed goblins emerged, one holding a black urn, the other a thick leather-bound book.

'By your leave, my lord?' croaked the book holder.

Harbin nodded.

The goblin moved to the pool edge and slowly opened the book, causing a gasp from onlookers. Dust rose from the pages, hinting it had remained closed for some time. Reido began reading a passage in an unknown language. The air tingled with sinister magic as he chanted. Leigh looked down as the water changed colour from black to a lime green. A soft glow rose from the bottom, illuminating the pool.

Reido closed the book. 'It is done, Lord Harbin.'

'Good. Very good. Continue —'

Meido moved forward with the urn and lifted it, now poised over the water. 'We are ready, my lord.'

Harbin pulled a knife from his belt. Grinning, he cut into his palm, letting the blood pool there. He then held out the knife.

'Gregorn!'

A goblin hurried forward and took the knife.

'Cut them,' ordered Harbin.

Gregorn leapt into the pond and yanked Leigh's hand forward. The knife slashed her palm, causing her to scream. Matt tried to grab the knife, only to be cut as well as Gregorn slashed carelessly in his direction. Blood ran down Matt's left cheek and into the water.

Harbin walked over to the edge of the pond as Gregorn exited the foul water. The Goblin king then held out his palm and his blood dripped into the pool.

The water bubbled and frothed almost at once.

'Bear witness, my brethren. Witness the age of the goblin

reborn! Witness the end of my solitude.' Harbin closed his eyes and, in a whisper, said, 'Witness my beloved queen …'

He turned to Meido and nodded. The wizard unscrewed the urn. Silence fell in the chamber as it slowly tilted downwards. All eyes were glued to that urn. Matt and Leigh watched as well, still not understanding what was going on.

Then specks of ash sprinkled out, floating downwards toward the water. As the first speck touched the bubbling water, the urn shook and ash flowed out at an incredible pace, as if glad to be free. In seconds, the urn was empty. Harbin moved back from the pond and watched. The water swirled around Matt and Leigh. It rose higher and higher, faster and faster, until both were hidden from sight. For an entire minute, the Goblins of Mount Taranaki watched in silent awe. Then the water collapsed as quickly as it had begun.

'Remove them,' ordered Harbin.

Arcmedan and Derrein hurried forward and yanked Matt and Leigh out of the now still water. Both swayed a little, eyes closed, but appeared none the worse for their ordeal.

'Did it work?' frowned Gregorn.

Animated chatter began from all the goblins.

Harbin turned to Reido. 'Well?'

Reido came forward. He lifted Leigh's head and pried her eyes open.

Staring deeply, he searched for …

'SUCCESS! HER EYES YELLOW AS WE SPEAK!'

Meido hurried over to Matt. 'This one as well, my lord.'

Pandemonium broke out as the goblins celebrated wildly. They passed goatskin pouches full of ale around as dancing and chanting got into full swing.

Harbin motioned Arcmedan forward. 'Take them back to

the cave for now. Provide food and water and bandage their wounds. No more rough treatment — they are now part of our clan. But don't be *too* gentle either.'

'Yes, my lord.'

Matt and Leigh were still out of it, so they were picked up to be carried back to their cave.

'Wait!' Harbin moved over to Leigh and produced a small green bottle from inside his vest. He scraped it across Leigh's bloodied palm, causing her blood trickled inside. Harbin then corked the bottle and said, 'Take them away.'

Arcmedan did as he was told, looking curiously at his lord. Harbin brought the bottle to eye level, gleaming at its contents. He then yelled over the loud singing, 'Artex!'

A smallish goblin quickly answered the summons.

'Yes, my lord?'

'I assign you to our new takings. Guard and teach as you have before — understand?'

Artex bowed. 'Yes, my lord.'

Harbin growled menacingly, 'You know what will occur over the next few days. Guard her well, for should any harm come to my new queen, I'll tear your heart out through your throat.'

'Y-yes,' stuttered Artex. 'Err … what shall they now be called?'

Harbin frowned and scratched his chin. He hadn't thought of names yet. 'Hmm, Leigh and Matt will not do.' He then grinned. 'They are now Leighandra and Maorten.'

Artex bowed again and left.

Harbin smiled as a pouch of ale was passed to him. *Yes, Leighandra was a fine name for his queen,* he thought as he gulped down the ale. *A very fine name indeed …*

***

Matt stirred. He opened his eyes and found he could see quite well; better than the last time he was in the cave. A sob caused him to wheel around.

'Sis?'

Leigh lay huddled into a ball next to the cave wall. Matt moved quickly over to her.

'Easy, sis,' said he huskily. 'It'll be alright.'

Still huddled over, Leigh said, 'Oh, Matt, I'm so scared I can hardly breathe. You know I'm not brave or anything. I can't take this anymore. I want to go home!'

'Hey, I'm pretty scared, too, you know.'

'Really?' said Leigh.

'Yeah,' said Matt. 'You'd have to be a complete moron not to be, geek,' using his nickname for his sister.

Leigh looked up and smiled timidly. But her smiled vanished as Matt recoiled in horror, scrambling away from his sister as quickly as he could. Leigh jumped up.

'Matt, what's wrong?'

'Y … Your eyes!'

'What about them?'

Her brother took a deep breath and said, 'They've changed colour. They're … they're yellow now.'

Leigh felt her eyes before realising what she was doing and dropped her hands. Matt moved back towards Leigh as suspicion dawned on him.

'Mine too, I guess?'

Leigh let out a sob and nodded.

'Well, of course, your eyes have yellowed. That is the first step on your new path.'

Both turned to that new voice. Outside the cave stood a

goblin they had not seen before. He was smaller than the others, with much finer hair on his arms.

'I am Artex, your guide, protector, and mentor. Lord Harbin has assigned me to aid you through your transition. Your other teachers will be the wizards, Meido and Reido. Over the next day, you will be allowed more freedom to move about, but for now, you will stay in the confines of the cave. Food and drink will be brought to you shortly.'

Matt looked at Leigh, who also had a similarly confused look on her face. Turning to Artex, he said, 'What do you mean by *transition*?'

Artex raised an eyebrow. 'Do you not know what has just occurred? The Ritual of Zulear was a complete success. Your transition has already begun.' He smiled at the bewildered looks staring back at him.

'First the eyes yellow, then your facial features broaden out. Your human skin will change to accommodate the green hair that will grow. Your nails will lengthen, your arms will stretch and fingers will point like arrows. Feelings of loyalty to humanity will die as memories of your old life fade. Intense anger will flow through you. And then, when the 4th moon is no more, the transformation will be complete and you will be true goblins. Loyal to Lord Harbin forever.'

Matt and Leigh stood frozen to the spot, barely breathing. 'It ... it's not true,' whispered Matt.

'But I haven't even told you the best part,' said Artex. 'You,' waving absently at

Matt, 'will join our clan as a warrior. But you, Leigh ... you have a very special honour. One not bestowed upon a human for centuries.'

Leigh trembled as Artex revealed her fate.

'You are to be our new queen, married to our Lord Harbin. And so, as our queen, you shall become the future bearer of thousands of new goblins to our clan. Welcome to your new life, Queen Leighandra, future mother of all Mount Taranaki Goblins.'

Matt barely caught his sister in time as she passed out.

— Chapter Seven —

Tane and Mana

'Where's Alan?' Bill asked, pulling the backpack he'd retrieved from his 4x4 from his shoulders.

The guild was in deep conversation, huddled around a large map spread across the coffee table. At his askance, Beccia looked up and said, 'He said he needed to pick something up from the visitor's centre.'

Bill frowned. What could Alan possibly need from … 'oh no!' He dropped his bag before sprinting out the door. As he raced towards the centre, he saw his fears were confirmed.

Alan was on his mobile.

'Jules, please sit down, love. I … I have something to tell you. Last night there was a storm here, a bad one. And … and well … something happened. I err … d-don't know how to quite tell you this but —'

Bill grabbed the phone out of Alan's hand.

'HEY!'

Bill ended the call and threw the phone back to Alan. 'Text your wife and tell her everything's fine. Tell her your call was about the road being blocked, but it's open now. Tell her the phone reception has gone flaky and you'l call when you can.'

'But —'

'Don't you get it yet? It's up to you, me and the guild to save your kids. No one else can know. You can't bring your missus into this, Alan. And not the police, or even the army for that matter. Just who we have here.'

Through near tears, Alan moaned, 'Bill, she can be here in less than 24 hours.'

'Do you want to put her in danger as well?'

'N-no,' he replied as he grabbed at his hair in frustration. 'Of course not!'

Bill said, 'Good, because sure as hell, that's what would happen if she turned up. As it is, we'll be lucky if no one is killed by the time this is all over. Come on, back to the lodge. I reckon the guild is ready to outline where we go from here.'

As they walked back, Bill added, 'Besides, your missus would probably think it's another one of your stupid pranks if you tried to explain all this.'

'Yeah,' Alan muttered, 'you're probably right.'

As they entered the lodge, Amiria gestured for them to join the guild.

'Did you close the park, Bill?'

'Yes. Our website now states the park and walking trails are closed due to storm damage. Digital messaging machine for the phone says the same thing. I'd like to put some of the plastic barriers along the road later on, but for now we won't have any day visitors to deal with.'

'Good. We have reviewed our last encounter with the goblins. Bill, what have you told him about their origins?'

'Very little, I'm afraid.'

'Then we'll start from the beginning,' said Amiria. She waited for Alan to be seated and began.

'As you now know, the goblins arrived here in 1841. At first, they were small in number, perhaps no more than a dozen. We are not sure. But what we do know is they were drawn to Mount Taranaki. It is a mystic place held in high regard in Māori culture, so it is natural they chose it. It also closely matches that of their traditional homeland, we believe. Over time, this forest has transformed into what you see today. Trees grow around and even through other trees. Lichen, moss, vines and ferns all grew rapidly after the goblin's arrival. It is a place where you feel you are being watched. And you *are* watched. Harbin has sentries stationed throughout the forest, hidden from sight — and of course, sunlight.'

'Why sunlight?' asked Alan.

Beccia said, 'Sunlight is the enemy of goblins, Alan. Exposure to direct sunlight will kill them.'

'Correct,' added her brother. 'Which is why they always come out to strike at night. And why it is so dangerous to be caught alone in this forest after sundown.'

'I don't understand something,' said Alan. 'Why haven't they taken over New Zealand? I mean, every night would have these creatures swarming out of their holes. The world would know. You can't hide this sort of thing in this day and age. There would be online videos, websites dedicated to these goblins, travel warnings and such. Yet, there's nothing. Come on, something doesn't add up.'

Ari answered. 'Māori magic is powerful, Alan. After the Day of the Red Tears, the Ariki and the Tohunga drew on the power of Tane to confine the goblins to Mount Taranaki. They cannot venture past the boundaries of the forest. Nor can they enter any dwelling without triggering the power of

Tane. That's why the world knows not of their existence. This will remain so, as long as Tane and Mahuta stand.'

'Tane?' said Alan. 'Mahuta?'

'Tane is the Māori forest god. He/They/She broke away from the sky god, Rangi, and earth mother, Papa, to allow space for a forest to grow. Many think this as myth, sort of like how many of your countrymen think of the Aboriginal Dreamtime. But always remember this: myths and legends are usually born from truth.'

'And Mahuta?'

'Lord of the Forest,' said Bill. 'A giant Kauri tree, the largest of its type in the world. Legend has it that this tree holds the power of Tane. The tree guards all the forests of New Zealand, even though it's a long way from here, way past Auckland, in fact. Its power still keeps the goblins trapped on Mount Taranaki after all these years.'

Bill leaned back and closed his eyes, sunlight playing across his tired face.

'Now onto the Hellier kids. I was only one month into the job when they were taken. We searched the woods in the morning with their father and mother. Police choppers scoured the area, volunteers searched on foot throughout the forest and the news media reported round the clock. It was pure bedlam.'

Bill opened his eyes and looked at Amiria with warmth in his eyes. 'Then Amiria arrived with the guild. At first, I was ready to throw them out of the park as kooks looking to cash in on the misery of others. I refused to believe it when she spoke of the goblins, as did Dave and his wife. But she sort of convinced us by finding a message from Harbin. The bastard likes to leave a calling card, it seems. Carved on a tree at the start of the trail were the words, *"They are mine!"*

'We had to get the volunteer searchers out of the forest before sundown,' said Amiria. 'To do this we enacted a Rāhui, which allows the Māori to restrict access to an area. After the forest was cleared of all others, we spent the night with Bill and the children's parents.'

'It was one of the longest nights of my life,' continued Bill. 'I learned that my view of the world was rather a narrow one. I learned of the goblin lore. I learned how to protect myself from them — and how to kill them.'

'With a shotgun on both accounts, hopefully,' muttered Alan.

'Guns have no lasting effect on them,' said Makoa. 'To kill a supernatural creature requires Mana.'

'Mana?'

Bill sighed. 'Mana is —'

A woman rose from sitting on the wooden floor. She had not spoken before.

'Kyeua, are you okay?' asked Amiria.

'A vision is coming,' she said. Without further notice, she left the group to walk outside.

Makoa saw Alan's surprised look and said, 'Kyeua is a Tohunga Matakite, Alan, a foreteller of the future. When a vision comes, she must be clear of all distractions. It will take some time for her to return. We should take advantage of this and prepare a meal.'

Alan looked up at the clock with some alarm. He turned to Bill and said urgently, 'Half the day's gone already!'

'The whole day will be needed, mate,' said Bill. 'You have much to learn before we enter the forest to take back your kids, so that won't happen till tomorrow morning. You're not prepared yet.'

'But ...'

'You go trudging through the forest now and you sign your own death warrant,' growled Bill. 'There are traps out there. Traps set by the goblins that will snag you like a fly in a web. Sun goes down — goblins come — one dead Alan. Get it?'

Alan shoved his hands into his pockets and strode out the door.

Amiria moved over to Bill and murmured, 'Watch him, Bill. Something is not right here. He's hiding something.'

Bill muttered, 'I'll see what I can find out.'

***

After a quick meal, Amiria pulled out a thick leather-bound book out of her bag and placed it on the desk.

'This book contains what we know of the goblins. It is *The Goblin Grimoire*. The knowledge in this book is gathered from many sources, from ancient to modern times. The goblins have roamed for centuries in France and Germany. And to a lesser extent, the United Kingdom. We have added our knowledge to this tome. But I'm afraid that our local knowledge is not as complete as we would like.'

Alan had returned to the lodge after a walk. He did not eat the prepared meal, but at least to Bill, it seemed he had himself under control.

'Why is that?' he asked. 'You had me believing you knew all there was to know about the goblins.'

'Know this, Alan. The Tohunga have been the keepers of knowledge, both spiritual and temporal, since the dawn of my people. The knowledge of our ways is passed from generation to generation. And done with great accuracy. With the coming of the white man to New Zealand, this changed. Like your own country, there were many clashes between the white man and the traditional owners. The English thought the Tohunga dangerous. This resulted in the Tohunga Suppression Act of 1907, which made it illegal for Tohunga to practice their arts.'

'Damn,' muttered Alan.

'Pretty much,' said Beccia dryly. 'The Tohunga watched their people embrace the new religions of the white man. They then declined to pass on their own knowledge to the next generations. This was disastrous for our culture. You see, the Tohunga pass their knowledge by voice, no written records were kept back then. The act was only repealed in 1962, but by that time the damage was done. A generation of knowledge was lost. Now we document everything we know, but there are gaps. And those who fought the green ones have left our world to be with their ancestors. We work to restore the Tohunga to their true place in Māori society, but it will be a difficult task in the world we now live in.'

'Perhaps some-day we shall prevail,' sighed Amiria. 'For now, we mainly lean on the knowledge of the foul ones from European sources as well as what we have pieced together from surviving Tohunga.'

'You were saying something about Mana before lunch, Makoa,' said Alan.

'As I said, guns will not kill goblins, and that Mana is required,' replied Makoa. 'Mana is one's own power, Alan ... power that resides in all of us. It can be inherited from your ancestors or born from character. If strong enough, we can transmit it through iron or wood. The power of Mana flowing through a sword, spear or club will defeat a creature of evil like goblins. The weapon *must* be an extension of your Mana. Guns cannot do this. It doesn't take much courage to wield a gun. They are weapons of the weak.'

Bill reached over and lifted up his backpack. Pulling the flap back, he pulled out a medium-sized sword. Sunlight through the windows danced along the blade, revealing scrolls etched in the metal. 'It doesn't get more personal than this, mate,' he grinned.

Beccia said, 'Those scrolls represent the Day of Red Tears, Alan. All weapons owned by the guild have them. The scrolls were engraved by Tohunga artists and carvers and blessed by an Ariki, the highest member of the Māori tribe of this area. We have more weapons in our vehicle, which we will —'

Beccia's voice faded as Kyeua came through the door. All eyes turned to her.

'My vison is over,' she said. 'The green ones will march on the rise of the 4th moon.'

'Why would they do that?' frowned Ari. 'And where on earth would they march to?' Then the light bulb went off. 'The 4th moon — the time when taken children are fully transformed into goblins …'

Amiria stood up, alarm on her face. 'For that to happen, the ritual *has* been conducted.'

'Yes,' stated Kyeua. '*If* my vision is correct.'

Alan leapt up. 'What are we waiting for, dammit? Let's go!'

'No, Alan,' said Bill. 'Like I said before, you're not prepared yet. And neither are the rest of us.'

Beccia said, 'And there is the fact that Kyeua's visions are not always set in stone.' She smiled at Kyeua and added, 'The future is never a foregone conclusion.'

Kyeua grinned back. 'Everyone has the power over their tomorrow by the choices they make today.'

'Yes,' said Amiria. 'Please sit down, everyone. Makoa,

unload the equipment from the van if you please.'

Makoa nodded and left the lodge.

'Kyeua, what else of the vison?' asked Beccia.

'The vision was clear at first, yet it clouded towards the end,' said Kyeua. 'Honestly, it was the strangest vision I have had to date. I saw the goblins on the march, but I also saw them enter homes without permission. That should not be. And before the vison ended, I saw —'

'What?' whispered Bill.

'I saw, through a clouded haze, the goblins advance on the town.'

'But that is not possible,' said Makoa, coming through the door carrying two large canvas bags. 'Tane's power keeps them confined here.'

Kyeua shrugged. 'As I said, the vision clouded at the end. I'm not even sure if I read it correctly. I only saw them on the march. I can't tell you why.'

Amiria looked deeply disturbed, but put aside further questions. They watched as Makoa dumped equipment onto the floor. He then started removing items from canvas bags.

'Alan, you can see here what we used in our attempt to retrieve the Hellier children.'

Beccia reached down and lifted a blue-bladed sword. 'This is mine. My brother uses a bow as his weapon of choice.' She then reached down and lifted another sword. Carefully, she turned the hilt towards Alan.

'This one is yours —'

Alan slowly reached out and embraced the hilt. 'But ... but I've never handled a sword in my life!'

'You will be trained,' said Beccia.

Alan stared at the blade as Makoa continued his inventory

check. 'Manilla rope for hauling people in and out of bolt-holes. Cyalume sticks, flares, camouflaged tarpaulins, knives, waterproof maps. Take note of the flares, Alan. They won't kill goblins like sunlight does, but intense light pains them greatly.'

Beccia turned to Amiria. 'We should begin his training immediately.'

Amiria said, 'No. First, Alan needs to know what he must do. Then we search the grounds for which path they took before night falls.'

She lifted the *Goblin Grimoire* and turned to a chapter. 'From sources in Europe, we know children are taken to add to a goblin horde should they have no queen. We also know that the change from human to goblin takes four moons. Once the transformation begins, it can only be stopped one way.'

Alan put down the sword and leaned forward to listen closely.

'Even if you manage to snatch the children back, Alan, they will continue to transform. The power of transformation comes from Harbin's blood. To reverse the change, *you* must kill the goblin king,' ended Amiria.

Ari added, 'And it can only be you. They are your children. Your blood flows in them, as does Harbin's. Kill him and the power of his blood is broken. The children revert to human form again.'

'And there lies the problem,' sighed Bill. 'A goblin king has not been slain for a very long time. Harbin is cunning, ruthless, and powerful. Taking him down is a tall proposition. The last man to kill a goblin king was a bloke called Arthur Wellesley.'

Alan frowned. 'Why have I heard that name before?'

Bill smiled, but it was a smile without warmth. 'Wellesley's official title was The Duke of Wellington. He was famous for defeating Napoleon Bonaparte at a place called Waterloo.'

He stood up and walked to the window. Staring at the peak of Mount Taranaki, he said, 'And he had a full army to help defeat *that* goblin king. We have seven people. The guild and myself.' Bill turned to face Alan.

'And you.'

— Chapter Eight —

Zulear

Under Mount Taranaki, the war council of the goblins had assembled and were now deep in argument.

'Yes, the queen will be ready in four days' time. And yes, our horde will swell in numbers, able to wipe out the humans. There is one slight problem, though. WE ARE STUCK ON THIS MOUNTAIN! That blasted Māori power keeps us from our destiny!' shouted Crawfin.

'I see no solution to this,' said Arcmedan. 'Not only that, but I see another issue. The mountain cannot sustain the numbers we seek to add to our horde. Only goats and a few pigs now roam here — we have devoured all other creatures. What shall we do with more mouths to feed? Survive on berries?'

The council heatedly objected.

'We need meat!' roared Derrein.

Crawfin leapt up from the ground and spat, 'I say we must defer from adding more kin to our ranks. I will not live on damned berries!'

'But you cannot defer if the queen wills it. Her word will be law,' whispered Artex.

'She is from human stock, she can be restrained,' said Crawfin.

The argument ceased at once as Harbin leapt down from his chair.

'What did I just hear you suggest?'

Goblins edged away from Crawfin as he trembled a little in the dim light.

'L-Lord Harbin ... I err ... meant to say that ... well, we should consider asking her to not birth. I-I would never lay a hand on your queen. Her word will be law, I humbly accept that and —'

In the blink of an eye, Crawfin found himself pinned against the chamber wall, feet dangling above the ground. With his free hand, Harbin drew his sword and pointed it at Crawfin's throat.

'I accept your apology,' he said. 'Do not let there be a next time that you forget your manners ...' Dropping him to the ground, the goblin king faced the council. 'Listen to me! The Māori witchcraft that keeps us here will soon no longer be a problem.'

The council gasped.

'How can that be, my lord?' asked a stunned Arcmedan.

'Meido, Reido — bring me the wheel.'

Both wizards scuttled off, returning with a thick circular rock of black quartz. Carved coloured white lines ran across its face. Harbin took the wheel and raised it above his head.

'Behold, the Wheel of Zulear. Forged in the fires of Nea Kameni. Retrieved from the human refuse that claimed it after our Irish clan were wiped out. Taken with us on our journey south all those years ago. You all believe this to be only to be a symbol of the rise of our species, but it is so much more.'

A buzz of conversation began amongst the goblins.

'How so, my lord?' asked Derrein.

'I will reveal all in time, my brothers. But let me say this: The time draws near where we will no longer be confined by Māori mischief. The human race will fall ... and the time of the goblin will be at hand. This world will be ours!'

The goblin horde sat stunned. Then they leapt up and roared in unison. A roar of evil delight that echoed throughout the underground world.

***

'The sods are happy about something,' muttered Matt, as the cheering sound faded. He shrugged and returned to the wooden gate, trying to find a weakness. But try as he might, the beams were too strong. He gave up and sat down next to Leigh.

'Wish they'd hurry up and bring that food. I'm starving.' Matt turned to his sister. 'You okay?'

Leigh just stared ahead, not speaking.

'Leigh?'

Eyes red rimmed, Leigh ignored her brother.

'Look, sis, I know it seems bad. Okay ... it is bad — as bad as it gets. But we're going to get out of this, I promise. And don't forget Dad either. You can bet he's looking for us as well. Knowing Dad, he'll have everyone from the police to the Marines out looking for us. And he would have called Mum.'

Leigh finally turned to her brother. 'I-I wish M-Mum were here.' And with that, Leigh burst into tears. 'I D-DON'T W-WANT TO BE A GOBLIN QUEEN! PLEASE MAKE IT ALL STOP, MATT — PLEASE!'

Matt quickly grabbed his sister and hugged her fiercely, his own throat tight.

'I won't let them hurt you, Leigh.' Then his voice changed, taking on a primeval edge as he roared, 'I WON'T!'

Brother and sister stared at each other, shock naked in their yellow eyes.

'Oh my god, it's happening,' whispered Leigh.

'Yes, it is. Do you think this is all make-believe?'

They turned to see two new goblins carrying food and water. They dumped raw fish, fruit, and berries outside the barrier and a leather water bag.

'I am Adoien and this,' pointing to the other goblin, 'is Bezenar. Artex ordered you to be fed.'

Matt's hands shot between the beams and snatched the food. Throwing the fruit to Leigh, he bit into the raw fish and chewed down hungrily.

'See? You even eat like us,' grinned Bezenar.

Matt stopped mid-swallow as a pained expression formed on his face. He slowly gulped down the fish and then took smaller bites. Leigh did the same with the fruit, taking small bites out of the apple she held.

'No use trying to deny your future. It will come regardless,' said Bezenar. 'Resisting your destiny can be quite painful. Eat up; we'll be back later to collect you.'

Both goblins walked off. Matt waited till they were clear before resuming the tearing apart the food to ease his hunger. Leigh went to take a huge bite out of a fish when she stopped. She stared at her hand, eyes wide, before dropping the fish in horror. Green hairs had sprung from her knuckles.

***

The wooden gate creaked loudly, causing Matt and Leigh to jerk awake.

'Out,' motioned a goblin waiting outside the cave.

Leigh whispered to her brother, 'I don't remember falling asleep …'

'Whispering is wasted, human. We goblins have excellent hearing … as you'll soon find out,' smirked the goblin.

'Where are we going?' said Matt.

'To the pit to relieve yourselves. Then Harbin wishes to speak to you. Now move!'

They rose from the ground and walked out of the cave, receiving a shove for not moving quickly enough. Through the tunnel they moved, disturbed that they could see their surroundings quite well despite the dimness.

Leigh started to whisper to Matt before remembering. 'Why did we fall asleep so quickly?' she asked her brother.

'I don't —'

'We sleep mainly during the day,' interrupted their guide. 'The night is ours to own. We hunt the forest dwellers during the darkness. And if lucky enough, stumble across campers who make excellent meals.' The goblin stopped and grinned over his shoulder. 'Harbin will be pleased your sleep patterns have changed so quickly. It seems your change may be much more rapid than the others.'

Onwards, they travelled through the tunnel. Many smaller tunnels lead off the main one and Matt and Leigh stared into them as they passed. Some had goblins sleeping inside. Others held weapons and food. Then, before the entrance into the main chamber, stood a small tunnel. The foul smell coming from it was almost thick enough to be visible.

'Inside … and do not linger. Harbin does not like to be kept waiting.'

In they went and after a few minutes Matt and Leigh returned, their faces green, which had nothing to do with the goblin DNA flowing through their bodies. Their guide led them into the main chamber.

There sat Harbin, relaxing in his stone carved chair.

'Approach,' said Harbin. 'We shall speak of things you will come to know.'

Matt and Leigh came forward to stand before Harbin.

'That will be all, Steworan.'

The goblin bowed and left.

Harbin motioned for them to sit. He pulled out a foul-smelling pipe and lit it with the flaming torch next to his chair, eyes fixed on his new takings. After a few puffs, he said, 'Night will fall soon and my clan and I will exit our lair to hunt. You will remain here with Artex, Adoien, and Bezenar. Your education will begin tonight. As each day falls, you shall understand more. There will be tests for you to undergo.'

'What sort of test?' said Matt.

'Weapons handling, tracking, loyalty, goblin lore, to name a few.' Harbin grinned evilly and said, 'And, of course, hunting humans. This will all be taught to you.'

'I will never do that!' yelled Leigh.

Harbin jumped down from his chair and casually strolled up to Leigh. She shrank back as he felt her hair through his scarred fingers. 'Oh, but it won't be a choice. It will become an instinct you will constantly crave, Leighandra.'

Matt frowned. 'Leighandra?'

'The name you shall now go by.' Harbin took Leigh's hand and kissed it. 'The name of my queen.'

Matt knocked his sister's hand out of Harbin's grip, only to find himself lifted from the ground by his throat.

'You are now called Maorten,' he said silkily, 'and you simply must learn to curb that temper of yours. A taking has been killed before during the transformation, you know. It would be such a shame if my queen did not have her brother to keep her company. '

Harbin released Matt and yelled, 'Meido!'

From a tunnel in the far wall behind Harbin's chair, Meido scuttled out, wiping the sleep from their eyes.

'Yes, my lord?'

'Prepare the book of Zulear. Instructions are to commence immediately.'

'As you wish, my lord.'

Meido led Matt and Leigh towards their wizard's den. As Harbin watched them go, he pulled a knife from his belt and fiddled with the point, contemplating if Matt was worth the trouble.

— Chapter Nine —

Harbin's Hunch

Beccia knelt, her hands feeling the displaced grass under the window.

'Hard to tell for sure, but I would say at least six goblins,' she said as she examined the footprints. 'And see here — human footprints, two sets.'

Alan squatted next to Beccia. His hands gently traced the imprints of his children's feet.

'Lead the way,' said Amiria. 'Time grows short, the sun will fade soon.'

Makoa joined his sister, and they tracked the path of the goblins away from the lodge. The others fell in behind except for Alan, who stood rooted to the spot where his children once stood.

'Come on, mate,' said Bill gently.

Alan stared at the footprints for a few seconds more before leaving.

Bill whispered to Alan as he caught up, 'They're trackers, mate, and damn good ones at that. They'll find where the goblins entered the forest.'

Beccia and Makoa followed the faint signs of the goblins

until the tracks turned towards the road before ending.

'Clever creatures,' said Makoa grudgingly. 'The gravel road hides their tracks. We need to split up and search the edge of the woods to pick up the trail. Ari, do you feel anything?'

Ari closed his eyes. After a minute he said, 'Not sure, maybe to the west. There is something … just not sure what.'

'Right then,' said Bill. 'Amiria and I will search the Manaia Road exit. Makoa and Alan search the area east of the lodge. Beccia, Kyeua and Ari take the area west. Yell out if you spot anything.'

The group split up and went their ways, searching the grounds leading into the forest. The storm damage got in the way at times, and branches had to be moved from pathways. Each group had a tracker, although Amiria was not as gifted as Beccia and Makoa. So far, no tracks were spotted coming away from the road.

Beccia's group reached the forest edge and followed it towards Makoa and Alan, searching intensely for signs.

Suddenly, Ari stopped. 'We're being watched.'

'It can't be the goblins,' said Beccia. 'Still daylight.'

Kyeua looked towards the sun and said, 'But not for long. Already dark patches are forming in the forest valleys. Dark enough maybe for scouts to peer out of their bolt-holes. We need to be careful.'

Beccia nodded and motioned for them to continue.

Over at Manaia Road, Amiria and Bill were following the edge of the road as it left the grounds, when Amiria noticed something.

'Bill, look at that area near the signpost.'

She made her way over to the post and bent down, staring keenly at the flattened grass.

'Something was here. But I'm not sure what. We need Beccia or Makoa to interpret this.'

Bill moved out on the road, cupped his hands and went to yell out when Amiria said, 'Bill, wait a minute.'

The ranger looked confused at the request.

She motioned for him to return. As Bill strode back, she said, 'They will be here in due time. I need to talk to you alone before they arrive.'

'What about?' said Bill uneasily.

'Leigh ...'

***

'The tracks are old; they are of no use to us.' Makoa stood up and faced Alan. 'The creatures didn't pass this way.'

Alan said, 'I guess we keep moving towards Amiria and Bill then. Hell, I don't even know what I'm looking for?'

'It takes many years to become a skilled tracker, Alan. And you have to have the knack of noticing what others don't. See these signs,' he said, pointing to the faint marks on the ground. 'What made them? How old are they? Can you follow them and if so, where will they lead? You can be taught the basics of tracking if you wish to learn.'

'Right now, though, all I want to learn is how to get my kids back,' muttered Alan.

Makoa placed his hand on Alan's shoulder. 'We'll do that. We'll also be going with you when the time comes.'

'All of you?'

'Ari and Kyeua may stay at the lodge. Their skill in hand-to-hand combat is somewhat lacking.'

'Does that mean that Amiria will come along?' said a surprised Alan.

Makoa grinned. 'Don't let appearances fool you. She may

be of advancing age, but she's highly skilled in warfare. Come on, Alan; let's join up with the others.'

They continued to walk along the trail before spotting Beccia, Ari, and Kyeua approaching.

'Anything?' asked Beccia.

Makoa shook his head. 'Nothing fresh. They had to enter the forest somewhere, dammit!'

Ari said, 'We'll check with Amiria and Bill. See if they have anything.'

But as the group approached the road, Makoa held up his hand, causing everyone to halt. The sound of Amiria's and Bill's voices reached them easily, and to Alan's shock, they were quite heated.

'What's going on?' he said to Makoa.

Makoa muttered, 'I'm not sure.' He yelled, 'Amiria, we're returning!'

The voices stopped.

The group exchanged glances before moving on. Meeting up with Amiria and Bill, they were surprised to see Bill's face was flushed, chest heaving slightly. Amiria looked composed, but her eyes gave her away; they blazed furiously.

'Beccia, Makoa, there are signs here,' she stated. 'It may be what we are looking for.'

Makoa moved to examine the ground, as Beccia came over to Amiria. 'What's wrong? Were you arguing?' she whispered.

'Nothing is wrong. Please help your brother.'

Beccia hesitated briefly before joining Makoa. Bill kept his eyes hidden as he regained control over himself.

Alan strode over to Bill. 'Everything okay?'

'Yeah, mate. Just a … a minor disagreement, that's all. Nothing to worry about.'

'Minor? It sounded more than that. What —'

'Everyone, come here, look at this!' said Beccia.

The group gathered around Beccia and her brother.

'This is where they entered the forest, no doubt at all,' said Makoa. 'But not just footprints, but a large indentation on the ground. Someone fell here.'

'Fell or …?' said Amiria as her eyes darted to Alan.

'No, just fallen. No signs of attack. But there are many prints here. It must have been a large raiding party that took the children.'

Alan walked over to the indentation. 'Too big for my little girl. It must have been Matt.'

Amiria glanced up to the skies and said, 'It's getting dark. Let's return to the lodge for the night. Tomorrow morning, we'll start early and follow this trail.'

'Amiria, I felt a presence when we searched,' said Ari. He frowned suddenly. 'And I still do. Someone watches us.'

All turned quickly, staring at different parts of the forest.

'Let's call it a day, back to the lodge everyone,' ordered Amiria.

As they entered Konini Lodge, the last rays of sunlight illuminated the white tipped peak of Mount Taranaki like a beacon. Shadows travelled far and wide, bringing darkness below. From the forest floor, eyes watched from hidden bolt-holes as the glowing peak of the mountain extinguished.

Twilight.

Goblin sentries scuttled down from their posts, down the long, narrow tunnels and into the goblin domain. Goat horns were snatched from carry pouches and raised to foul lips. Throughout the chambers, tunnels, bolt-holes and sleeping caves, a piercing whine woke those who slept and excited those who were awake.

'Raiding party to the chamber!' commanded Derrein, as he walked through the larger tunnels. 'Come on, come on, gather your gear and get to it.'

The goblins saddled their packs and fastened their swords to their belts before moving off to the main chamber.

'What's happening?' said Leigh, watching the horde amble past their cave of instruction.

'Why, the nightly surge into the forest, of course,' grinned Reido. 'Our brothers gather to Lord Harbin to receive tonight's orders. With two extra mouths to feed, it should be a good hunt tonight. Surely you are both hungry?'

'No, we're not,' said Matt, but the growl from his stomach betrayed him.

Meido chuckled. 'Tomorrow will be day two of your transition. You will find your ability to deny your future becomes much more difficult. Speaking of which, next chapter Artex.'

Artex turned the page. 'Chapter six, the superior mind of the spiritual creature.'

He began reading whilst Meido and Reido paced behind Matt and Leigh, chanting softly. Despite trying their best not to listen, the words caressed their ears into accepting. And soon, their newly formed yellow eyes glazed over in compliance.

In the main chamber, Harbin gazed over at the assembled goblins. 'Tonight, we do something different.'

A murmur of voices rose from the assembly. Harbin raised his hand for silence.

'Derrein, take ten with you for the hunt. Make the bounty plentiful tonight, for we feast in honour of our change of fortunes. Crawfin, take six with you and inspect the observation posts. I want their concealment checked. Should they be noticeable, cover them and dig new ones. All others will follow me.'

'Where to, my lord?' questioned Arcmedan.

Harbin said, 'I have a hunch. We travel to the human shacks.'

'But, my lord, we cannot get within the human abodes without being invited?'

'I know that!' snapped Harbin, causing the front row of goblins to take a step back. After a minute, Harbin smiled. 'As I said, I have a hunch. A hunch that one of them will come to us tonight ...'

***

In the lodge, the fire crackled merrily, warming the room. Yet a chill still lingered in the air. And Alan was in no doubt on the reason. The argument between Amiria and Bill had not been normal; he had figured that out for himself. The tension in the lodge was palatable. Even now, the two avoided eye contact.

'If everyone's finished eating, I'll clean up,' said Bill.

Seeing no response, Alan stood up and said, 'I'll give you a hand.'

'Amiria, that presence I felt disturbed me. It can't have been goblins. But it was something alien in nature. Perhaps we should break out the grimoire to see if there is any way they can be out before sundown. I can't see how, but ...'

'Quite right,' sighed Amiria, pushing herself up from the overstuffed chair by the fireplace. 'I thought I knew that cursed book like the back of my hand, but ... but it is worth another look.' She pulled the grimoire from her backpack and placed it on the table, the rest of the guild eyeing it with subdued expressions.

In the kitchen, Bill began running the sink as Alan piled plates up.

'I know what you're going to say, Alan,' muttered Bill. 'Ask after we have your kids back, okay?'

Alan whispered, 'Answer me one question then, Bill, and I'll shut up. Tell me that argument had nothing to do with my son and daughter.'

Bill began busily cleaning plates, avoiding Alan's eyes. 'Like I said, mate, ask me afterwards.'

Alan dropped the tea towel. 'No need to, you already answered,' he said and walked out.

Bill cursed under his breath. Maybe he should have lied. But to tell the truth would also have been disastrous. If Alan even found out what Amiria had suggested ...

Chapter Ten

Enter the Trap

'What is the first law of the goblin race?' asked Meido.

In the cave of instruction, Matt and Leigh stood staring blankly ahead and replied in a toneless voice, 'Loyalty to the goblin lord.'

'What is the price of cowardice?'

'Death.'

'What are humans best for?'

'Dying and eating.'

'Good,' said Meido, 'very good.' He moved over to a wooden box and pulled out a sword. Placing the sword on the ground in front of Matt, he moved clear. He then nodded to Reido, who ducked outside.

The minutes passed, Matt and Leigh still motionless. The candlelight producing flickering shadows in the cave. Then —

'A human has entered! Defend the horde, Maorten!' yelled Meido.

Matt grabbed the sword and spun around to see a dim figure leaning against the cave wall. He charged the figure and slashed at it, his sword slicing through the branches, leaves and clay that made up a human dummy, destroying it in seconds.

Matt leapt backwards to adopt a crouched position, sword levelled, chest heaving, eyes blazing yellow.

Reido clapped. 'Oh, very good! He learns fast this one. I sense he will be an excellent warrior. Maybe even as good as Arcmedan.'

Meido snorted. 'Don't let Arcmedan hear that. He'll —'

'Grub is up!'

Derrein appeared at the entrance and unloaded a blood-soaked sack. 'Goat and pork tonight, and lots of it.'

Reido raised his hands and chanted a spell. Leigh's eyes came into focus. Matt looked down at the sword in his hand, then at the straw figure, letting the weapon fall to the floor. Before he could say anything, a hunk of pork landed at his feet.

'Eat, both of you. We continue the lessons after the meal.'

The goblin wizards departed. Matt and Leigh didn't talk, make eye contact or even join back up together. They chowed down instead, eyes gleaming at the food, nostrils sniffing in appreciation at the raw odour of the kill.

Artex looked on with a most peculiar expression on his face before leaving to have his own meal.

Meido and Reido, meanwhile, had met up with the raiding party in the main chamber.

'The hunt was good tonight,' said Meido as he licked the blood off his hands.

'Oh yes indeed,' said Crawfin with a belch. He picked up the leftover bones of the meal and threw them into the black water pit. 'The storm last night created much confusion for our forest meals. They are still scattered from their usual areas

— easy pickings.'

'What of Lord Harbin's group?' asked Reido.

'Harbin waits in place, ready to strike,' said Crawfin. 'Soon, very soon ...'

***

'Try to use two hands at all times, Alan,' said Beccia. 'By only using one, a heavy attack from a goblin can knock a sword out of your grip, and could even snap your wrist.'

'Right,' panted Alan. He still held on to the sword, but his wrists ached from the last strike, not to mention his shoulder.

'Okay, one more time. Take the stance and nod when you're ready.'

Alan planted his feet firmly and crouched down, holding his sword with both hands. Eyes fixed on his opponent as they taught him, he nodded. Before he knew it, his legs buckled under him and he was flat on his back, looking at the point of an arrow touching his forehead. Makoa had come in from the side and swept his legs from under him.

'Hey! That wasn't fair!'

Beccia grinned and moved forward to help Alan up as Makoa de-tensioned the bow and put the arrow back in his quiver.

'Goblins don't fight fair, Alan,' said Makoa. 'Yes, keep your eyes on your opponent, but use your peripheral vision on your flanks. I took you down because you were too fixated on your target. Tunnel vision is a bad thing in an all-in brawl. Goblins will usually attack in pairs. I can guarantee you at least one will try to skewer you from the side.'

'True that,' said Beccia. 'One thing you can count on is goblins will use every trick in the book to kill you. Like tripping you with branches, blinding you with dirt in the eyes, digging pits for you to fall in, vines to entangle you, just to name a few. The only rule you need to remember when fighting goblins is there are no rules.'

'Seems I have a lot to learn,' said Alan painfully.

Beccia smiled. 'And *that* is a good attitude to have. In my book, if you stop learning, you stop living. In any case, you will not face them alone, so your flanks will be covered, but keep in mind what I said.'

Amiria said, 'It's getting late. We should call it a night. Tomorrow will be a long and dangerous day. Starting at first light, we'll begin the search.'

They all began to pack it up when Ari said, 'Wait!'

'What is it, Ari?' frowned Amiria.

'I … I don't know. I felt something just then.' He moved over to the nearest window and peered outside. 'There is a presence nearby, I think.'

Makoa joined Ari, peering outside as well.

'Goblins?'

'I don't know,' replied Ari.

Alan looked towards the windows, fingers flexing around the hilt of his sword.

'It does not matter,' said Amiria. 'We are safe behind Tane's barrier. If it is a goblin, they cannot enter.'

'You never fully explained that to me,' said Alan. 'Just how did my words let them in?'

Makoa answered. 'As powerful as they are, the goblin race has limits. They cannot enter a human abode unless invited inside. It is known that by saying a name of someone you know and the word goblin together six times is an invitation for them to enter. How this rule occurred is vague.'

'You lowered Tane's barrier, Alan,' said Beccia. 'It wasn't

intentional ... but the result was still the same.'

Amiria said, 'goblin magic is powerful ... and so secretive that we have little true knowledge of how it works. We know they have wizards that practice magic, but that's about it.'

'It's still all so much to take in,' said Alan. 'And to believe ...'

Kyeua said, 'Alan, believe that anything is possible in this world. That way you are prepared should you one day face the impossible. And that time is now.' The seer took on a sad look as she added softly, 'Those who go through life thinking bad things won't happen to them get hurt the most when it does.'

Alan didn't reply. He just put his hands in his pockets and looked down at his feet.

'Well,' coughed Bill, 'as Amiria said, tomorrow's going to be a long day. Alan, Makoa and I will sleep down here. Amiria, Beccia, Ari and Kyeua should take the upstairs rooms. Let's break it up, eh?'

Amiria led her group to the stairs leading to the upper floor as Bill broke out pillows and blankets from the closet to make two extra beds in the living room. Makoa added a few logs to the fire as Bill sorted out the sleeping arrangements. Alan stood in the kitchen alone for a while, staring out the windows, occasionally glancing at his sword on the kitchen table.

***

Bill woke with a start. He raised his wrist to see 2 am on the luminous dial of his watch. The room was almost dark, the dying embers from the fire casting barely any light. Bill rolled over onto his side, vaguely wondering what had woken him. He glanced over at the sleeping form of Makoa on the floor and then to the couch.

Alan was gone.

'DAMN!'

Bill leapt up, wide awake now.

'Makoa, get up!'

The young Māori warrior was up and alert in seconds.

'Alan's gone,' said Bill over his shoulder as he hastened to check the ground-floor rooms. Makoa made for the stairs when Bill cursed again.

'Oh crap!'

Makoa halted to see Bill staring at the kitchen countertop. Alan's sword was missing.

Bill raced to the door and flung it open. He scanned the darkness but saw nothing. Turning to Makoa, he said, 'Get the others!'

***

Harbin sat on his haunches, chewing on a pig bone. Around him, goblins sat sharpening their swords with stones or talking quietly amongst themselves. The mood was not good. The night was waning with dawn not far off. For the first time in eons, Harbin doubted himself. For hours they had camped in the forest near the human settlement, but no signs of any humans. Could his recent excitement of his new queen have clouded his judgement? Harbin pondered this unwelcome thought.

Adoien burst through the tree line, panting heavily.

'Lord Harbin, a light to the east!'

Throwing down the pig bone, he stood up. 'Stay in the tree line, keep quiet and ready your weapons.' Harbin grinned from ear to ear. His foresight was still intact.

***

The light from the torch played over the imprints of Matt and

Leigh. Alan bent down, placed his sword on the ground and again felt where his children once stood.

'I'm coming, kids,' he whispered. He pointed the torch towards the pathway that led in to the forest, picked up the sword and moved on. As he moved towards the dense foliage, Alan stupidly held to a flickering hope that this whole thing was not real, despite all that happened so far.

He moved deeper into the forest, losing track of time. The tree branches swayed in the wind. To Alan, it was an uneasy sound, like a warning.

The bushes to the left of him rustled heavily, swaying back and forth, causing Alan to swing the beam of light that way.

'Matt? Leigh?'

The bushes stilled their movement.

Alan yelled, 'KIDS? IS THAT YOU? IT'S ME, DAD!'

'Nope. Guess again, fool!'

Arcmedan leapt out of the bushes, his sword flaying through the air. Alan screamed and fell backwards as the blade cut through the air where his head once was.

'Stand down, Arcmedan!'

Harbin strode into the open as Arcmedan backed off, pouting he had missed taking the human's head.

Alan's eyes bulged in horror as more goblins emerged from the bushes. And now ... finally, at the end, he believed.

Everything was real.

Every story, every word, every minute since Bill has said *"goblins have your kids."* All the truth's combined to deliver the final blow to Alan Dwyer. He gave out a surrendering groan.

Harbin looked at him with smug eyes. 'Well, well, now what do we have here? Last time I saw you, I was about to slit your throat as you slept. But I didn't kill you the night I took your children. I wanted you to feel despair — the despair only a failed, worthless father would feel. Now I'll take your severed head back to my queen to show her how weak humans really are.'

Alan scrambled to his feet and ran. A hastily swung blade from Arcmedan cut him as he flew past, causing blood to flow from his shoulder. Terror had him cannoning through the rest of the goblins and into the forest. They tore after him, screeching in glee.

'Capture him, but do not kill him!' yelled Harbin. 'That is my pleasure alone.'

He grinned, trotting casually behind his chasing horde. This would be easy, as the cowardly fool still carried the light. The goblins followed the swaying light through the forest with ease.

Outside the lodge, the guild hastily scanned the forest in different directions.

'There! Over there!' shouted Beccia, pointing towards a rapidly shrinking pin-prick of light to the east. 'Where the hell is he going?'

'Not just that … listen,' said Amiria. The whoops and hollers of goblins giving chase echoed through the trees. 'The goblins are here. Alan is being hunted.'

'Oh crap!' cried Bill.

Without a word, Makoa and Beccia took off towards the fleeting light. Bill followed, but could not match their speed and was quickly left behind.

Amiria turned to Ari and Kyeua. 'We'll stay close to the lodge. Ari, prepare yourself.'

***

Alan ran blindly, branches scraping his face as he tore through the thick growth. More than once he tripped over tree-roots, only to get up and run in a different direction. He was hopelessly lost and knew it.

'Ahhh ... gaagh!'

He came to a shuddering halt as he became entangled in the hanging vines of a large tree. The creatures were closing, their gibbering voices getting louder and louder by the second. Alan could not get free of the vines. He knew now he would not get away. They had him. He was about to die. A terror filled scream tried to escape him but his voice failed.

'Give me the light, you!' urged a low voice.

Alan looked down at the voice and almost passed out. A small hairy creature with large round eyes looked back at him.

'There is no time, human. Quickly now!'

Alan dropped the torch out of shock.

The creature picked up the torch and hurled it far away. He pulled a small dirk out from his belt and cut the vines free.

'Run with me. Come, come quickly, tall one.'

The creature took off. Alan felt reality slipping away as the goblins burst into view. He swayed. Then pain erupted from his shin as the creature ran back and kicked him.

'Move it or die, stupid!'

That did it. Alan chased after the creature like a man possessed.

The small furry being pulled out a flute as he ran and blew into it. From the treetops, a shrilling cadence replied. Alan snatched a look back and was astounded to see a dozen of the same little beings swing down from the trees and land on the goblin's backs, beating them furiously with rocks.

The creature stopped and pointed south. 'Go that way. Get to your home, you. Do not come back here ever again. Go!'

Alan finally found his voice. 'W- what are you?' he croaked.

'Friends of the forest, enemies of the goblins.' He blew the flute again. 'We go now. Before they come, go. Go quickly. Go now!'

The furry little creature scurried off and was lost to the forest in seconds. Alan blundered towards the pointed direction, creating a hefty racket as he ran.

***

'I think I see the flashlight,' said Makoa. 'This way!'

'No, stop! Something's approaching from the right,' said Beccia. She raised her sword at the oncoming threat.

Makoa strung an arrow and waited. Bill finally caught up and took position next to him, gripping his swords tight, his face pale but determined.

Alan burst into view.

'RUN! THEY'RE COMING!'

He skidded to a stop, chest heaving, his shirt a bloody mess. 'T-There … must be dozens of them,' he managed to spit out. 'We got to go!'

'Back to the lodge,' urged Bill. 'We don't have —'

Makoa's arrow flew past Alan's shoulder and thudded into a goblin emerging from the scrub. It screamed and tumbled out of sight.

'Let's go!' cried Beccia, and the group took flight.

Makoa kept turning as he ran to fire arrows into the darkness. Sometimes, a scream of pain could be heard through the sounds of thundering feet. After what seemed like an eternity, they were in a clearing next to Manaia Road. They stopped for the briefest moment to get their bearings.

'Keep running!' yelled Amiria. 'You're not safe yet!' But even as they turned towards the lodge, Harbin burst through the tree line with his pack. That briefest moment cost them dearly.

'Get them!' roared the goblin king. He batted away Makoa's incoming arrow with his sword and then rushed forward. Bill met his incoming blade with his own and sparks flew.

'Well, well, little Billy the ranger,' sneered Harbin. 'Long time no see. Have you missed me? How's the scar I gave you? Want another?' He flicked his blade towards Bill, who ducked and then kicked Harbin's legs from under him. Bill's sword slashed and drew blood as a surprised Harbin fell backwards, clutching his cheek.

Bill's eyes lit up with savage pleasure. 'I've learned quite a bit from the Māori since our last meeting, you evil son of a bitch.'

Harbin got up, eyes slits of rage. He felt the cut on his cheek. 'You'll pay for that, Ranger.'

'Get to the barrier, Bill, we can't hold them!' yelled Beccia.

Out of the corner of his eye, Bill could see Makoa and Beccia fully engaged with three goblins with many more emerging from the trees, howling battle-cries. Alan was unarmed, trying to wrestle a goblin who was intent on trying to bite into his neck. In seconds, the group was surrounded, their haven of the lodge now cut off.

Harbin raised his sword. 'Now you die!' he snarled and lunged towards Bill.

From the lodge Amiria commanded, 'NOW, ARI, NOW!'

Ari raised his hands and a powerful chant rent the air.

HINE-NUI-TE-PO, GODDESS OF THE NIGHT AND UNDERWORLD. THE UN-HUMANS OFFEND YOUR

FATHER'S FOREST! RELEASE YOUR POWER, SAVE THE MORTALS FOR YOUR OWN JUDGEMENT!'

The night sky took on an instant reddish aura. The very air seemed to sizzle with some hidden electricity. Then the ground rumbled and shook. Humans and goblins engaged in battle were thrown apart from each other like rag dolls. Amiria and Kyeua ran towards the stunned group as the red aura faded from the night sky.

'Get up!' yelled Amiria. 'Before the goblins recover. RUN!'

Beccia and Makoa got up and staggered towards the lodge.

Bill got to his feet too and grabbed Alan, who seemed to have trouble recovering from the blast.

Of the goblins, Harbin recovered first. He grabbed his sword and charged after the fleeing group. He was within feet of Bill and Alan when he slammed into an invisible barrier and fell backwards, clutching his face. Tane's barrier revealed itself with patterns of electric blue sparks glimmering around all the dwellings.

They were safe.

'Human cowards, hiding behind your unfit gods. Come out and fight!'

Amiria moved up to the shimmering blue field and said, 'We will foul one, we will. But on our terms, not yours.'

Harbin slashed with his sword in frustration, the blade carving red sparks along the blue veil. 'Foul Māori witch! Your time will come soon enough.'

'How's that cut feel, Harbin?' taunted Bill. 'You want to fight? One on one then, just you and me. Tell your gibbering jackals to back off and I'll show you some more tricks I've learnt.'

Harbin barked, 'You think I hurt you last time, ranger? Well, you have not—'

'My lord, dawn comes soon. We must return now to make it back in time.'

Harbin spun around and struck Gregorn, sending him flying backwards. 'SILENCE!' he roared.

Arcmedan lowered his head and said, 'It is true, my lord. Look to the east.'

The goblin king did so. Pink and orange hues rose from the horizon, reaching upward with every minute.

'Bah!'

He turned to the guild and growled, 'Another time then.' He grinned wickedly at Alan and added, 'I'll tell your kids you said hi ...'

Harbin raised both fists and crossed his arms. The pack of goblins responded and retreated to the forest, Arcmedan helping a groggy Gregorn to the tree line. The rustling of the retreating goblin pack through the trees was heard for a few minutes before silence fell in the clearing.

Amiria turned furiously on Alan. 'What were you thinking, you absolute blithering idiot! You could have gotten us all killed!'

Alan tried to speak but only managed a groan.

Makoa moved fast, but not fast enough to catch Alan before he collapsed on the ground.

Chapter Eleven

Wood Elves and Warriors

Under Mount Taranaki, sentries sounded the call as Harbin's group entered.

'Food!'

'At once, my lord,' bowed Crawfin, who scurried off. Within a few minutes, sacks of meat and berries were brought in and dispersed to the hungry party. Harbin ate quietly, a sour expression on his face.

Reido applied herbs and tree sap pasted onto a large leaf to the goblin king's face while Meido quietly chanted, causing the concoction to glow yellow as it healed the wound. Harbin winced and then continued to eat.

'What happened, my Lord?'

Harbin growled, 'Our little friends turned up.'

Reido frowned. 'The gremlins? But they have not troubled us for some time.'

'We had the father. Had him trapped in the forest, scared out of his wits, bleeding and whining. Then those little runts ambushed us. By the time we threw them off, he had reached the Māori. Then, they cowered behind their magic.'

Derrein said in a greasy voice, 'But the gremlins could not

hurt you, my Lord.'

Harbin felt the leaf and said, 'The gremlins did not do this. That bastard ranger did.'

A murmur of whispers broke out.

'Bill is still there?' asked Meido. 'But he was a pushover last time, my lord. If not for the Māori woman, he would have died from your hand.'

Harbin jumped down from his chair and paced before his assembled horde.

'That was five years ago. Much has changed, it seems,' he muttered. 'The ranger was untrained back then. The Māori have been busy with him. His skill with the blade has improved tenfold.'

Crawfin stepped forward. 'Let me seek him out at the next moon then. Let me kill him and bring his head to you.'

Harbin shook his head. 'They will be alert now. The father will not be so stupid to wander in our domain at night.' A smile formed on his foul lips. 'But then again, maybe he is. Meido, bring my queen and Maorten before me, then tend to the wounded.'

'Yes, my lord,' said Meido and departed.

Harbin continued to pace as the idea formed. He halted. *Yes,* he mused, *with the right bait, all sorts of stupid can be coaxed out of a human.* He walked over to the meat sack and pulled out a goat rib. As he chewed, he figured it would be an excellent test for his new taking as well. *Oh yes. A fine test of the state of the transformation,* chuckled Harbin.

He looked up from his meal as Meido approached with Matt and Leigh. He grinned in delight at what he saw.

'Greetings,' said Harbin. 'You both look very fine today. A very fine pair of goblins indeed.'

Matt and Leigh couldn't bear to look at each other anymore. Fine green hair covered their entire bodies now. Their feet and hands had stretched out painfully, nails twice as long as before. The eyes had fully developed the night vision that went with goblin DNA. Leigh's hair had changed colour to a dull dirty orange. The old Matt would have cracked a joke about having a sister as a ranga, but Matt's sense of humour was long gone. Even since the sword instruction, he had resorted to brooding silence. Leigh could not get her brother to talk much, which frightened her.

Seeing as Matt hadn't replied, Leigh said, 'What do you want?'

'It is not you I want, my queen — not yet, anyway. It is Maorten who interests me.'

'His name is Matt!' said Leigh.

Harbin laughed. A mocking laugh that was repeated by other goblins nearby. He turned to Matt. 'What is your name?'

Matt remained silent.

The goblin king strode forward so his and Matt's face almost touched. He repeated the question.

'What is your name, my warrior?'

Matt eyed his new master. He then growled, 'My name is Ma … Ma … ORTEN!'

Leigh's hands flew to her mouth. 'Oh no!'

Harbin roared with laughter. 'Oh yes, my queen. And by this time tomorrow, you shall also be using your new name with pride.' He turned to Matt. 'Now, my warrior, the next moon will be a special night for you. For you will accompany the hunt to the forest. And if you are very lucky, you may even meet your daddy.'

Leigh looked thunderstruck, realising she hadn't thought

of her father since yesterday.

Harbin read her face easily. 'And before long, Leighandra, you will not think of him again. Take them away. In fact, upgrade them to a normal sleeping chamber.'

Meido and Reido came forward and led brother and sister away. Harbin yawned and said, 'Right, to rest, my brothers. We plan tonight's foray one hour before sunset.' The goblins retired to their sleeping quarters, passing Matt and Leigh's new abode. Leigh waited till they were gone before talking.

'Matt, you might be able to escape tonight. Please fight it. You could even get to Dad ...'

'Dad? Yeah, right. So, where is he then?' muttered Matt. He got up from his new vine and leaf bed and spoke forcefully. 'Is he even looking for us? We've been here nearly two days and no sign of him. It's because of him we're in this mess. His stupid prank, his stupid idea. His stupid fault!'

'He couldn't have known this would happen,' said Leigh. 'He —'

'I DON'T CARE! I really don't! Scaring you all the time was his business and you always let it happen, but dragging me into it sucks. Now, because of it, I'm becoming a god-damn goblin!'

Anger stirred for the first time in Leigh. 'Oh, so it's my fault now?'

'Yeah, it is. If you weren't such a wimp, he wouldn't have bothered with his idiotic pranks in the first place.'

'I AM NOT A WIMP!' roared Leigh. Her eyes started radiating their own yellow glow. 'You take that back!'

Matt advanced on her sister. 'No, you are a wimp. A sooky little mummy's girl who should have stayed —'

Leigh's arm shot out and lifted her brother as easily as the wind does a leaf. She threw him against the cave wall and yelled in triumph as he bounced off the wall and hit the ground.

'Don't mess with me, you fat tub of lard!' she thundered, breathing hard through flaring nostrils.

A slow clap began. Leigh wheeled around to see Harbin standing at the entrance, eyes gleaming in pleasure.

'The power of a queen is the strongest of all goblins, even my own. You have taken your first step towards a new future, Leighandra. Admit it. That felt good, didn't it?' Without waiting for a reply, Harbin strolled away with a spring in his step.

Leigh's heart pounded and her chest heaved as she watched Harbin leave. She turned to the sound of groaning and saw her brother trying to get up. The yellow glow faded from her eyes and she raced forward to help Matt up.

'Oh, Matt, I'm so sorry! I … I didn't mean for that to happen. I couldn't help it. Please forgive me.'

Matt leaned against the wall, naked fear in his eyes. Leigh burst into tears.

Matt took a deep breath, wincing as he did so, and put a furry arm around Leigh.

'It's okay, sis. I'm sorry for what I said. I don't know what came over me. It's like … I dunno… if I feel angry or upset, it feels good and I want more. Feeling angry at Dad felt so right. I didn't want it to stop. And when you tried to defend him, I hated you for it. I wanted to —'

'Shhh!' said Leigh as foot-steps approached.

Artex entered with Adoien and Bezenar. 'No need to hush, Leighandra, your words carry quite far.'

'We want a word before you slumber,' said Adoien.

Matt eyed them warily. 'What about?'

Bezenar said, 'Tonight, Adoien and I will be by your side as your guardians, Maorten. We will teach you trail lore as we hunt. But be warned. Any attempt to escape and you will be killed. Is that clear?'

Matt nodded.

Leigh kept her eyes on Artex. There was something in his look, something different from the others. Her questioning gaze was returned by Artex before he looked away.

'Leave us,' he said.

Adoien and Bezenar turned sharply to Artex. 'But we have more to discuss with the humans on tonight's raid.'

'I will do that. Leave … now!'

Both goblins hesitated briefly before turning away, muttering between themselves.

Artex gave it a few minutes before sitting down and motioning for Matt and Leigh to do the same.

'When you rise this evening, more changes will occur. Mainly a change in attitude. I warn you both to be prepared.'

Leigh frowned. 'Why are you warning us at all?'

'Because tonight Maorten joins the hunt as a warrior, my queen,' said Artex. 'Lord Harbin will use Maorten to lure your father into the woods again. If your father ventures into the woods, Bill will follow him, which is who my lord really wants. Once he kills Bill, your father will be next.'

'Well, then I won't co-operate,' said Matt.

Artex gave Matt a grave look. 'As I said, changes will occur when you have awoken from today's slumber. You will find not co-operating most difficult. In fact, tonight you may find your feeling towards your father rather different than they are now …'

Artex rose and made his way towards the cave exit. But before he left, he halted and over his shoulder he said, 'If you value your father's life, Maorten, use whatever strength you have left in your heart tonight to warn him off.' Then he was gone.

Matt retired to his bed, deep in thought.

Leigh watched him for a minute before saying, 'Something's not right about Artex. All the goblins have been horrible to us most of the time, but not him. He talks to us differently too, but I'm not sure why.'

Matt yawned. 'Maybe he fancies you?'

'Not funny. Not funny at all!'

A larger yawn escaped Matt, and he closed his eyes. 'Whatever. I'm hitting the hay.'

Leigh lay down on her bed too, too. She whispered, 'You will try to warn Dad if he comes, won't you?'

Matt mumbled something incoherent and rolled over. Leigh sighed and closed her eyes as sleep came for her. It would not have come so easily, had she known the conflict bubbling inside her brother. For Matt slept with visions of hugging his dad one minute and savagely wringing his neck the next.

***

As his kids drifted off to sleep, Alan stirred from his. Voices washed in and out of his fogged mind, but none of them made any sense.

'We are in no condition to search today. All of us need to rest.'

'We are losing time that we can ill afford. Remember what is at stake here.'

'What choice do we have? Alan's in no condition to come

with us. And he needs to.'

'A little higher and he would have taken that sword hit in the throat. God knows how he got away from them. I wouldn't have thought it possible?'

'Either way, with time running out, we must face the possibility of having to do the unthinkable.'

'NO, Amiria!' came an angry shout. 'I told you to forget that. I will never be a part of it!'

That was enough to jolt Alan awake. He sat up at and instantly regretted it, letting out a loud groan and clutched his shoulder.

Bill came into his view. A gentle hand came to rest on his good shoulder. 'How do you feel?'

'Awful. W-what happened?'

'You passed out. Not surprising, considering the amount of blood you lost. You took a nasty gash to your shoulder.'

Alan tried to stretch his left arm out but winced in pain and gave up. He looked around to see Amiria gazing at him.

He stood up and swayed a little. 'How long have I been out?'

'A few hours,' said Bill. 'We carried you in after the goblins retreated. Ari stitched up your shoulder. Might sting for a while, mate.'

Kyeua walked in from the kitchen with a cup of strong coffee for Alan. Taking it, Alan said, 'Thank you.' He nodded to Ari and added, 'For both.'

Ari said, 'You ought to be in hospital. I also used a healing chat to that will heal the wound fast, but I can't guarantee infection won't set in.'

Amiria grumbled, 'Not only that, but we will lose most of the day, thanks to your foolish effort.'

Kyeua frowned. 'This doesn't help matters, Amiria. What's done is done.'

Alan looked to the floor and mumbled, 'I'm sorry I messed up so badly… and for putting you all in danger.'

Kyeua said, 'You will need to rest today. Makoa and Beccia are in town picking up a few supplies and will bring back antibiotics for you. Rest up today and tomorrow you'll be good to go. Go out now with us in your weakened state and you'll be a liability. Understand?'

'Okay,' muttered Alan and drained his coffee in one go.

Bill said, 'Tell us what happened out there, Alan. And why you went out alone. Was it Harbin who cut you?'

'I don't know,' said Alan. 'A goblin leapt out from the bushes and took a swipe at me. Then more turned up. A big one then told the others to back off. He called me a worthless father and that I was about to die. I took off in a panic and one of them sliced me as I barged through them.'

'We saw the light from your torch,' said Bill. 'Makoa and Beccia reacted first to get to you. But then you came out from the opposite direction?'

Alan grimaced. 'Yeah, I got trapped in some vines. I was a dead man. Then a little furry creature turned up and threw the torch away. He then cut me free and told me to run.'

'WHAT!' cried Amiria.

'There were a whole bunch of them,' said Alan. 'They looked like little furry gnomes. Umm, they called themselves "Friends of the forest, enemies of the goblins." Anyway, this one cut me free of the vines and blew into a flute of sorts. Next minute, those things were jumping out of trees and attacking the goblins. Allowed me just enough time to get away.'

Silence hung heavily in the lodge. 'What? You don't believe me?'

Bill said, 'Alan, I've been here a very long time and I've never seen anything like what you described. Are you sure you're not imagining it? You know you took a fair bump on the noggin when you collapsed.'

Alan shook his head. 'No, it was real. As real as the pain throbbing through my shoulder. Bill, I would be dead if they hadn't intervened.'

Amiria stood up suddenly. 'No ... It can't be ... it just can't!' She strode into the other room, grabbed the grimoire off the other table and came back. She flicked to a chapter mid-way through and laid out the book for the others.

They all stared at the heading.

THE WOOD ELVES

'Alan, was this the creature?' she asked.

Alan leaned forward and stared at the drawing under the title. The image showed a small creature, similar to a miniature furry human-being. The eyes were quite large, fingers overly large and ears slightly pointed. The creature wore a green vest, brown trousers, and carried what looked like a slingshot.

Alan looked up. 'I guess so. Too close to be a coincidence,' he said.

Ari and Kyeua exchanged stunned looks.

Amiria said, 'There are no records of wood-elves being encountered in New Zealand before. So, what you saw was not them.' She suddenly smiled. 'I believe they may be the Te-Tini-O-Hakuturi.'

Ari looked dumbstruck. 'This would be a wonder if true.

The Māori have not had contact with Tane's offspring for eons.'

'Okay, what the heck are Te-Tini-O-Hakuturi?' demanded Alan. 'Jesus, just how many mythical creatures do you have running around this place?'

Amiria replied, 'The Te-Tini-O-Hakuturi are the guardians of the forests, also known as the offspring of Tane. They are small creatures who, unlike their wood elf brethren, are shy and avoid humans. They prefer to be left alone. It is said they are of a softer nature than wood elves and, most of all, loathe goblins.'

Bill asked, 'So if they avoid humans, why did they save Alan?'

Kyeua said, 'Something has changed to cause them to reveal themselves to us. Something that maybe threatens *their* existence?'

Alan said excitedly, 'Leigh! Leigh being taking has put them in danger. They said they were the enemies of the goblins. If they know Harbin has my kids and one is a girl, a new army of goblins would be an enormous threat.'

'Exactly,' said Kyeua.

Beccia said, 'They may be our allies and help get the children back.'

'Perhaps we should go out today to try to make contact?' suggested Ari. 'We can also do some scouting of the forest, check for more bolt-holes and such. We won't need Alan for that.'

Amiria went to say no, but halted. She took on a thoughtful look for a few minutes before saying, 'That's a good idea, it will save us time. We'll take the old map with us and plot any new bolt-holes we find. It will put us in good stead for tomorrow.'

'Right then,' said Ari. 'Let's get organised before Makoa and Beccia get back.'

Bill pulled out his pipe and stuffed some tobacco into the bowl. He stood and said to Alan, 'Come outside for a minute, mate, I want to have a chat.' Without waiting for an answer, Bill moved towards the front door. Alan followed suit.

On the front porch, Bill sat staring at the mountain, puffing his pipe, deep in thought. Alan gingerly came up and sat down beside him. 'I didn't know you smoked, Bill?'

'Only when I'm stressed,' grunted Bill. After a few minutes, he said, 'I need to tell you my story. Five years ago, the guild and I fought to save the Hellier kids. We failed to retrieve them before they turned into goblins.' He glanced sidelong at Alan. 'We failed because *I* failed.'

'What do you mean?' asked Alan.

'I was a touch arrogant and kind of headstrong back then. The guild trained me and Dave Hellier as best they could, but I fancied myself in a fight. Did a bit of boxing at school so I thought I could take care of myself. And of course, there was a big part of me that still didn't believe the guild over this goblin business — just like you. So, I took the training with a pinch of salt, paid attention of course, but didn't really absorb the lessons from Makoa and Beccia.

'So, the following day, we located a bolt-hole and squeezed into a cave that led to the goblin lair. There were bones everywhere and flickering lights in the tunnels. I got a bit uneasy, you know? Things were a bit more serious now. We travelled for what seemed like hours. Then, out of a tunnel to the right of us, emerged a goblin. Now it's all horribly real to me, Alan. I nearly soiled myself when I saw it. The goblin tried to raise the alarm and got an arrow in his throat from Makoa for his trouble. Amiria urged us to hurry and find the kids while she went with Dave, Ari and Beccia go to find Harbin. We search as fast as we could, trying to keep quiet. We found them. Two kids in a small cave with wooden bars at the entrance.'

Alan listened intently, the pain of his shoulder forgotten as Bill unloaded his guilt.

'It was horrible. They looked all green and ugly, and to me, desperate to get out of there. When they saw us, they started yelling for help. Makoa tried to warn them to shut up, but it was already too late. Before I knew it, goblins poured out of tunnels, including Harbin himself. It all seemed so surreal, you know? He went straight for me and … and I froze. I was terrified beyond all reason. I didn't even get my sword up to defend myself. He sliced me bad.'

Alan reached over placed a reassuring hand on Bill's shoulder, remembering the deep scar Bill had showed him.

'Makoa couldn't help me; he was fighting for his own life. Harbin went to finish me when Amiria and the others came rushing out from another tunnel. She is very good with a sword, mate, better than most of the goblins. She held Harbin at bay long enough for Makoa to throw me over his shoulder. Ari then let off a flare and threw it at the goblins to distract them, then we took off. We got out of there by the skin of our teeth. Dave never got the chance to kill Harbin because of me.'

'Jesus, Bill,' was all Alan could say.

'I'd lost so much blood,' continued Bill. 'The guild got me back to the park and bundled me into my car. On the way to the hospital, Ari stabilised me. Without him, I wouldn't have made it.'

Bill stood up and walked a few feet away. Over his shoulder he said, 'That was the end for the Hellier kids. The goblins had them now. It was my fault, Alan. You hear me? My fault for not listening. Dave and his wife lost their kids because of me! And Harbin let me know too. When I'd healed enough to return to work, I found carved on a tree near the Wilkies Pools: *"Come back soon, Billy"* The bastard even knew my name.'

Noticing his pipe had gone out, Bill reached into his pocket for his tobacco pouch. As he worked the makings of another pipe, he said, 'I wanted you to know my history, mate. And the consequences of not thinking things through. Of acting prematurely or trying to do things yourself. These goblins are killers at the best of times. Now that they have a queen in the making, their savagery in guarding the Hellier kids will pale compared to what they will do to guard your daughter.'

There was a long silence between the two as Bill stared ahead, smoking his pipe.

Alan finally spoke. 'I get it. I shouldn't have gone off on my own.'

'So why did you?'

Alan shrugged.

'Shrugging doesn't cut it, mate. I need to know,' said Bill. 'We all need to know.'

Bill waited. Alan took a deep breath and then blurted, 'I still had hope that this was all a...'

'A scam?'

'Yes, err no — oh hell, I don't know. It's just that a part of me waited to be ridiculed for believing in this goblin tale. So, I went out to find them myself. To prove no one would sucker me in. Or, or hurt me.'

'Eh? What do you mean "hurt you?"' asked Bill.

Alan's long hidden fears opened like a floodgate.

'I copped so much ridicule early in my life. I was a very scrawny kid, so I got bullied a lot. Teased, tricked, you name it. And things got far worse as an adult when I was in the military. I was a screw-up as a kid and that didn't change into adulthood when I wore a uniform. People would play pranks on me, nasty ones that were quite humiliating. It wasn't long before that turned into physical assaults. The Navy of the 80s was a rough place. It seemed that when I trusted someone the most is when they would turn on me. I became quite introverted, vowing never to be taken for a ride or trust anyone again. I vowed never to be hurt again.

'Last night I went out full of piss and wind, thinking I've got this. No one's going to humiliate me! But the further I moved into the forest, that old fear returned. I doubted myself. But when that goblin charged out of the bushes, I froze too, mate. In that second, I knew I was wrong about everything. The kid's lives flashed before my eyes as did mine. Oh god, Bill, I am so sorry about everything. I just wanted to get away from that thing. Then more of them charged out to get me. It's like they were waiting for me.'

Bill frowned. 'They must have been watching the lodge to pick you up so quickly. Amiria will need to know that.'

'I'm sorry I stuffed up everything, Bill. I'll do anything to fix this and get Leigh and Matt back. Whatever it takes.'

'As I said, they'll guard Leigh with all the rage they can muster. We'll have to tread very carefully when we're out in the forest from now on.'

A car appeared from Manaia Road. 'Looks like Makoa and

Beccia have returned,' said Bill. 'Let's go back inside. You look like you could do with some more rest. I'll talk to the guild to see what the plan is now. I'd say we'll be gone for a couple of hours at most ...'

Alan rose and winced. 'Okay, and, Bill, thank you for that. I've never spoken to anyone about that before, not even my wife.'

'It's never good to keep stuff bottled up, mate. When it finally comes out, it can cause a lot of heartache. Been there and done that. And I get never wanting to be hurt again, I really do. I've been taken for a fool, lied to and taken advantage of in my time. I've been burnt too many times to remember. Which is why I'm a park ranger. Trees make better friends than people.'

As they moved toward the door into the lodge, Bill said something that halted Alan in his tracks.

'Alan, this is not meant to hurt you, you've been through a damn rough ride so far, but as a friend, I need to say this.'

'Say it, Bill. I feel like I'm going to deserve it, anyway.'

Bill paused and then said, 'I wonder how Leigh felt when you played pranks and tricked her. Was she as trusting of you the most as her father, just before you scared her with pranks? Is she becoming more introverted? Did *she* feel humiliated? I'm not trying to make you feel bad, mate, honestly, I'm not. But now maybe you should look to your own past to see what sort of future you should have with your kids when we get them back. Sorry, mate, but now was the time to say that when what happened last night was still raw in your memory.'

Bill squeezed his friend's good shoulder and walked back into the lodge.

Alan Dwyer stood there for some time, staring at the

mountain, searching his past … and his heart. What he found was not pretty. A tear ran down his cheek as he sat back down to be alone for a while.

Chapter Twelve

The Natawidu

'Will he follow orders tonight?'

Meido looked over at the sleeping form of Matt. 'Yes, my lord, his humanity fades fast. Your queen is a different matter, though.'

'Explain,' growled Harbin.

Artex came forward and spoke. 'My lord, Leigh is —'

'Leighandra!'

'Ah, yes, my apologies, Lord Harbin. Leighandra resists the change. A girl-child has never been taken by the horde before. We do not yet know how or why she has not progressed as far as Maorten.'

Reido said, 'We will know more when she wakes this evening.'

Harbin ordered, 'Separate them. When she wakes, move her to her new quarters,' before storming out.

Artex sighed and turned to Leigh. Her face was peaceful as she slept. Traces of humanity remained in her features, which saddened him.

Reido noticed this and warned, 'Remember, Artex, you are here to train her and no more. Should Harbin sense otherwise, your life may be forfeit.'

Artex said indignantly, 'I know that. I serve Lord Harbin's wishes and his only.'

'See that you remember that,' growled Meido before he and Reido left.

Artex covered Leigh with a rough blanket. He glanced at Matt before leaving, noting Matt held very few of the traces of humanity that Leigh still carried. Tonight, he understood Matt would most likely taste blood.

Who's though, was another matter.

***

Alan rested in the loft for most of the morning as the pain medication did its job. But it was a restless sleep as Bill's words plagued his dreams. In the lounge room, Bill whistled appreciatively as Makoa showed off a new gain from the town visit.

'Where on earth did you get that?'

Makoa grinned as he wielded his new toy.

'Multi-shot crossbow. I know a person who makes them. It can fire four arrows before reloading. The arrow shafts are wood, so Mana will guide them true. We need more firepower and this will do the job.'

He handed the weapon over to Beccia, whose hands caressed the gleaming wooden stock with a sense of awe. He then picked up his old bow and said to Amiria, 'You were once pretty fair with a bow. When we go out today, I suggest you carry this. We'll need everyone armed when in the forest.'

Bill's face showed a glimpse of worry before masking it.

'They have grown strong,' said Amiria, as she came over to take the bow. 'Their power exceeds what we faced in the past. Do you all agree?'

Ari nodded. 'Yes, and the reason is also clear,' and waited.

Bill stated, 'Leigh.'

'Correct, my friend,' said Ari. 'Harbin and his horde have their prize. They will defend it to the death. Knowing what she is about to become has empowered them to greater strengths.'

'They're watching the lodge too,' said Bill. 'Last night when Alan messed up, the goblins were on him in a flash. That could only happen if they're camping nearby during the night. Tonight, when the sun goes down, they'll be back.'

Beccia said quietly, 'We need more people.'

Amiria shook her head. 'I *could* send a message to Vincent and the others, but I doubt they would get here in time.'

Kyeua brightened and said, 'We don't have more people, but we *do* have allies. The Te-Tini-O-Hakuturi.'

'How do we contact them?' asked Bill.

Amiria said, 'Kyeua, see what it says in the grimoire about the contacting the wood-elves, it might work for the Te-Tini-O-Hakuturi. I'll make a call to the others.' As she strode outside and up to the visitor centre, Kyeua grabbed the thick volume and laid it out on the table. All gathered round as she flipped to the correct chapter. After a few minutes, Amiria returned.

'The others will come, the other Tohunga. Will they get here in time?' She shrugged and moved over to the table. 'What's it say?'

'Nothing about contacting them, just this,' said Kyeua and read,

Blood enemies of the goblins, the wood elves have received various names over the centuries — fairies, gnomes, gremlins, to name a few.

They avoid battle with the goblins unless absolutely necessary. They will not aid humans or any other creatures unless under the direst of circumstances.'

'Doesn't get more dire than this,' muttered Bill.

Amiria nodded in agreement as Kyeua continued to read.

'There have been four noted occurrences of aid being offered: 1069, 1615, 1708 and 1819. The goblin uprising of 1819 stands apart from the others as the wood elves made contact with the Duke of Wellington whilst he was surveying the Dartmoor lands for military purposes. With the aid of the wood elves, he raised an army and launched an attack. The Duke himself skewered the goblin king. All involved were sworn to secrecy afterwards.'

'I would have liked to have been a fly on the Duke's wall when they made contact,' mused Beccia. 'He must have thought he'd lost his marbles.'

'Wow, look at that!' exclaimed Bill, pointing to a drawing of Dartmoor Forest below the chapter.

'It's a twin of our forest,' whispered Ari. All were silent for a minute and they stared at the drawing. Moss-covered trees, vines, creek-beds and narrow tracks bombarded their senses. The Dartmoor National Park in Devon, England, was without doubt another Goblin Forest.

'I thought our forest was unique,' frowned Makoa.

Kyeua said, 'If you read more, it details all the sightings in Dartmoor. Spectral hounds, pixies, and a strange one here that just says hairy hands, all known to attack people at the two bridges of Dartmoor.'

'It all fits alright,' said Beccia.

Amiria said, 'It fits, but it is still fraught with danger. This book is a joining of ideas, beliefs, and knowledge of many cultures. These can mix to cloud one's judgement. It comes down to whether the Te-Tini-O-Hakuturi are of the same nature as the wood elves.'

Bill turned to Amiria. 'We're going out soon, right?'

'Yes, we must plot any traps, and locate the bolt-holes. We must find the best way in, mark it on our map and combine all this in our plan to enter their lair. And we must try to contact the Te-Tini-O-Hakuturi.'

'Can we wait for the help to arrive?' asked Ari.

Amiria shook her head. 'No, there is no guarantee the other Tohunga will arrive in time. And time is something we do not have. We must carry on without them and hope the Te-Tini-O-Hakuturi aid us if we can make contact today.'

She turned to Bill, but her eyes stayed on his chest. 'Perhaps you should stay here, Bill? Keep an eye on Alan in case he wakes up and tries to do something else stupid.'

'No!' said Bill quite loudly, causing the others to frown. He chuckled and said, 'Sorry about that, just a bit jumpy, I guess. What I meant to say is I have had a long chat with Alan. He won't do anything. You need all the people you can get.' He stared at Amiria until she was forced to make eye contact. 'I'm coming.'

'Right then,' said Ari. 'I'll make us some lunch, then we can then sit down and plan this afternoon's foray into the forest.'

'I'll help,' said Bill.

As he turned to the kitchen with Ari, he glanced at Amiria, who looked away.

In that glance was a warning. A warning that Bill hoped Amiria would heed.

***

At one pm, the Konini Lodge door swung open. One by one they emerged, carrying backpacks and weapons, faces set. Ari led, followed by Amiria, Kyeua, Makoa, Beccia, and Bill, bringing up the rear.

Ari halted and help up a hand, causing everyone to stop. Amiria came up to stand next to him.

'What is it?'

Ari stood still; eyes closed. He seemed to be almost sniffing the air. Then his eyes opened. 'We are being watched. North -west I think.'

'The Te-Tini-O-Hakuturi?'

'Maybe,' replied Ari.

'Lead on,' said Amiria, 'but everyone be on guard.'

They continued on, approaching the tree line. Makoa and Beccia then took the lead as they merged into the forest.

***

'Wake up, it is time for your watch,' said Arcmedan. Crawfin rose from his pallet at once and dressed. Derrein, however, yawned and rolled over on his side.

Arcmedan reached down and flipped the pallet over, ejecting Derrein onto the floor with a thud. He leapt up, cursing as Crawfin looked on with a smirk.

'One day, your laziness will cost you dearly,' growled Arcmedan. Derrein said nothing as he gathered his clothes, a sour expression on his face. Arcmedan nodded to Crawfin and left.

'He's right, you know,' said Crawfin. 'I for one am tired of covering your big lazy ass.'

'Oh, shove off with the lecture,' snarled Derrein. 'I can take care of myself!'

Crawfin marched up to Derrein and poked a finger into his chest. 'And therein lies the problem. You take care of *yourself* too much. The horde comes first.' He moved back as Derrein glowered. 'I'll take the north-west post, you take the south-east. And stay awake this time.'

'*Yeah, whatever you say, kiss-ass,*' he muttered under his breath before pulling on his boots. Yawning again, Derrein had a quick bite of leftovers before trundling down the tunnel leading to his post. Eventually, he entered a largish chamber lit by a single sunbeam coming through the south-east bolt-hole.

'You are late,' accused Gregorn.

'I was awoken late!' whined Derrein.

Gregorn eyed Derrein suspiciously before handing over the watch. 'Nothing to report. No movement from the traps, nor any sounds noticed from outside. The sun will set in four hours. Harbin has ordered that even the slightest sound is to be reported at once, understand?'

Derrein absently waved a hand and took up his position. Gregorn picked up his gear and moved off, leaving Derrein in charge of the bolt-hole. As Gregorn disappeared from view, another large yawn escaped from Derrein.

***

The guild stopped to rest and get new bearings. Amiria pulled out the map and laid it on the forest floor.

'Okay, we still have the old bolt-holes marked, and the 4 new ones we have found so far, but there is no telling how many new tunnels they have dug or which would be the best one to enter. When we do enter tomorrow, we will not have much time.'

Ari said, 'And the longer we are in their domain, the greater the chance of being discovered. We need to be in and out as fast as possible.'

Bill squatted down next to Amiria and pointed to a red X. 'That's the one we entered that led to the cave that held the Hellier kids, remember? Could it still be there and if so, could Matt and Leigh be there? In the same cave?'

'I don't know, Bill. It's been 5 years. This is going to take longer than we realised.' She sighed and picked up the map to roll it up. She then turned to Ari. 'Try again, please.'

Ari stepped away from the guild and raised his hands slowly. He closed his eyes and spoke in a loud, commanding voice.

'Enemies of the goblins, hear us. We seek an alliance with you. We wish you no harm, only to end the rise of a new goblin queen. We are the Māori and we have battled the evil ones for over a century, but we need your help. Te-Tini-O-Hakuturi, aid us, please. Help us both in our hour of need.'

The others watched the woods for any sign, except for Beccia, who had her arms crossed, deep in thought. Then her face brightened.

'Bill, you said the goblins were onto Alan in quick time last night, right?'

'Yes,' he said over his shoulder as he looked for any movement.

'And they left after being unable to penetrate Tane's barrier because dawn was approaching. They would need to get underground before then, right?'

'Agreed,' said Kyeua. 'What are you getting at, Beccia?'

'Well, would it not also make sense they would not risk travelling far with dawn so close, their best way back underground would need —'

'— To be close to the lodge!' exclaimed Amiria. 'Beccia, you're on to something here.'

Makoa beamed and slapped his sister's back.

Beccia blushed at this praise.

Amiria laid the map back down and all gathered around again.

Bill traced a line through two of the new bolt-tholes to the south-east.

'What's the bet if we follow these two south-east, we'll find another one closer to the lodge?'

'No contest, Bill,' said Ari.

Amiria said, 'We head that way, agreed?'

Everyone nodded.

Beccia led the group on with Makoa behind her, carrying his crossbow across his chest. After a rather long trek, they could now see the lodge in the distance. Two more bolt-holes were discovered, but these were very well hidden. If you were not looking for them, you could easily walk past and not notice. To be sure, they carried on searching, but no more were located. They backtracked to the last bolt-hole and stared down at its blackened entrance, listening closely for any sign below.

'This would be the one to use,' whispered Ari. 'When Alan is well enough to join us. We will have to start early tomorrow because, as Amiria said, we do not know how many tunnels are there. And if we run out of time …'

Bill muttered, 'I can't even remember how many tunnels we went through before finding the Hellier kids.'

'Not to mention you were bleeding badly and half dead at the end of all that, Bill,' said Makoa. 'That's enough to mess with anyone's memory.'

Amiria moved away from the bolt-hole, motioning for the others to join her. After she was happy with the distance, she stopped and waited for the others. Bill eyed her warily as she cleared her throat and spoke.

'Time is slipping away from us. We really only have tomorrow to search the goblin lair, find the children, and kill Harbin. It is too great a risk to put all our eggs in one basket. We *must* put preparations in place beforehand to ensure a better chance of success.'

'Oh?' said Kyeua. 'Is that not what we are doing now?'

Amiria eased the backpack off and placed it on the ground. She reached in and pulled out a sack of white pebbles and a length of rope.

'No, Amiria! We would put them on guard if spotted. We wait till tomorrow when Alan is with us.'

Others looked at Bill with a puzzled expression.

'It is a risk, Bill, but one that must be taken. As leader of the guild, it is my decision to make.'

The others now realised what Amiria proposed.

Ari said, 'Are you sure, Amiria? Bill could be right.'

Amiria began pulling out flares and torches as she spoke. 'We're just going down there to map as much as we can of the tunnel system. This save time tomorrow. We won't venture far. We will drop pebbles at intervals to provide a trail back to this bolt-hole. We will be careful to make no noise. It is daylight, so the goblins are most likely sleeping, apart from a few sentries. These we will avoid as best we can.' She pulled some red electrical tape out of her pack. 'Cover the torch lenses with the tape. It will dull the light and allow us to keep our vision in the dark.'

'This is dangerous, Amiria,' said Kyeua. 'I agree that this would help for tomorrow, but if we are spotted, it could end any chance *of* a tomorrow.'

From above them came, 'And endanger my race's survival.'

Makoa had his crossbow up in a flash whilst the other grabbed for their swords. Amiria looked up sharply and gasped. A troubled, small face eyed them curiously.

'Well, fine show of hate this is. First ask for aid, and then draw weapons, you?'

Makoa lowered his crossbow as they all realised what was happening.

Contact was made.

Ari spoke quickly. 'Please forgive us. We mean no harm to you. I am Ari. I was the one who called. We thought you were a goblin.'

The little creature swung down from the tree and landed in front of the guild.

'A good start, this is not. Goblins and the light of day make not good companions… do not know this, you?'

'Yes, we know. I guess we were a little startled somewhat,' replied Beccia, a little defensively.

The creature waved a furry hand in dismissal. 'And startled will be the least of worries should you enter. Bad things await you down there.'

'Who are you?' stated Amiria.

The creature smiled, showing white but uneven teeth. 'I am what call you "Te-Tini-O-Hakuturi." That is your name given to us. We are the Natawidu, I am Howelia. I lead many.'

He pulled out a flute that Alan would have recognised and blew into it, causing a complex yet flowing melody to pierce the air. After a few seconds, Howelia waved a welcoming hand

and grinned.

'My many.'

The guild looked around and were stunned to see a hundred odd small faces now staring back from only a few metres away.

They had never heard a sound.

***

The guild brought Howelia up to speed on events and why they were here. If he looked troubled before, it was nothing compared to his face now.

'We felt a change in the natural order of things,' he said. 'The air carries dark feelings and bad intent. I never have in time felt such change. It put my race to alert. This confirms much of what I have spoken of, you. A goblin queen *must* not happen!'

'Will you aid us?' asked Ari.

Howelia stood from his squatting pose and said, 'It is needed, so it is given. First time we have given aid, you. First time also we are revealed. Once the queen is no more, this reveal must be withdrawn. Your word is asked. We will not be revealed to others.'

Ari said, 'Howelia, you have our word that your secret will remain hidden by us for all time.'

The Natawidu leader nodded. 'So taken.'

Amiria said, 'Time is growing short. We either go into their lair now or it will be too late.' She stood up and stared at Howelia. 'Do you agree with my plan?'

'Yes, but I will go too. The Natawidu feel when the goblins are near. Need me down there, you, I think.'

'Just you and not more of your clan?' said Kyeua.

'Less the better. More down there, more to be observed by

goblins.'

'He has a point,' said Bill. 'Maybe Kyeua should stay up here with the rest of the Te-Tini, err, I mean the Natawidu. She is unarmed and if things go wrong …'

'Agreed,' said Amiria, heading over to her backpack and throwing it over her shoulders. 'Let's go. Beccia, you lead, Makoa, right behind, followed by Howelia. Then me, then Ari. Bill, you guard our rear.'

Bill went to say something when Howelia said, 'I lead. I sense goblins before you do. Much warning far better.'

He leapt up with surprising ease and landed in front of the bolt-hole. Amiria hesitated briefly before forming up with the others. Makoa checked the safety lock on his crossbow whilst the others checked their swords. Ari unfolded a large piece of wax paper and then checked his chinagraph pencils, ready to map the goblin lair.

Howelia scampered down the hole, out of sight.

Kyeua said with great concern, 'Watch yourselves down there, my friends, you hear me?'

Beccia gave her a thumbs-up, though no smile accompanied the gesture.

One by one, they followed Howelia and dropped into the bolt-hole.

— Chapter Thirteen —

Betrayal

Alan came out of his sleep and gingerly sat up. He moved his shoulder slowly and found the movement quite good. Already the swelling had subsided more than he thought possible. He threw on a t-shirt and made his way downstairs, eager to hear if the guild had made contact with the *Te-Tini-O-Hakuturi*.

'Ari, you're a miracle worker!' said Alan as he exited the stairs and walked into the living space, only to find himself alone. He looked up at the clock and frowned.

'Damn, they've been gone longer than they said they would be,' he said to himself with a touch of unease.

***`

Inside the start of the tunnel, they waited for Howelia to lead. Bill looked around. He had forgotten how big they were, more like caverns than tunnels. Memories came flooding back, painful memories. He went to speak to Amiria when Howelia put a hand up fast. Then he pressed a finger to his lips

Everyone froze.

He pointed to a large bundle laying close by, then to his ear. Sure enough, sounds of snoring were coming from the bundle.

Howelia whispered, 'Sentry it is. But it sleeps. A good sign. They expect none to come or more would guard. We move past. Silence a must now.'

The little Natawidu slinked past, with the guild following. Ari kept staring at the sleeping goblin as he walked and failed to watch ahead. He ran into Amiria and dropped his paper and pencils on the ground. The sound wasn't much, but it was enough.

The goblin stirred.

Makoa levelled his crossbow at the bundle as it rolled over. But after a tense minute, the snoring began again.

Ari bent down and picked up his lost items as quietly as possible, glad the darkness hid his reddening face.

They moved on, with Amiria opening her sack and breaking out the pebbles to lay the trail.

Up ahead lay what looked like a large cave coming off the tunnel. Bill turned on his torch and moved up with Howelia as they advanced to the cave edge. The dulled red beam showed stores, barrels, and weapons, but no goblins. Bill gave a quick thumbs up to those behind the trio and the guild lowered their weapons. They moved inside, where Ari began drawing the layout to this point.

Beccia said, 'Makoa, keep your crossbow pointed towards the exit.'

Amiria motioned for the others to come together behind a line of barrels. 'Whispered talk only from now on,' she said. 'This is how we will continue to do it. Find a large enough area like this to bunker down so Ari can sketch the tunnel system. We will try to remain concealed behind any stores we see in case any goblins come in.'

Bill said, 'And when it is time to move, Howelia can look

outside to see if the coast is clear. With his size, he won't be spotted as easily as we would be. He is our lead anyway and our best chance of avoiding those green bastards.'

'That is good, you,' said Howelia, eyeing Bill curiously. 'Fought goblins before?'

'Yeah, we've met,' said Bill.

'Okay, got it down,' said Ari. 'Ready to move on.'

Howelia moved to the cavern entrance. There he waited, sniffing the air. He then waved his hand and moved out into the tunnel. The others followed.

They moved deep into the system, sometimes having to stop when finding multiple tunnels branching off the main cavern. Sometimes they risked being in the open whilst Ari drew as fast as he could. They passed the second bolt-hole, noticing it was smaller than the other one.

'Looks like they have a main bolt-hole and a backup one,' said Makoa. 'Not what I remember from last time. I don't recall smaller ones.'

Howelia quietly chuckled. 'Smaller holes have slippery vines placed around it, not larger ones. Animals slip on vines, fall in … food. Can be used to come and go, but not main purpose. Understand, you?'

They continued on.

'Oh, what is that smell!' hissed Beccia, as they approached one tunnel.

'Don't know,' said Makoa. 'But Ari should take note *not* to ever go down that one.'

Howelia stopped. He tuned fast, alarm on his face.

'They come! To the tunnel!'

The guild darted inside. The smell was overpowering, but they had no choice.

Howelia stayed just inside the entrance, hidden in darkness.

Flickering light flooded the cavern, followed by, 'We will have to build more storerooms once the queen starts birthing. We don't have enough as it is.'

'True, Gregorn. I will raise this with Lord Harbin after tonight's hunt.'

'Ah, yes, Arcmedan. Tonight will be an excellent test for Maorten's prowess. The rest think he will make a great warrior.'

Arcmedan grunted a reply. The guild caught their breath as the two goblins walked past the tunnel, not looking inside. The flickering light faded, but not before they heard, 'Ugh! And we may need a new waste pit. That one smells like it has reached its usefulness.'

The light was now gone. Bill gagged. 'Oh crap, we're in … well, we're in theirs!'

'Come,' commanded Howelia. 'They will return. Must hurry!'

The guild came out of the tunnel, their boots slippery. Beccia said, 'I'm burning these boots after this is all over.'

'Yeah, make that all my clothes as well,' said Makoa.

'Let's go,' commanded Amiria as she dropped more pebbles to mark the trail.

Howelia moved forward, continually sniffing the air. The guild followed, with Bill now guarding Ari. He drew as he walked to save time, Bill holding his torch to provide a dim light. The minutes ticked by as the darkness slowed their passage. The torches were used sparingly. More tunnels were marked and then …

'Uh-oh,' whispered Makoa. They had reached the end of this cavern. Six tunnels ran off here in a semi-circle pattern.

'Which one to do we take? Or should we split up?'

Howelia turned to Amiria. 'All stay together, all *live* together! Understand?'

'But we don't have time to search them all,' she said. She looked at the luminous dial on her watch. 'Sunset is just over an hour away. We need to be back at the lodge before that.'

The Natawidu frowned, knowing the truth in this. Whereas his race can easily stay safe in the trees at night, the humans could not. Howelia moved to each tunnel and sniffed at each entrance. Then he faced his allies.

'This tunnel,' he pointed, 'has most goblin trace. Map this one.'

Bill said, 'If that is the primary way, then mark it on Ari's map and let's get out of here. It's a miracle we haven't been spotted yet. No more pushing our luck.'

Amiria shook her head furiously. 'But what if it isn't? What if it's just their sleeping spaces? We can quickly check and *then* leave.'

'And we quickly go in and run into the goblins.' mimicked Bill. 'Amiria, we can't do anything without Alan and you know that.'

'I —'

'Shhh, goblins come again, behind, you!' warned Howelia.

The guild wheeled around, looking back up the way they came. The very faintest of a light reflected off the walls.

Howelia urged, 'Choose a tunnel. Hide till they pass!'

Beccia made the call. She strode over to the outer left tunnel and the others followed. Deep inside, they readied their weapons. If Beccia had chosen wrong, they would have to fight. Howelia again stood near the tunnel entrance, but this time, it was much harder to hide. He cursed under his breath.

The light of the goblin torches became stronger. Then the same two goblins walked past their tunnel. They breathed a sigh of relief. Until —

'Stop, Gregorn.'

'What? What's the problem?'

There was a pause.

Enough for Amiria to ease off her bow and pull an arrow out of her quiver.

Arcmedan sniffed, his heavy nostrils making a guttural sound. Howelia moved further back into the tunnel.

'Ugh, that damned smell from the waste pit has followed us. After the hunt tonight, arrange for that tunnel to be collapsed and a new one dug for the pit.'

'It will be done,' said Gregorn. 'I'll have that lazy ass Derrein do it.'

Arcmedan chuckled. 'Come on, we'll be waking the others soon. I need to report to Harbin the state of the stores and what we need tonight.'

They continued to talk, but the voices receded. Howelia sprung out of the tunnel and watched the flaming torches disappear down the tunnel.

The same one he had marked.

The guild left the tunnel, weapons still drawn.

'Howelia, lead on please,' said Amiria. 'Beccia, behind him with your sword. Makoa and I, crossbow and bow behind Beccia. Bill and Ari, watch our backs.'

***

It was past 4 pm now and Alan observed the sun was moving towards the horizon. He paced back and forward, occasionally testing and moving his shoulder to ease the stiffness. He had even done some practice with his sword, but this was more to take his mind off the worry.

He left the lodge and strode up to the centre. After a few minutes, a couple of bars of signal allowed him to check the sunset time again. Then came a flurry of texts from Julie. He was tempted, sorely tempted. To hear her voice would mean everything to him, but Alan knew that voice he loved so much would make him blurt out what was happening. He put the phone away.

Alan continued to pace, wishing he hadn't checked the sunset time after all. Something wasn't right, and he didn't know what to do.

***

'Where do you think the other tunnels lead to?' whispered Ari.

Bill said, 'More large caverns like the one we went through, I reckon. Notice how there are no bolt-holes around here, so I doubt this is the main sleeping chamber.'

'So where does this lead?' wondered Beccia.

'I don't know,' replied Bill. 'But we'll find out shortly.'

The tunnel began to enlarge. 'Shorter than I thought,' he muttered.

Howelia raised a hand for them to stop, but there was no need. They stood and gaped in awe at what had to be the main chamber of the goblins. It was enormous. Flaming torches along the walls lit the area just enough for human eyesight.

Makoa whispered, 'Look at the size of those stone chairs!'

'Harbin's is one,' said Amiria. 'I guess we know who's the other one will be …'

Howelia pointed to the far right of the chamber. 'Look there, you. Caves — many caves. In one would be your missing children. This doubt there is none.'

'We got what we needed,' said Ari. 'Now we need to get

out of here.'

'Ari's right,' said Bill. 'Amiria, we don't' have much time before sunset. We need to go now!'

Howelia said, 'Move back into the tunnel. Check caves, I will, quickly.' And before anyone could say anything, the Natawidu leader raced to the far-right wall and sped to the first tunnel in a shocking show of speed. He spied into the cavern and moved on to the next.

And the next.

And then, there she was, the biggest threat to his race in memory — the goblin queen, fast asleep. He went to run back along the wall edge to re-join the guild, but froze when a guttural yell rang out.

'INTRUDERS! BEWARE! INTRUDERS!'

Crawfin had appeared.

Makoa wheeled round and yelled to the guild, 'Get down!'

Everyone dropped as he raised his crossbow. Crawfin yelled, 'INTRUDER!' one last time, before an arrow flew through the air and tore his throat out.

Leigh awoke with a start to see Howelia starting at her. 'What on earth are you?' she asked.

'A friend. We will be back for you.'

Before Leigh could reply, Howelia was gone from sight.

Leigh hurried out of her cave and in the direction of the little creature as other goblins rushed out of the caves, half asleep.

Bill saw Leigh at the same time she saw him. 'LEIGH, WE WILL SAVE YOU! WE WON'T GIVE UP!' he yelled.

More alarms sounded throughout the caves. Matt appeared from another cave and saw the humans. He drew his sword and darted towards his sister.

'Makoa, take the shot!' urged Amiria.

'What shot?' What the hell are you talking about?' he yelled back.

'SHOOT THE QUEEN!'

'NO!' yelled Bill. 'Makoa, no! We can still save her. Don't you do it!'

'You have to. If she lives, all is lost!' cried Amiria.

Makoa lowered the Crossbow. 'I ... I can't.'

Howelia pointed at the tunnel and yelled, 'We go! We must flee!'

Everyone except Amiria turned towards the tunnel and started running.

'Come on, Amiria!' urged Bill, looking back to see her rooted to the spot.

The guild leader raised her bow at Leigh.

'Damn you, no!' roared Bill and tried to get to her to knock her aim.

Amiria pulled back the bow and fired.

The arrow soared past the advancing goblins and stuck home with a sickening thud. Bill furiously grabbed Amiria and yanked her towards the tunnel.

A powerful, ugly scream filled the goblin chamber.

Bill took one last look over his shoulder before entering the tunnel and moaned at what he saw.

Leigh was unharmed. She was on her knees holding Matt, who lay on the ground. A red patch forming quickly from the arrow sticking out of his chest.

***

'Keep running, they're gaining on us!'

Makoa moved to the rear, occasionally turning to fire his crossbow. But there were too many. They passed a side tunnel, and a goblin barrelled out of it, sword slashing. Ari cried out as his chest spurted blood. Bill took the goblin's head off with one swift stroke of his sword. He then lifted Ari up and carried him fireman style.

'Get your torches out and follow the trail,' yelled Beccia. 'Stealth means nothing now!'

The yelling and gibbering behind them got louder. Ari was slowing them down too much.

'We're not going to make it!' yelled Bill. 'Run and leave us!'

'Not a frigging chance!' Beccia screamed back.

Howelia pulled out his flute and began blowing furiously. 'Not far, the exit, keep going!' he urged.

They rounded a corner to see a goblin approaching, rubbing sleep out of his eyes. He never had a chance to understand what was happening as Beccia slashed at him, causing him to fall backwards. But it was only a glancing blow, and they didn't stop to finish him off.

'The bolt-hole!' yelled Makoa, pointing to the distant light from above. It was not a strong light.

'Sunset not far away, you. Move fast!' urged Howelia.

Suddenly dozens of Natawidu came flooding down the hole and flew past the guild, holding little wooden carved knives, yelling in unison.

'My clan gives us time,' said Howelia. 'Up we go, you.'

Makoa turned and faced the tunnel. He strung an arrow and waited.

Bill yelled up to the outside, 'Kyeua, Ari's hurt! Give me a hand.' He dragged Ari up the bolt-hole as Kyeua appeared at the top. She reached down and grabbed him as Bill shoved hard. Ari stifled a groan as he cleared the exit and collapsed on the ground outside.

'Ari's out!' yelled Bill. 'The rest of you, get outside fast!'

Howelia blew his flute again, and his Natawidu returned, minus one. They flew up the bolt-hole, followed by Amiria and Beccia. Makoa fired a volley of arrows as the goblins turned the corner, striking two. He then darted up the hole.

Bill then climbed out, yelling to Howelia, 'Move your furry little butt, Howelia!'

The Natawidu leader stared at the oncoming goblins, hate in his eyes. 'Foul ugly ones, this is not over yet.' He then hissed at them and leapt up out of the tunnel.

***

'Ari, can you walk? We need to go, sunset is close,' said Beccia.

He groaned as Kyeua wrapped a field bandage around his wound. 'Yeah, but I don't think I'll be much use after this for a while.'

Howelia said in a muted voice, 'Go now, you. I will come later. I must care for my clan.' He gave out a sob. 'One has fallen to the foul ones.'

Bill bent down to Howelia. 'I grieve for your loss, as do we all. Your people saved us by attacking. We are in your debt.' He didn't know if it was allowed, but placed his hand on Howelia's thin little shoulder. The Natawidu leader looked up with watery eyes, then leapt up into the trees and was gone.

Amiria said in a subdued voice, 'Head to the lodge.'

Bill didn't look at Amiria but replied, 'Yeah, let's get the hell out of here.'

They made a decent pace back to the lodge, the fresh air helping Ari find some of his strength. As the sun's rays faded behind Mount Taranaki, they emerged into the clearing.

Alan came running, waving his arms in exasperation. 'What

the hell happened? I thought you were just going to —' He then saw Ari sag to the ground and surged forward to help.

'What happen to Ari?'

'We'll explain everything once inside the lodge and safe,' said Makoa.

'Hey, he's been wounded … is that by a sword? How can you have met the goblins? It was daylight. You said you were only going to scout outside the bolt-holes!'

Kyeua muttered, 'Please, Alan, wait until we are inside and Ari has received aid.'

They moved towards the lodge with Ari being held up on one side by Makoa and Beccia, the other.

Alan couldn't help it and said, 'Sorry, but cripes, do you all smell really bad.'

As they entered the door, Bill snarled, 'That's not the only thing that stinks either!'

The shock then hit him. He slumped down into a chair and teared up as he realised what he would have to tell Alan.

His son Matthew was most likely dead.

— Chapter Fourteen —

Alan's Torture

Harbin stood with Meido and Reido as they surveyed the dead. Crawfin's loss pained him the most. He had been one of his best warriors. It was he who has sounded the warning.

He was furious. Harbin had not anticipated the humans entering his abode to seek out his queen. He had been bested, *and* he had almost lost her but for Maorten's sacrifice.

'Can he be saved?'

Reido bent down to his queen, who was holding her brother, tears streaming from her eyes. 'My queen, please release your grip. I will see what can be done.'

Leigh eased off, but still held her brother's hand.

After a minute, he looked up and said, 'He lives, but barely. The arrow bites deep. He will expire shortly.'

Leigh looked up at Harbin and said, 'He saved me! He saw that woman about to shoot that arrow and he pushed me away.'

Harbin didn't reply.

Leigh's faced turned cold. In a first, she yelled at the goblin lord. 'You would not have a queen if it were not for him. YOU OWE HIM! AID HIM!'

Harbin turned to Meido and Reido. 'Heal him with your arts if you can.'

'Yes, my lord,' they replied. They both eased Matt clear of Leigh and carried him away.

Harbin shifted his attention to Derrein. His laziest goblin stood before him; eyes lowered to his hairy, green feet, a hand covering a bloodied gash on his arm. He looked up and eyed the goblin lord with apprehension as he approached.

'You were guarding. Speak of what occurred upon their entry.'

'My lord, they were able to knock me out as they entered, so I could not sound the alarm.'

'Yet you are wounded, Derrein,' smiled Harbin curiously. 'Just how did that travesty occur?'

'I ... err, came to in time to attack them on their way out. I ... I managed to wound the ranger as he passed, but another struck me with her sword.' He then lowered his eyes again to avoid Harbin's gaze.

'Well, that is something, the ranger no less! Well done, Derrein,' boomed Harbin. 'With Crawfin dead, I will need an able replacement in the senior guard and you might just be worthy.'

Derrein looked up, pleased with the news. 'Thank you, my lord, oh thank you. I will not let you down.'

'Go to the aid cavern and seek treatment from the wizards as well.'

'Yes, my lord,' bowed Derrein and turned for the aid cavern. As he passed Arcmedan, Harbin nodded. In the blink of an eye, Arcmedan drew his sword and ran Derrein through. The goblin screamed and fell to his knees, clutching his stomach. Blood spurted through his fingers.

Harbin drew his sword and casually walked over.

Derrein looked up at Harbin, gibbering in fear.

'Do I look like a fool, Derrein?' growled Harbin. 'Sleeping is what you are best at, it seems, so let me help you sleep forever.'

Derrein's scream cut short as Harbin detached his head from his body.

He re-sheathed his now bloodied sword and turned to face his horde, his gaze sweeping across the subdued crowd. 'I hope this lesson is taken? Forfeit your duty … forfeit your life.'

No one spoke as the goblin king picked up his queen and carried her to her quarters.

***

Kyeua came down the stairs and into the subdued living room. 'Ari is resting. I have done my best, but I am no healer.'

She sat down, averting her eyes from the sobbing man in the chair.

Bill refilled the glass with the scotch he had hidden in the visitor centre and nudged Alan, who slowly removed his hands from his face. He took the glass, and for the second time, swallowed its contents whole.

'Alan, I-I am so sorry. We … I felt —'

'Shut it, Amiria,' said Bill in a strangled voice.

'Bill, Mother was wrong in her actions,' said Beccia as he gave Amiria a withering look. 'Very wrong. And she knows it. We are all so very sorry it happened.'

Alan looked up through red-rimmed eyes. 'Mother?'

'Yes, Alan, both Makoa and I are her children.'

Bill got up, hands on hips, his face an ugly shade of red. 'So, this is what it came down to, eh? The Māori Guild of

Mount Taranaki now kills children for the greater good. Is that it?'

Amiria paled. 'Bill, please ...'

'IS IT? How would you feel if it were *your* children to be executed because it was an easier option? Do you even frigging care if they are saved?'

Amiria stood up. 'How would *I* feel? I feel it every time my children go underground, wondering if they will come back up alive.'

'Easy everyone,' said Kyeua.

Amiria looked at her children. 'They think like all youth. They think they are invincible and everything's an adventure. Only when it's too late, do they realise that folly. Graveyards are filled with the young whose adventure came with too high a risk and they paid the price. I feel like it's my fault they are like this. I feel like I put them in danger by them just being my children, despite them saying it is their choice to fight. I feel one day *they* will pay the price of just being my children and I will have to bury them. If that ever happens, Bill, I could not go on. So yes, I do care for Matt and Leigh... more than you will ever know.'

Beccia quickly went to Amiria and put her arms around her mother. The guild leader burst into tears.

Makoa turned fiercely on Bill. 'What about you, Bill? Do *you* care, or are you looking for redemption for the past? We all were there too, you selfish bastard!'

Bill slumped back in the chair, unable to look at Makoa. His words had bitten deep.

For a while, no one spoke. Then Alan managed to say, 'How ... how sure are you all that Matthew is ...'

'He was hit by the arrow, Alan,' murmured Makoa. 'We ran

soon after for the tunnel. I saw him lying there with your daughter holding him.'

'But you didn't see him actually die?'

'Well, no,' he admitted.

'Then I refuse to believe it,' stated Alan. 'He's alive until I see proof saying otherwise.'

Amiria said through sobs, 'Alan, my actions were inexcusable. I am so deeply sorry ... so sorry.'

Alan simply replied, 'He's not dead.'

Bill stood up. 'I'll make us some coffee. Then, we'll make a new plan to rescue Matt and Leigh tomorrow. And then, kill that little green slimebag.'

***

Leigh paced the rough floor of her quarters, waiting for news. As every minute passed, her anger grew. Those yellow eyes of hers glowed with a hate she had never experienced before. She liked how it felt.

'You are troubled, my queen?'

Leigh whirled around to see Artex standing outside her cavern. 'Troubled? That is an understatement! My brother lies at death's door and *I* was the target. I did not know who they were, but I recognise one. His name is Bill.'

'Ah, yes, the ranger. He is well known as an enemy of the goblins. He was part of the group that tried to save the human children from the last taking.' Artex shrugged as he added, 'He failed.'

'So, this time he and his friends decide to kill me instead?' said Leigh, her anger mounting.

'I ... I don't know.'

'But I do ...' Leigh and Artex spun around to see Harbin standing there. Artex bowed.

'Leighandra, have you not noticed something?'

'What would that be?' growled Leigh.

Harbin grinned widely, showing all of his jagged yellow teeth. 'Why, the fact that your father was not amongst them. Ask yourself why that is.'

Leigh frowned. She had not noticed that.

'It is because the Māori and Bill were sent to kill you. Your dear daddy was too squeamish to come along to see. He obviously waited just outside to hear the news before leaving these lands. He has abandoned you both.'

Leigh said, 'Both?'

Harbin whistled. A few moments later, Arcmedan arrived and with him was —

'MATT!'

Leigh launched herself at her brother, who hugged her back fiercely. Her tears ran freely as he soothingly said, 'Hey now, sis, ease off. I'm okay. I'm good.'

'I w-was so w-worried, Matt. I thought you had d-died!'

'It was close,' said Meido, who had joined Harbin, 'very close. But the spell worked to stop the bleeding. We removed the arrow and healed the internal damage. We then sealed the wound with a healing potion. There will be some stiffness there from now on, but Maorten is healed.'

'Fit enough for some payback?' asked Harbin slyly.

'How so, my lord,' frowned Maorten.

'Tell him, my queen.'

Maorten searched his sister's face. 'Tell me what?'

Leigh broke free from her brother and moved back a little. She locked eyes with him and then spoke. 'That arrow was meant for me, Matt. The park ranger, Bill, was a part of it. Dad wasn't with them. I think … I think he has abandoned us.'

'And wanted you dead,' injected Harbin. *'Both of you dead.'*

Maorten clenched his fists a few times before he said, 'My lord, if payback is to be given, I want to be a part of it.'

'Part of it? No, Maorten. You will *lead* it.' Harbin turned to the wizards. 'Take Maorten to Arcmedan to be briefed, then come back here with the wheel.'

'What wheel?' said Leigh.

The goblin king just smiled.

***

'The question is, how do we get inside again without alerting the goblins?' said Beccia, sipping her tea. 'They'll have more than one guard at the entrances now. More like a dozen.'

Kyeua said, 'We need to find another way in, but I don't see how that is possible?'

'Well, at least we know where the children are now,' said Amiria. She unrolled Ari's map, pulled out a red marker, and marked an X over it.

A new voice said, 'A new way in is the only way in. All others will be death now.'

'HOWELIA!' exclaimed Kyeua.

The little Natawidu seemed to appear out of nowhere. 'I return as said I would,' he said, a sad smile on his face.

Alan jumped up excitedly. 'It was you! You save me that night!'

'Indeed, I did. It is grand to see you whole again.'

'How did you get in here?' asked Makoa.

'Unlike the goblins, need no invitation, do I. Rarely do we venture into places like this, you. The forest is our place. And besides, an unlocked door is no challenge.'

The group grinned rather sheepishly.

Beccia asked timidly, 'Your warrior who was lost?'

'It is our way not to speak of these things with outsiders. But, he is at one with the forest now.'

There was an awkward silence as no one knew what to say to this.

Howelia helped them by asking, 'How fares the one named Ari?'

'He is resting,' replied Amiria. 'The wound was not deep. But he is, or was, our healer, so we had to use traditional bandages and medicines as best we could. We will get him to a hospital as soon as possible.'

'Hospital?'

'Ah, a place where human healers reside,' said Kyeua.

Howelia nodded. 'So, where stand does tomorrow?'

Bill said, 'As you heard, we cannot use the bolt-holes. Any ideas?'

'No. Only that a way in new must be found.'

Alan said, 'Of course, that's it! A new way in — why can't we *create* new ones? Goblins dig upwards to form these bolt-holes to come and go from their lair, right? So, what's stopping us from digging our own hole *downwards*?' He moved over to the map and began tracing his finger through the known tunnels. The others gathered around, with Howelia jumping onto Bill's shoulder to see.

'These smaller tunnels should lead to other caverns, right?'

'Makes sense,' said Bill.

'So, it's my guess that these small tunnels are just used to transit between the main areas. They might not have guards inside them at all if they just connect caverns. Maybe just the occasional goblin passing through?'

Makoa interjected, 'I get it. If we can dig our own entrance into a tunnel instead of the cavern, we have a better chance of getting in undetected.'

'It's going to be hit or miss though,' said Beccia. 'Ari's map, through no fault of his own, is not that accurate. We only know the approximate area of the tunnels from the surface only.'

'Choose a tunnel, early dig. If miss, dig another.'

'Howelia is right,' said Amiria. 'We'll know soon enough if we've missed the tunnel. And seeing as we are starting out early at first light, we have time if we don't hit pay-dirt straight away.' She turned to Bill. 'You have shovels in the centre?'

Bill said, 'Yeah, we have gardening and landscape stuff in the sheds.'

Kyeua snapped back from the map. 'I'm getting a vison,' she said and left quickly to go outside.

'Keep close to the lodge, Kyeua,' reminded Amiria.

'That could be a good omen,' said Beccia.

'What is *vision*?' asked Howelia.

Amiria explained Kyeua's gift as the guild's seer, which he found fascinating. 'The Natawidu sense when wrongness is afoot, but visions we do not have. More we have to learn from each other, you.'

Alan said, 'Bill, should we start gathering the gear for tomorrow?'

Bill shook his head. 'Not tonight, mate. The sheds are at the far clearing, outside Tane's barrier.'

Alan went back to the map, studying the tunnels. But his eyes always came back to the main cavern, specifically, the cave his children were in …

***

Meido and Reido, as commanded, placed the Wheel of Zulear

before Harbin and Leigh.

'Come, Leighandra, gaze upon the ancient artefact of your new heritage.'

Leigh looked at the stone wheel and felt a strange longing to touch it.

'It's beautiful,' she breathed.

'Yes, it is. And *you* will be the one to activate it.'

'Activate it? But it is just stone.'

Harbin grinned. 'It is so much more, Leighandra. Notice the channels carved into the black stone? They represent the lineage of the goblin race. The six being the northern, southern, eastern and western clans and the mountain and forest Clans. Zulear himself forged this wheel in the fiery lava of Nea Kameni over a thousand years ago. Notice the lines do not touch?'

Leigh said, 'Yes, they only point to some sort of symbols on the rim.'

Harbin nodded. 'The ancient lost language of the Goblin race. All Wizards throughout our world work tirelessly to restore this.'

Leigh traced the lines with her fingers as Harbin watched her fondly. She asked, 'What is the eye in the middle for?'

'Ah, that is where *you* come into it, my queen.'

'Me? How?'

'As I said, the lines do not touch. That is for a special reason. When a new queen is about to begin her reign, a window opens up on Zulear's wheel. Look closely at the eye.'

Leigh bent forward, her eyes mere inches away. After a moment, she leaned back and said, 'It's hollow.'

'Yes, your blood and mine will be drawn. Combined, the wizards will pour a small amount into the eye. Our blood will run down all the lines, revealing what is hidden *under* the eye. Then, my queen, you will see something to behold.'

'What? What will happen?'

Harbin shook his head. 'You must wait to see. And see you will ...'

***

The guild had their plan pretty much completed. They knew it would take a good deal of luck to work, but at this stage, it was all they had.

'So, it is settled. As long as we are able to rescue Leigh and get her clear, Harbin will chase. Makoa, your aim will have to be true, you must *wound* only,' said Amiria.

Alan said, 'Remember, there are two children here. We have to take out any goblins that are with Matt as well.'

There was an awkward silence at the mentioning of Matt.

Bill cleared his throat loudly and said, 'How soon will they revert to human once Harbin is dead?'

Amiria shook her head. 'The grimoire is vague on this. It only states that children will revert to human form when the last breath of the goblin king is taken. That could mean immediately, but we won't know for sure till it happens.'

Howelia said, 'Then prepare we must to take them after the goblin lord is no more. Forcibly if needed.'

'That won't be easy,' said Bill. 'Goblins are strong. We may have to tie —'

The door opened and Kyeua entered, her face ashen.

Everyone stood with Amiria rushing over to her. 'What is it Kyeua, what's wrong? The vision?'

Kyeua's voice croaked, 'Yes ... but there is something else.' She looked past Amiria to Alan. 'We have visitors outside. They wish ... they ah, wish to speak to Alan ... alone.'

'No, Alan, wait!' yelled Bill, grabbing Alan as he made for the door.

'Kill the lights!' urged Amiria.

Makoa hurried over and flicked the switch, plunging the room into darkness.

Amiria whispered, 'Head to the windows, everyone, but no one goes outside yet. Let's see what we're up against first.'

Beccia whispered, 'This is bold, they've never done this before.'

'Exactly,' said Amiria. 'We must be cautious.'

They all moved to the long line of windows facing the visitor centre. As they stared, Amiria gasped. Tane's barrier glowed blue, as it did when goblins were near. Outside the barrier, over a dozen goblins stood, holding slain rabbits and wild boar carcasses.

'We can see you without light, stupid humans!' said a mocking voice outside.

Howelia murmured, 'Goblin eyesight sees all when no light inhibits others.'

'Tell the one called Alan that his son would like to speak to him … alone.'

'He's alive!' said Bill. He turned to Alan with joy. 'He's okay, mate!'

Amiria staggered to a chair, her relief overwhelming her.

Alan said, 'Turn on the lights, Makoa, it doesn't matter now.'

The lights came on and Alan turned to everyone, his eyes already tearing up. 'I'm going outside. Anyone tries to stop me and they will regret it.'

Bill moved to Alan and placed a hand on his shoulder. 'Stay behind Tane's barrier, Alan. Do not let them trick or bait you into going past it, no matter what they say or promise. They will kill you if you do.'

Howelia added, 'Devious are the goblins. Remember, your son is not your son. More goblin he is now.'

Alan nodded and turned to the door, his hands shaking a little. Beccia moved to the kitchen and grabbed Alan's sword, but he shook his head in denial.

Alan Dwyer went out to meet his son for the first time since he was taken.

***

'How far to go, do you think?'

The man driving the bus turned to the woman in the next seat and said, 'We'll reach Stratford in about twenty hours, I think.'

'Can't we go any faster?' asked another.

The man looked in rear vision mirror at the people in the bus. All were sharpening swords and the tips of wooden staffs, despite having done this a dozen times already. The Tohunga were nervous, knowing time was running out. New Zealand National roads had been upgrading the highway and had closed it to install a pre-fabricated bridge. The detour had been long and excruciating.

It had also put them way behind schedule. They should have been arriving at the lodge by now.

The driver said, 'Any faster and I would put us in danger. Then what good would we be to Amiria if we crash?'

The woman next to him cursed under her breath as she looked at her watch. The Tohunga could only stare out the window, wondering what would happen to their native land if they arrive too late.

***

They watched from inside the door as Alan slowly made his way to the glowing blue barrier. Makoa had his crossbow loaded but hidden.

'This isn't going to go well,' said Beccia, trying to keep the croakiness out of her voice. 'They will be brutal.'

Silence descended around the park as Alan stood before Tane's barrier. The blue glow casting enough light for them to see.

The goblins leered at him, showing their horrible teeth. They were formed in ranks of two. Then, they slowly parted to reveal a lone goblin.

'Greetings, Father.'

Despite knowing what he would see, Alan still groaned in misery.

'Why the groan, Father? Look hcw I have I grown!' Maorten ran a long-nailed finer along the barrier, causing little blue sparks to erupt. 'Surely you have missed me? Come through the barrier and give your son a hug.'

'Matt, I- I am so sorry. I never meant for this to happen.'

'Sure you did, Father, you just *love* pranks. Isn't this the pinnacle of your career? And my name is Maorten now, my forever goblin name.'

Tears rolled down Alan's eyes. 'I love you so much, Matt. I won't give up on you, son, not ever.'

Maorten's eyes clouded for a fraction before narrowing. 'Then come through the barrier and embrace me. Show me your love, *Dad.*'

'I-I can't!' Alan dropped to his knees. 'You know I can't.'

'Leigh sends a message: she looks forward to marrying our Lord Harbin, but is sad her father won't be there to give her away.'

Alan scrunched his eyes closed as a wave of dizziness overcame him. 'I'm sorry, I'm sorry,' was all he could say as he buried his face in his hands.

'But not sorry enough to stop your friends from trying to kill my sister, eh? I have a scar on my chest to prove it, Father dear. But that doesn't matter anyway, as *you're* dead to us both!'

'Maorten, we're hungry. Leave this pitiful human and let's go,' growled Gregorn.

'Yes, I am done speaking, we return home,' said Maorten. As the other goblins departed, he bent down to his father's hidden face and said, 'Goodbye, Alan Dwyer, tell Mother you don't have children anymore, just like you always wanted.'

Alan looked up, not really seeing his son through tear-streaked eyes, and held out his arms, his hands reaching out to Tane's barrier. Maorten reached out with his.

'NO, ALAN!' screamed Bill.

Their hands were so close. Then Alan slowly dropped his before slumping down and buried his head into his knees.

Maorten looked down at him and snarled before fleeing to join his comrades. As he ran, though, he could not stop a small tear escaping from one eye.

All was quiet now, apart from Alan's sobs. Bill went down the steps, followed by Amiria, Beccia, Kyeua, and Makoa.

They bent down to Alan and, one by one, embraced him as he cried. The glow on Tane's barrier faded out. Howelia went inside and jumped to the light switch, flicking it off, plunging the area into darkness.

For once, darkness was not the enemy, but a much-needed friend for a broken father.

— Chapter Fifteen —

The Eve of Battle

Harbin listened to the report as he ate. He guffawed as he heard what Maorten had said to his father and slapped him on his back.

'I could not have said it better myself, Maorten. In time, you may indeed become one of my best warriors.'

Maorten grinned.

'Did he cry?' snickered Harbin.

'Yes, my lord, like the coward he is.'

'Good, very good. Eat now, my brothers, then be ready for my summons. We have work to do before the night is done.'

Maorten left to enjoy the spoils of the hunt. Harbin then called for Meido and Reido to bring Zulear's wheel to him.

As they laid it on the ground, Harbin growled, 'Go over this time difference again. I want no confusion this close to success.'

Meido said, 'My lord, once the sun has set, the last rays of light must be gone before activating the wheel. Then the moon will be in its fourth cycle and then the power of Zulear can be unleashed.'

'Good,' grunted Harbin. 'Go over the ceremony plans and

run through of the activation process again.'

'But my lord, we have already—'

Harbin gave a low growl.

'Yes, my lord, right away!'

***

'He didn't mean it, Alan. You have to understand it wasn't Matt talking, but a goblin. That wasn't really your son.'

All Alan wanted was to chug the bottle of scotch, but the guild wisely reminded him that tomorrow would require fresh minds, not alcohol damaged ones.

'I know, Beccia, I know,' said Alan. 'It doesn't make it any easier though.'

Bill said, 'Harbin's game and a sick one, mate. He did something similar to me after the Hellier kids were full goblin. Left little carvings all over park trees for me to read, the gutless little dickhead!'

'Bill!'

'Sorry, Amiria,' replied Bill, not really sorry at all. Remembering something, he turned to Kyeua. 'What was your vision about, Kyeua?'

'Oh dear, I had forgotten about that,' said Amiria.

The seer stood up and slowly paced in front of the kitchen. 'I, I don't know what the vison was. It was something I have not seen before. Something no one has ever seen before, I think. It … it was …'

'Take your time, Kyeua,' said Makoa.

She took a deep breath. 'A light of enormous power came out of the mountain. The colours were both terrible and yet beautiful. The light felt … not nice. Then, as in my other vision, once again, goblins roamed the lands at will.'

'I know not of this light,' said Howelia.

174

Everyone looked at each other with uncertainty. Amiria said, 'I'll check the grimoire for any mention of this.'

'I doubt you will find much,' said a weak voice from above.

'Ari!' exclaimed Beccia and raced up to help him down the stairs. He winced at every step.

'Damn, I'm getting too old for this.'

'Nonsense,' said Makoa, his usually strong voice a touch hoarse. 'You'll be back to normal before no time.'

Ari pained a smile as he hobbled into the living room. Kyeua grabbed a solid backed chair from the kitchen for him to sit.

'Thank you for getting me back, everyone. And whoever did the first-aid did a great job. I can't heal myself, but this is the next best thing.'

Amiria said, 'We'll get you to the hospital at Stratford as soon as we can, Ari, but …'

'I know, Amiria, that can wait. It *has* to wait. I can still help, but I won't be able to enter any bolt-holes for some time.' He turned to Alan. 'I heard what was said out there, Alan, which is why I made my way down here. You showed great courage in meeting them. They wanted you to breach the barrier and figured you would. But you held strong, and that was very tough to do. I don't think Matt would have attacked you, but he would not have stopped the others.'

'Yeah,' croaked Alan. 'I reckon I'll never forget what he said.'

Ari smiled, 'Rest assured, Alan. Once he is rescued and returned to human form, your son's love for you will return.'

Alan blinked his eyes furiously.

Ari turned to Amiria. 'I also heard Kyeua. It is my belief her vision centres around Leigh successfully transforming into the queen. If the vision is correct, it could foretell us failing.'

'Oh, crap on that!' argued Bill. 'Visions are not set in stone, are they, Kyeua?'

'Well … no, but they are a powerful predictive tool,' replied Kyeua.

'So long as we follow our plan and all goes well tomorrow, the vision shall not influence the outcome,' said Amiria. 'Ari, we will work out what you can do tomorrow without entering the bolt-holes. Everyone else should get some rest. We rise at 5:30 am.'

Howelia said, 'Then I return to my clan. Tomorrow I will be outside.' He gave a slight nod and left the lodge.

The guild and Alan headed to the upstairs bunks, with Alan wondering how on earth he was supposed to sleep after his confrontation with his son.

Bill stayed behind to have a quick word with Amiria. 'Look, if that vision comes true, the last thing we want is for Ari to be out in the open in his current state.'

'I know, Bill, I won't risk it either. Ari will stay behind.'

Bill nodded and headed up the stairs for a spare loft bunk. He could not stop Kyeua's vison repeating in his mind. He knew he was scared. Scared, Ari was right.

***

'I saw Dad at the lodge. He wouldn't even give me a hug! Some father,' laughed Maorten.

Leigh said, 'Did he say anything?'

'Yeah,' he replied, as he bit into a chunk of rabbit. 'He was *so sorry.*'

'And did he say anything about those people trying to kill me?'

'No, and I didn't ask. What's the point? They're the enemy now. They proved that. And how about *kindly Bill the ranger*? He was with them. He was a part of it. They're *all* the enemy now, including Dad.'

Leigh sighed. 'I guess you're right, Matt.'

'My name is Maorten now. Please honour my new name as I honour yours.'

Leigh didn't say anything for a while as she watched her brother eat. There was still something in her brother that scared her, not realising it was the reflection of her own change she could see.

'Maorten, have you finished your meal?' Arcmedan had arrived outside.

'Yes, what orders?'

'Lord Harbin has requested a meeting of the inner defence. Come, the meeting starts shortly.'

Maorten turned and bowed to Leigh before leaving.

Leigh sat down in her chair and stared at her hands before burying her face in them.

'You are troubled again, my queen. Can I offer anything?'

Leigh looked up to see Artex. 'No, I am fine,' she croaked.

Artex looked left and right before entering the cave. He sat in front of Leigh. 'My queen, it is not for me to speak of certain things, but what you feel is natural.'

Leigh roared, *WHAT DO YOU KNOW HOW I FEEL!'*

Artex winced. After a minute Leigh said, 'I am sorry, Artex, that was not called for. It's just that … it's just that …'

'May I speak freely?'

Leigh nodded.

'You are not fully goblin yet. You still feel longings for times past and families lost. All takings go through this.'

'So why does Matt not feel it anymore?' asked Leigh.

'Maorten is male, and also had warrior like tendencies before being taken, I believe.'

Leigh whispered, 'How could you possibly know that?'

Artex said through a rather sad smile, 'I am the teacher of the goblin race. I teach all takings, so I get to know about human feelings. I also teach pure blood goblins in human ways. What Matt is going through is the usual transition. However, you, my queen, are different. You somehow cling to your humanity when others did not. But seeing as you are the first ever female taken, we expected differences. It … it has been noticed by others. Hide these feelings, my queen, for your own good.'

'What happens tomorrow tonight, Artex? Talk to me about what happens. My Lord Harbin will not speak of it.'

'I- I cannot.'

Leigh's eyes flared yellow. 'Artex!'

The goblin eyed Leigh for a short period before saying, 'At sundown, the Wheel of Zulear will be activated.'

'Yes, Lord Harbin told me about my blood activating the wheel. But what happens after that?'

'Well, I am not fully sure, but I think it will —'

'Do what is ordained,' said Meido. Leigh and Artex looked around to see the wizards outside. They did not look happy.

'You may go now, Artex,' said Reido.

For the first time, and to Leigh's astonishment, anger flared in Artex's face. He bowed to her and wheeled around, striding out of the cave.

Meido and Reido watched him depart, not hiding their displeasure at his insolence.

***

In the main chamber, Harbin outlined the coming day. 'The primary observation posts will remain open. Ten goblins are to guard, each with five awake at *all* times. I want no fires in place at the bases, so those above think it is unguarded. All guards are to be hidden from sight. Rotate the guard every two hours. I want a patrol up at all times, moving between posts. All other posts are to be collapsed. Are we clear?'

Maorten said, 'I know humans, my lord. May I also suggest some sort of spike pit?'

'And what is that, Maorten?' smirked Gregorn. 'Some lame human trap?'

Maorten growled, 'Dig a hole at the base, close to the entry point. Place spikes in the hole with the tips only an inch below the surface. Mark the tunnel walls where this is, for our benefit. Humans come, impaled through their feet, cannot run, dead humans.'

Arcmedan said, 'My lord, this is sound thinking. I like it.'

'Agreed,' said Harbin. 'You all have your jobs, make it happen. Make no mistake, the humans *will* return tomorrow. I want them all dead in my lair and then devoured. Anyone caught slacking or asleep will suffer the same fate as Derrein. Now get to it!'

The goblins broke into teams. As Maorten headed off, he gave Gregorn one of the last traits of his humanity in a one-fingered salute.

A bewildered Gregorn turned to Adoien and Bezenar and said, 'What the hell was that?'

***

For the next few hours, the goblins prepared their defences. Once completed, they bedded down for the coming sunrise with the guards set.

At the lodge, the guild slept whilst Alan tossed and turned, tormented by his dreams.

The Tohunga coming to aid the guild were asleep on the roadside in their bus, the driver beyond exhausted and needing rest.

At Stratford, the town was also at peace, with Sergeant Simonka snoring loudly in his bed, to the annoyance of his wife Teresa.

Dawn's rays kept marching across the lands of New Zealand. They then hit the peak of Mount Taranaki, signalling a new day was about to begin.

A day that would end in tragedy.

Chapter Sixteen

The Fallen

'You look like hell, mate.'

Alan smile faintly as he came into the kitchen. 'I'll be okay, Bill. But after I have the kids back, I'm never going to dream again if I can help it.'

'Bad, eh?' sympathised Bill, handing him a mug of coffee.

'Yeah ...'

As they chatted, other members of the guild made their appearances, except for one.

'I have left Ari in bed,' said Amiria. 'He is still too weak to come out, so he will stay here.'

'I bet he didn't like that,' said Bill.

Makoa smiled. 'You have no idea. We would have locked him in the room except it doesn't have a bathroom.'

Kyeua said, 'His power will be missed, but should things not go well today, he would be unable to defend himself. It's not worth the risk.'

'Yeah,' said Beccia. 'It's a miracle we haven't lost anyone yet.'

'Now that's what I like to hear, unbridled enthusiasm,' said Bill with a hint of sarcasm.

'Just being a realist, Bill,' stated Beccia.

Alan put down his empty mug with a noticeable thump. 'Okay, so when do we go?'

Amiria looked to the nearest window. 'We leave a 7am.'

***

The phone woke Sergeant Simonka from his sleep. He squinted at the clock and cursed. Picking up the receiver, he grumbled, 'Sergeant Simonka.'

'Sarge, it's Constable Spurrett. We got a small problem here.'

'At six am, it had better be a big problem!'

'Err, yes, sarge. Umm, well we got a call from a Sergeant Macey, an off-duty bloke from Hamilton on his way to Wellington. Says he pulled over a bus outside Tahore that was driving too fast. He says he was just going to give the driver a warning to slow down, you know?'

'Yeah.'

'And something didn't sit right with him, so he searched the bus and found all sorts of weapons.'

Simonka was wide awake now. 'What sort of weapons?'

'Swords, crossbows, spears, knives an' stuff. No guns, though. Macey's detained them all, about ten men and women, and wants us to take them in, as we're the closest town.'

Simonka swung his legs out of bed. 'Alright, Spurrett. Tell him to bring them in. I'll be there in about half an hour.' As he hung up, Simonka thought, *there goes my quiet day …*

***

'All quiet?' asked Arcmedan.

'Yes, no signs of anyone outside.'

The patrol waited around as Arcmedan spoke to the head goblin of this bolt-hole guard.

'It is light outside now. If they are coming, it will be very soon. Remain alert and swap out your guards as ordered. Sound the alarm immediately if you hear something, understand?'

Without waiting for a reply, he swung about and motioned for his patrol to follow him to check on the next bolt-hole. They passed Artex, who was returning from the storage cave with a ewer of water.

'Going to wash the queen's feet, Artex? What a good little servant you are,' sniggered one goblin.

'Quiet!' growled Arcmedan, giving Artex a nod before moving on.

Artex sighed and continued on, used to the snide remarks. He was no warrior and knew it. He passed the caves of sleeping goblins and stopped cold at the entrance of the queen's chamber.

A faint singing came from the cave.

He listened for a while. A strange look washed over his face before he shook his head and said loudly, 'My queen, fresh water, as you asked.'

The singing stopped abruptly and Leigh said, 'Enter!' She took the ewer from Artex and gulped down the water.

'Leighandra ... what was that tune?'

Leigh looked startled before eventually replying, 'A song my father sang to me as a little girl. It's called *King of the Road*.'

'It- it sounded nice.'

Leigh looked down at the floor to hide her eyes, specifically the wetness forming in them.

'I ... I've been singing it to myself a lot since ...'

Artex now realised why Leigh had resisted the transition better than her brother.

'My queen, that doesn't help. You *must* let go of your humanity. The change is coming whether you like it or not. Do you not feel it coming?'

Leigh didn't look up. 'Yes, I feel it. I long for it, and yet I'm also terrified of it.'

Artex quickly looked left and right and then laid a hand on Leigh's shoulder. She looked up, startled.

He said, 'You will feel much better after you transform. This is a tough time for all who change. But you will be a new power after you are one of us, and you will like it.'

Artex removed his hand and left Leigh with her thoughts.

***

At seven am, Alan, Bill and the guild stood outside the lodge, fully dressed and armed, each with a shovel or a pick. They eyed the forest carefully, their thoughts hidden. Ari hobbled down and watched them depart.

'Be damned careful down there,' he said. 'Take chances only if there is no other alternative.'

'Listen to him telling *us* to be careful!' laughed Kyeua nervously.

Makoa said, 'The gods are with us, Ari. We will return with the kids, and Harbin's scalp.'

Amiria hitched her backpack and in a muted voice said, 'Let's go finish this.'

'Hey, Howelia isn't here,' stated Alan.

'He'll have to catch up,' replied Bill. 'Time is something we don't have, so let's roll.'

They began walking toward the forest. One by one, they merged into the green canopy and disappeared.

Ari fought the urge to join them and instead began a protective chant for his friends. It was all he could do to ward off the sudden fear he felt in his heart.

The guild marched on through the forest, each keeping sound to a minimum. They passed the first bolt-hole closest to the lodge. Then before long …

'My goodness, they've collapsed some of the bolt-holes!' exclaimed Beccia.

Where the second bolt-hole had lain was now nothing but a pile of dirt. The third also was no longer there.

Amiria said, 'Okay, let's stop and have a look at this.' She laid out the map on the ground and all gathered around.

'Hmm, looks like they have removed all but the one closest to the lodge,' said Makoa.

Bill frowned. 'Why would they do that?'

Alan said, 'The fewer places to guard, the more you can concentrate your forces.'

'Correct, you,' said Howelia as he thumped down in front of them from the nearest tree. 'Apologies I give for my lateness, preparations take time. My people lay in the woods ready. They will remain hidden and await my flute.'

'You're a sight for sore eyes, Howelia,' beamed Beccia.

The little Natawidu grinned in pleasure.

Makoa said, 'Alan's right though. What's the bet all but a few bolt-hole are still intact?'

'Come, I show something. Come, come!' said Howelia with some excitement. He trampled off, and the guild had to run to catch up with him. After a few minutes, they came through a dense part of the forest to find Howelia next to a bolt-hole. He had a finger to his lips and gestured them forward.

'Look, you, closely at the edges,' he whispered. Howelia then pulled at the moss. Sticky sap stretched away from his hands. 'Slippery for any creature to get close. Too close and then, in you go. Small ones had similar if you remember, now does the big ones.'

Amiria nodded and moved back, with the others following. In a hushed voice she said, 'Absolutely no noise from now on. If they are concentrating around the openings, they will be alert. We will head to the target site and begin our diggings.'

The guild moved on with Howelia disappearing into the bushes now and then before re-joining them. It took longer than expected as they walked carefully over broken ground, avoiding anything so much as a twig.

Amiria raised a hand, and they came to a halt. She pulled out the map again and whispered, 'Here.'

They lowered their packs to the ground. Alan took one last look at the map and moved three metres away and chose a spot. Then he started to dig. The others picked spots a few metres on either side of Alan and began digging as well.

***

'You're not going anywhere. You'll stay behind bars until you see a judge and bail is set. And if you keep up with this ridiculous story, your chance of bail will be zip!'

'Look, sergeant, why would we make this up? We are obviously not street thugs looking for a good time. And Bank Robbers don't normally use swords. I'm telling you we are needed urgently at Konini Lodge. If you don't let us go, we are all in terrible danger.'

Simonka snorted. 'I know Bill Gardiner personally. How about I give him a call then, eh?'

The sergeant expect their faces to fall, instead he got, 'Great idea! Please call him now and tell him that the other Tohunga are at Stratford and you're sending them up right away.'

He looked at them curiously, then shrugged. 'Be back in a few minutes.' As he left the cells, he muttered to Constable Spurrett, 'Keep an eye on these nutters, but keep your distance.'

***

At the lodge, Ari had taken more medicine and was feeling better. To keep worry from making him do something stupid like heading out, he kept busy by preparing food and blankets for the kids. He also prepared his own healing materials, just in case. As he passed the lounge area, he passed a bunch of mobile phones on charge, all showing no signal on their screens.

***

Simonka hung up and returned to the cells. 'No response, so you're out of luck. Now seeing at its Saturday and the local Court is shut, you'd better get comfortable. Lunch will be at 1pm.'

He went to leave when the eldest of the group said, 'Please, may I have a word, sergeant?'

The Sergeant wondered over to him and said, 'Go ahead.'

The man said in a low voice, 'I know you don't believe, few do. But we speak the truth. I am a veteran and old enough to be your father, so I only ask one thing. Please keep trying to contact Mr. Gardiner. Because if we do speak the truth, you can either help save New Zealand or be partly responsible for destroying it.'

Michael Simonka, police sergeant of Stratford, stared at the man with amusement, only for a steady gaze to be returned. He smirked, 'Okay. But should I get through, it will make for an interesting conversation. "*Hey, Bill, ya had any goblin problems lately, mate?*"' Simonka chuckled and left the cells.

The old man muttered, 'You naive fool.'

***

'The map is near useless, and we're losing time!'

'Keep your voice down, Bill,' said Makoa.

'Sorry,' muttered Bill. 'But we've dug till our hands bled and we've hit nothing so far.'

Alan said, 'We know the map is vague, but it's all we have. We've got to keep trying.'

Amiria was exhausted and had to stop her part of the digging. Everyone else took turns resting, which slowed down the progress.

Howelia said, 'Time turns against us. Be back shortly, you.' He left the group and disappeared into the forest. They then heard his flute. Within a few minutes, he returned with a stiff piece of flat bark.

'Help ... and more,' he grinned. Dozens of Natawidu appeared from the deep growth, all carrying bark. Howelia spoke in his native language and shortly, they were all digging at fever pitch.

Beccia grinned. '*That* will make a difference,' she said and drove her shovel into a new spot.

The Natawidu dug like possessed creatures. The guild could barely keep up. It was not long before ...

'Humans, come quick!'

They raced over to the excited Howelia. Kyeua pulled out a torch and shone through the smallest of holes. Bill peered in and yelled, 'I see a flat dirt bottom. This is it!'

'Lower your voice, dammit!' hushed Amiria.

'Okay,' whispered Makoa. 'We need to enlarge the hole and setup the tarp.'

Howelia gave a signal, and his clan fled to the safety of the forest. Makoa and Bill carefully enlarged the hole with their hands whilst Alan, Beccia and Kyeua gathered thick leaves to spread out over the tarpaulin.

'Howelia, are you ready?'

'Yes,' he said and moved over to the hole. With a little wriggle, he popped through and was gone. After a minute he called up, 'Clear, it is, of goblins. Continue to dig. A warning will be given if needed.'

Bill and Makoa laid down flat and enlarged the hole so they could enter, with Howelia smoothing out the dropping dirt with his feet. The tarpaulin was then laid over Bill and Makoa. Amiria and Kyeua spread large, leafy foliage over it, trying to block out the sunlight from entering the hole. Beccia set out the knotted ropes and tied them to the nearest tree. All the while, Bill tried his best to keep Howelia in sight despite the darkness below.

Suddenly, Howelia began frantically waving and stomping his feet.

'Goblins are coming!' hissed Bill as loudly as he dared. 'Makoa, move!'

They scampered out from under the tarp, letting it drop flat. More leaves and dirt were piled over the top.

'Shh, stay still,' whispered Amiria.

Nobody moved, the only sound coming from the slight wind passing through the trees. They all strained to hear any sound from below. The minutes ticked by. Then the tarp bulged up. The bulge moved towards the edge of the tarp. Makoa readied his crossbow.

Howelia popped clear. 'Close, that was,' he said.

Makoa said, 'Now that had my heart racing! Give us a bit of a warning next time, Howelia.'

The Natawidu leader smiled and pointed up towards the sun.

'Guess I'm on edge a bit,' said Makoa, a little embarrassed.

'So how many were there and how on earth didn't they see you?' asked Kyeua.

'I left the tunnel. A rock in the next cavern I stayed behind. I hid till they passed. Six there were, armed in battle dress of some kind.'

'They're definitely expecting us then,' said Amiria.

Beccia asked, 'Howelia, is there anywhere we can hide if they return?'

The Natawidu shook his head. 'If they enter the tunnel, nowhere to hide. Your size will give you away.'

'Not much we can do but hope they don't come back for a while,' said Bill. 'Amiria, we need to enter now. We're running behind schedule.'

Amiria took a deep breath and said, 'We went through this many times last night. Is everyone ready?'

'We're ready,' said Beccia.

Makoa and Alan lifted the tarp, and Beccia grabbed the ropes and fed them down the hole.

Howelia leapt down, ignoring the ropes.

One by one, Bill, Alan, Makoa, Beccia and Kyeua passed themselves down. Amiria then covered the tarp up again with leaves, checking that the branches would keep it from moving. Then she whispered, 'Good luck,' and made preparations for their return.

***

Maorten stirred, his stomach growling in hunger. He sat up and looked around at the other sleeping goblins. Picking a way out to not disturb them, he left the cave. Outside, he yawned loudly, stretching his hairy arms and then casually made his way towards the food storage area. He passed various caves and the occasional tunnel before reaching the one he wanted. As he turned to enter —

WHAM!

He cannoned into the patrol. Swords were raised before Arcmedan identified him. 'Maorten! What are you doing?'

'You're not allowed to roam at will yet!' growled Gregorn.

Maorten said, 'More food. I am still developing, so my hunger is great.'

Arcmedan said, 'Get your food and then get back to your allotted cave. I will let this pass … this time.'

Maorten replied, 'As you wish, Arcmedan.' He moved off to the provisions store and grabbed himself a big hunk of pork. Walking back to his cave, his teeth sank into the flesh, biting off large chunks.

He passed cave after cave without bothering to look anywhere but ahead. A tunnel approached on the right. And then —

WHAM!

He went reeling as he bounced off his father. His eyes bulged when he saw who was with him. He got up fast, trying to spit out the food to yell when Bill crash tackled him.

They swarmed Maorten, with Alan saying, 'Son, it's me! We're going to save you. Please stop struggling. Matt, stop it, please!' Alan tried to cover his son's mouth with his hand, only for Maorten to try to bite it.

Then Beccia hit him over the head with the hilt of her sword, knocking him out.

Alan turned fiercely on Beccia and yelled, 'Don't hit my son, damn you!'

'Quiet, Alan, for god's sake quiet!' whispered Kyeua.

'I'm sorry, Alan,' said Beccia. 'I had no choice. He was about to start yelling.'

'Tie him up,' said Bill. 'We can take him back to the hole. Kyeua can stay with him until we return with Leigh.'

Makoa pulled some rope out of his pack and tied Maorten's hands and feet with Beccia tying a gag around his mouth. Howelia said, 'This is good. Easier now. Kill the king, take the girl, return and leave.'

'Oh yeah, so much easier,' said Kyeua, not bothering to hide her sarcasm. She hauled Maorten up over the other shoulder and sagged. 'I'm going to need a hand to get him back to the exit.'

Alan and Bill took him off Kyeua. 'Howelia, scout ahead please to the main cavern. We'll be back in a few minutes.'

The Natawidu scurried off, hugging the side of the cavern as he left. Alan and Bill carried Maorten with Kyeua following. They lowered him next to the hole. Bill said, 'If that patrol comes through here again, Kyeua, leave Matt and get yourself out fast.'

'Will do, Bill,' said Kyeua.

'Shouldn't we haul him up now then?' asked Alan.

'No, Alan,' replied Kyeua. 'We have to keep him out of sunlight until the last possible moment. The tarp won't give much protection and he could suffer great pain up there, even death.'

Alan leant down and touched his son's face. 'Soon, Matt,' he whispered, 'soon.'

'I don't like leaving Kyeua alone,' said Makoa, as Bill and Alan returned.

'If you have a better suggestion, I'm all ears,' said Bill.

Makoa shrugged. 'Guess not. Come on, we better catch up with Howelia.'

But Howelia caught up *with them instead*.

'Patrol returning! Hide!'

There was nowhere to go. If they left the tunnel and the patrol then entered it, they would run into Kyeua and Matt. They edged further into the tunnel and drew weapons.

'Keep going past,' whispered Alan.

The sound of the patrol approaching got louder and louder. Makoa levelled his crossbow at the entrance.

Then the patrol appeared — and marched straight past the tunnel.

The sound of marching feet lessened and Bill dared to whisper, 'I think I need to empty my bladder.'

Beccia replied, 'Join the club!'

Howelia darted out of the tunnel, looked around, and gave a sign that all was clear. 'On we go now, you,' he said and scampered away, the guild running after him, as silent as possible, to keep up.

***

Leigh felt better. She couldn't say how or why and didn't really care, anyway. She only knew her terrors were fading as the day moved on. She brushed her orange, matted hair with an old human brush and smiled. In the corner, on a chest, lay a green dress with leather straps around the shoulders. A brown belt with an ornate orb in the centre lay next to it.

She picked up the thing that drew her in the most. A tiara made of goblin gold, with a black crystal in the centre. Leigh longed to put it on but knew it was not yet time. She sighed and put the tiara back down. Turning around, she found herself face to face with Howelia.

'You again?' Who *are* you?'

'I am Howelia. Back I am, yes. We take you away from all this. Your human form is to be returned.'

Leigh frowned. 'I -I don't understand. Who are we?'

Alan stepped into the cave. 'Hello, Leigh.'

'D- Dad?' gasped Leigh.

Alan did his best to keep the shock out of his voice. His beautiful little girl, relegated to this. But he couldn't stop his eyes from tearing up.

'Yeah, it's me,' he said. 'I never gave up on you, sweetie. The guild and I have been trying for days to get to you. Now we're going to take you from here and make you better.'

'How?'

'We already have your brother. Now I'm going to kill Harbin, which will return you and Matt to human form. Do you know where he sleeps?'

'I ... I do, but I can't tell you. You can't kill him!'

Bill stepped inside. 'We don't have time for this. Leigh, if we don't kill the goblin king, you and your brother turn into full goblins tomorrow. Do you understand?'

'I do, but ... but I ... please don't — you can't hurt him!'

Beccia overheard and came inside. 'She is almost totally under his spell. Her loyalty to the cruel one is very strong.'

Alan stared at Leigh for a moment before saying, 'Leigh, your mum misses you so very much. She wants you and Matt to know she cries every night, not having you back in her arms. She loves you so much, sweetheart, as do I.'

Alan's words hit home.

Leigh went through a huge internal struggle as she screwed her eyes up. Eventually, she lowered her head and said, 'He is in the last tunnel, past the stone chairs. Follow that to the end.

There are two caves, the one he sleeps in on the left. The right has his personal guard.'

'That will complicate things,' said Beccia. 'We'll have to take out the guard as well.'

Bill thought for a second before saying, 'Makoa takes out the guard as silently as he can with his crossbow, Beccia wounds Harbin instead by sword, then Alan finishes him off.'

Howelia nodded his approval. 'I will lead. To Harbin we go.'

They moved out, with Bill taking Leigh with him.

'Stay with me, Leigh,' he whispered. 'It will be all over soon, and then you can kick your dad's backside when you're human again. I'll even hold him down for you.'

Leigh tried to smile, but found herself filled with dread as they approached Harbin's tunnel.

Howelia entered. After a minute, so did Alan, Makoa and Beccia. Bill stayed with Leigh.

'Is there no other way?' whimpered Leigh. 'Lord Harbin is … is a good goblin. He takes good care of me.'

Bill shook his head sadly. 'No, dear child, this is the only way.'

Leigh fought the urge to race into the tunnel and yell a warning to her king. A battle she was losing by the second.

***

'Have you heard anything?' demanded Amiria, lifting the tarp ever so slightly.

'No, still nothing. They've been gone for ages,' said Kyeua.

Amiria looked up at the sun and grimaced. Time was becoming short. 'They'd better be out soon. My nerves are taking a battering.'

'Mine too. Won't be long now I hope,' said Kyeua and

returned to looking down each way of the tunnel. 'Better not be long,' she muttered. 'That patrol is sure to come through here again.'

With the blindfold around Maorten's eyes, she did not see them flick open. He tried to move his hands but couldn't. He also found out he could not see. Then he remembered why this was so. A nail sprung out, and he started working on the ropes. However sturdy Manila rope might be, it's no match for goblin nails.

It parted.

He heard a human pacing about and carefully eased an arm up and pushed the blindfold up just a little before lowering his arm. With an eye now clear to watch Kyeua, he moved a hand down his side to the ropes around his legs when she was not looking.

***

Howelia raised a hand. 'This is not good.'

'*Three caves*,' whispered Beccia. 'We've been had!'

'What do we do?' said Alan.

Beccia said, 'Leigh is almost full goblin. Her feelings for Harbin … my god, she's trying to protect him!'

'Quickly, back outside!' urged Howelia suddenly. 'The girl is bonded to him. She will —'

A loud howl came from behind, followed by the sound of running feet.

'Oh hell, she's free!' yelled Makoa.

Alan charged back down the tunnel, and crash tackled his oncoming daughter. But she screamed, 'NO! DO NOT HURT MY KING!' before he could cover her mouth.

It had the desired effect.

'I don't know how you got in, scum, but you're never

getting out again.'

They wheeled around to see Harbin and his guard coming towards them.

'Get them!' snarled the goblin king.

***

Maorten cut through the last rope and leapt up. He barrelled through Kyeua, knocking her down with a thud, and ran down the tunnel.

Kyeua staggered to her feet and yelled up to Amiria, 'Matt is loose!'

'INTRUDERS! INTRUDERS! WE ARE UNDER ATTACK! SOUND THE ALARM!' yelled Maorten over and over as he burst into the larger cavern.

The patrol was too far away to hear him — but the goblins guarding the nearest bolt-hole were not. Five of them rushed to see what was happening, blowing their warning horn as they dashed towards the yelling.

At the entrance to Harbin's tunnel, Bill stood up groggily, clutching his head. Leigh had turned and hit him so fast he never saw it coming. Then he heard the horns and paled as he realised what was happening. He yelled into the tunnel, 'The goblin alarm is sounding. They're onto us! Get out of there!'

'They are inside my cave!' roared Harbin. 'To my cave at once!'

The goblin king launched an attack against Beccia, his sword clashing with hers. Beccia used all her skill to keep him at bay, but she was being pushed sideways by his strength.

Makoa had killed one guard with his crossbow but could not line up the other one as Howelia had jumped on the guard and was pounding him with his little fists.

Beccia yelled down the tunnel, 'Run, Alan! Take Leigh and

run!'

Harbin's eyes widened. He roared in rage and intensified his attack, pushing Beccia back away from the tunnel exit.

'Watch out, you!' shouted Howelia. 'The king tries to get past!'

The guard threw Howelia off, who hit the cave wall with a thud, giving Makoa the opening he needed. An arrow thudded into the guard's head.

Bill arrived and yelled, 'We're about to be surrounded! We have to go. Alan has Leigh, let's move!'

Harbin roared, 'My warriors! To the main chamber. Kill the humans! Save the queen!'

Makoa aimed his crossbow at Harbin. 'No!' screamed Bill, 'it has to be Alan!'

'It's too late, we're screwed anyway!' cried Makoa and fired.

The arrows missed. Harbin moved too quickly.

'MOVE!' ordered Bill, 'Or we all goners!'

They turned and ran, Beccia scooping up the hurt Howelia on the way out.

They raced up the cavern towards the tunnel, Leigh screaming, 'LET ME GO! MY LORD NEEDS ME. LET ME GO!'

Beccia ran behind Bill and tried her best to gag Leigh, but received a nasty bite from her sharp teeth. She gave Leigh a backhand in return.

Alan said nothing as they ran. Behind them, Harbin closed in fast.

As they reached the tunnel, Maorten appeared with the five guards from the bolt-hole. His eyes widened as he saw Leigh.

'NO! The queen! Save my sister!' he yelled.

The goblins drew their swords and surged forward. The

guild darted into the tunnel, with Makoa desperately trying to reload his crossbow on the run.

Kyeua heard them coming. She cupped her hands and yelled up, 'Amiria, clear the hole! They're coming out fast!'

'Do they have both the children? Is Harbin dead?'

'I don't know. It's all gone wrong, I think. Hurry, Amiria!'

A few moments later, a shaft of sunlight burst into the chamber. Kyeua paled as she saw her friends running towards her with Leigh. Then she groaned as she saw Leigh was still a goblin.

Beccia yelled, 'Get out, Kyeua, they're coming!' But she stayed put.

'Bill, get up there,' Kyeua urged. 'We'll pass up Leigh and Howelia, get the tarp ready to cover her or she'll die from the sunlight.'

Bill went to protest, but Kyeua screamed, 'Now, dammit!'

Bill grabbed the rope and pulled himself up.

'You next, Alan. Bill will need help with Leigh.'

Alan nodded, pulling himself up. Then spears came flying up the tunnel.

'Watch out!' yelled Beccia, knocking one clear with her sword. Makoa had finally reloaded and fired all his arrows down the tunnel, which resulted in goblin screams.

Kyeua pushed Leigh up through the hole, who immediately began howling in pain as the sunlight hit.

She went to pick up Howelia, but he came to and groaned, 'I recover. What happens, you?'

'Get out of here fast,' ordered Kyeua. Howelia did not question, but jumped up clear of the tunnel.

Beccia said, 'Get up there, Kyeua, quick as you can.'

Makoa lit a flare and threw it down the tunnel towards the

goblins, who screeched in pain.

Beccia grabbed a rope and yelled, 'PULL US ALL UP! HURRY!' Then she shot up and disappeared out of the hole as the rope was pulled at a frantic pace from above.

Kyeua went to grab the second rope, but suddenly fell awkwardly. She got up a bit dazed and grabbed the rope to be hauled clear.

Makoa turned quickly to grab the last rope. As he was hauled up, the last image he saw was Maorten coming through the flare's smoke, running at him. His hands just missed his ankles as he was pulled clear.

Maorten shrieked as the small beam of sunlight touched him, and he scuttled backwards from the hole.

Outside, Alan said, 'The hole, cover it quickly!'

'Don't' bother,' said Bill. 'They can't come up here.'

From below, they could hear the screeching of the outraged goblins.

They all tried to catch their breath, lying slumped on the ground.

Makoa panted, 'Well, that did not go well. What a frigging disaster!'

'We're still alive though,' said Beccia, taking in deep breaths. 'It could have been worse. And we got the queen, at least.'

Alan heard the low moans of pain from his daughter, who was wrapped heavily in the tarp.

'She's hurting. The sun is burning her through the tarp!'

'Yeah,' said Amiria wearily. 'We need to get her into the lodge and into a dark closet or something. The tarpaulin is only offering limited protection. She'll die if she stays out here too long.'

'Right, let's leave,' said Bill as he stood up. 'We can work out what to do next at the lodge.'

'Amiria,' whispered a weak voice.

She turned from Bill to the voice.

'Kyeua, what the—'

'I'm so sorry, everyone.'

Amiria's eyes travelled down to Kyeua's hands, which were holding her stomach. The guild leader's eyes widened in shock to see a broken off spear end protruding between Kyeua's hands. Redness seeped through her fingers.

'Oh no ... no, no, no!' Amiria leapt for Kyeua as she fell sideways.

**

Harbin sat in his stone carved chair, brooding. All the Goblins of Mount Taranaki were in attendance. *They have the queen* they all muttered in muted conversation.

Harbin raised his hand for silence.

'Meido, Reido, what will they do with Leighandra?'

Meido came forward to speak. 'My lord, it pains us to say this, but they will kill her. It is the only logical thing to do.'

Reido added, 'They have already tried once. Now she is in their domain without our protection, it will be swift.'

Harbin screwed up his eyes and began shaking. The few goblins close to him took a step back as his rage threatened to explode and engulf anyone nearby.

Then a voice said, 'My lord, I ... I wish to be heard.'

Harbin's eyes snapped open to look down at Artex. 'What is it? Speak fast!'

Artex looked squarely back at Harbin and said, 'My lord, as you know, I have conducted much of the training with your queen. I know humans. They may not kill her.'

'Explain why!' demanded Harbin.

'The reason is that some of her humanity still exists.'

'Impossible!' snorted Meido.

Harbin raised a hand for silence. 'Go on,' he ordered.

'I have discovered Leighandra has resisted the change by singing songs her father taught her. This has kept a part of her humanity intact. I did not know this was possible. In fact, in all takings, this has never happened before. It explains much.'

Harbin was incredulous. 'And they will not kill my queen for this?'

'I think so, my lord,' replied Artex. 'It will come down to the will of the father. The Māori will wish to kill her, the father will not, nor will the ranger. In my opinion, she will live for the moment whilst they argue, but should the will of the Māori prevail …'

'I still say they will kill her swiftly,' argued Reido.

Artex flicked a glance at Reido and retorted, 'If they wanted to do that, they would not have taken her and she would lie dead in the tunnel. Remember, they also tried to take Maorten.'

He returned his gaze to Harbin. 'My lord, Māori magic is strong. Stronger than our European brethren have ever faced. Could this magic of theirs be used to undo the changes? Is that why they took the queen?'

Harbin turned to the wizards. 'Well? Is it possible?'

Meido and Reido looked at each other, thinking fast. Then Reido said, 'Lord Harbin, I cannot agree with this. This has never been documented before.'

'Only by other clans, though,' said Arcmedan thoughtfully, adding to the discussion. 'We are unique in this land they call New Zealand. We face an enemy no other goblin clan has.

Who is to say what is possible?'

Harbin leapt down from his chair and paced, occasionally flicking a glance at Artex, the wizards and Arcmedan. Then he stopped, a small smile forming on his face. 'They think they can reverse the process,' he said. 'If not, they would have killed my queen the moment they had her. This I believe.'

'So, we may have time,' said Arcmedan. 'Time enough to take back Leighandra, my lord.'

Harbin nodded. 'The Māori do not know about the Wheel of Zulear. We activate it at sundown and attack when the Māori witchcraft is blasted clear. All warriors are to be ready. Arm yourself with strong battering weapons to smash their doors down. We will go through the windows as well.'

'But how can we get into their homes, my lord?' said Gregorn. 'The Māori witchcraft prevents this.'

'Not anymore,' said Harbin, and he explained why. As he did so, the goblin horde began to cheer. Harbin held a hand up for silence.

'The best thing is *we* have the element of surprise this time. They will not know we can enter until we stand over them, slitting their throats.'

The goblins began stamping their feet in excitement.

'Now depart, my horde, and prepare yourselves,' ordered Harbin.

One by one, they left. Artex, too, went to the weapons cave to draw a weapon for himself, for his knowledge of humans would be needed tonight.

Harbin pulled Arcmedan and the wizards aside. 'Meido, how many hours till dusk?'

'Around three, my lord.'

'Then prepare the wheel. I want it activated the second we

can do so. You and Reido will stay here with a detachment and guard it afterwards.'

'Yes, my lord.' Meido and Reido departed.

Harbin then turned to Arcmedan. 'I want Bill and the father killed first, understand?'

The goblin second in command bowed. 'It will be a pleasure.'

***

Ari ran out of patience and dressed for the trek into the forest. He tested his bandaged wound and winced. Not the best of bindings, but it would do. He went outside and laid his backpack on the ground. Lifting his hands to chant to the forest god, he stopped when the guild came bursting out of the forest.

'Ari, we need you! Kyeua's been hurt!'

Ari's eyes bulged as Makoa and Alan carried Kyeua between them, whilst Bill and Beccia carried a rolled-up tarp. Amiria walked behind them all, looking dazed.

He hurried as best he could to them.

'What happened?'

'Not time to explain,' said Makoa. 'We need to get her into the lodge.'

Ari then saw the broken spear sticking out through Kyeua's hands.

'Get her inside, hurry!'

They staggered into the lodge, with Bill saying, 'We'll put Leigh into the kitchen pantry and cover the edges with blankets to block out the light.'

'What the hell happened in there?' demanded Ari.

'Just help Kyeua and worry about that later,' urged Bill.

Makoa and Alan lowered Kyeua down as gently as they

could. Ari said, 'Get my kit from the kitchen and boil some water.' He gently removed Kyeua's hands and paled at what he saw.

Makoa hurried into the kitchen as the pantry door started banging. Alan said, 'I'll deal with Leigh,' and tried to calm his goblin daughter through the door.

Amiria looked on in tears. 'How ... how bad, Ari?'

'Doesn't matter how bad, I can heal her.'

Kyeua smiled weakly and reached for Ari's hand. 'It is too late my, dear, dear Ari. Your healing powers cannot help this time.'

Makoa and Beccia heard this and rushed over.

'No! I can save you, Kyeua,' stammered Ari. 'Please hang on. Please!'

She replied, 'The last vision I had. I did not tell you all I saw. This was meant to be. I saw my fate.'

Amiria bent down, tears falling on Kyeua's face. 'Visions can be wrong. You said that yourself so many times, so don't you dare leave us!'

Kyeua smiled weakly up at Amiria. 'I'm so sorry ...'

'No!' said Ari. 'Don't you let go! Don't you —'

Ari's voice cut out.

Kyeua's eyes saw no more. Her smile remained frozen in time. Ari's hands shook as he gently lowered her eyelids before bursting into tears.

Alan stared in muted shock before slowly sliding down the pantry door to slump onto the floor.

Makoa and Beccia moved over to Amiria and held her as she sagged to the floor. Bill stood frozen, unable to accept what had happened.

Howelia felt their pain, having lost his brothers and sisters to the goblins before. He moved slowly outside and blew his flute. His clan approached the lodge. The Natawidu leader lowered his head and spoke soft words. All the small warriors circled the house and lowered their heads in sadness.

Howelia sang a song... their ancient song of mourning for the fallen Kyeua.

Chapter Seventeen

The Heavens Shook

'Sarge, you wanna come outside for a second?'

Simonka looked up in annoyance from his computer. Arrest forms always taxed his patience, and having ten people to process at once did not help his mood one bit.

Simonka followed Spurrett outside, where she pointed to the west.

'Damn, now where did that spring from? The weather is supposed to be fine today.'

They both stared at the angry, dark clouds forming on the horizon.

'The temperature's dropping too,' said Spurrett. 'If I didn't know better, I'd say a ripper of a storm is coming.'

'Yeah,' said Simonka. He went back inside, with Spurrett following. He then went over to the barometer hanging on the wall. 'Damn, that's dropping too. Mel, get on the phone to the local weather station. I want an update on the forecast, please.'

'Will do, Sarge,' said Spurrett and moved over to the phone.

'Dennis,' said Simonka. 'Come to my office.'

From the front counter of the police station came, 'On my

way, Sarge.'

As the sergeant slumped into his chair, Constable Anning came into his office.

'What's up, Sarge?'

'Dennis, check the emergency gear in the shed. Make sure it's good to go. Check *everything*, you understand?

'What for, Sarge?' he frowned.

'I dunno, a feeling, that's all. Just do it, right?'

'Yes, Sarge.'

Simonka leaned back in his chair as Anning left, wondering why he suddenly felt uneasy. His eyes moved to the cells. The people in there stared right back.

All over the town of Stratford, people occasionally looked west at the darkening skies and frowned. Others hurried to get their shopping done. In homes, people stuck their heads out of windows, almost looking like they were sniffing the air.

They all had the same uneasy feeling. The storm clouds that were not forecast were approaching fast.

***

Bill had the kettle on and boiled strong coffee for everyone. No one spoke, the grief was too raw. The rumble of the approaching storm frayed nerves already stretched beyond capacity. Every flash of lightning caused a screwing up of red raw eyes.

Time dragged on, with the occasional sob breaking the silence.

Bill looked at the clock on the wall. He had to break the silence despite not wanting to.

'So, what now?' he asked. 'Sunset is soon.'

'I don't know,' Amiria said eventually. 'I just don't know anymore.'

A still stricken Alan said, 'She knew she would die, yet she still went.'

Howelia nodded. 'Bravery so deep, it was. She will be remembered in our lore for many times to come.'

'I have spoken to Leigh through the door,' said Alan. 'She's demands to be called "Leighandra" and returned to Harbin. I-I wish none of this had happened. A good person has died because of me. Words cannot describe how sorry I am for everything. It should be me laying upstairs under that sheet, not her.'

Makoa moved away from consoling his sister and started pacing. 'It can't be over. We need to finish this or Kyeua will have died for nothing.'

'And how do we do that?' said Bill. 'We have done our dash, mate. We cannot get back in to kill Harbin or get Matt. They're fully alert now. Night is almost here, they'll be out again, just outside the barrier. In the morning, both kids will be goblins forever. We have Leigh, so New Zealand is safe. There won't be a new goblin army. But we still failed.'

Alan muttered, 'You don't have to be so final about it, Bill.'

'I'm sorry, Alan.' Bill eased over and put a hand on his shoulder. 'Believe me, I'm so very sorry, but I can't see any way out. We have to admit we've lost.'

Amiria thumped a hand on the desk. 'One way or another, we are still going to kill that bastard Harbin!'

They all looked at her in surprise. It was the first time they had ever heard Amiria swear.

Throughout this, Howelia stayed silent, lost in his thoughts. His knowledge of the goblins went deep, deeper than those in this room.

'It is not over, you,' he said, joining the conversation at last.

'They are coming.'

'Eh?' said Bill, looking confused.

Howelia jumped up on the small coffee table, gaining everyone's attention.

'Know this. Harbin wants his prize back. He thinks you will kill his queen.'

Alan stiffened.

'So, when the sun is gone, he will come. They *all* will. They will try to return her to the goblin clan. That is what I think.'

Amiria answered, 'How do you figure this? He can't get past Tane's barrier.'

'He has waited an eon for a queen, yes? Think, you that he will just wait and hope another girl human wanders into his clutches?' Howelia pointed to the pantry cupboard. 'No, wants that prize, he does and that prize only. He is bonded to her now. He will come. He will wait close by and hope for some way in. And that is to our advantage. If he is close by, killing him is possible.'

Makoa argued, 'We can't fight him out in the open. He won't just come alone, you know that. The minute we step past Tane's barrier, we'll be overwhelmed. We have no advantage, Howelia.'

'*Six times uttered …*'

They all looked at Alan like he had lost his marbles.

'Alan, what did you say?' said Bill.

'Six times uttered of name and kin shall open the path for the goblin,' said Alan as he stood. 'How about this? We invite Harbin *inside* by lowering Tane's barrier again. We can control the environment of the lodge better than outside. Set a trap beforehand to immobilise him, then I can kill him.'

Beccia shook her head. 'Harbin is too smart for that. He would know it's a trap.'

Amiria said, 'But if Howelia is right and he wants Leigh that badly, he would not care.'

Bill gave a slow nod. 'No, he wouldn't. He's arrogant enough to think it won't matter and he'll wipe everyone out inside, anyway. By god, Howelia and Alan are right. We may have one last chance here.'

'So how do we do this?' said Makoa.

Beccia said dryly, 'Carefully. You wouldn't just be inviting just Harbin in; you'll be inviting *all* of them in.'

'That's true,' said Amiria. 'It's a huge risk. And even if Alan does kill Harbin, it won't finish there; the rest of the goblins will continue to fight.'

Ari spoke for the first time since the tragedy. 'Maybe not. I think there is a chance that Harbin's death may lower the barrier. We are inviting their king in. If he dies, Tane may return his protection.'

'And if not?' said Bill.

Ari shrugged. 'Then we are in trouble.'

Amiria stood and walked to the window. She stared at Mount Taranaki for some time. Nobody spoke as the guild leader thought hard. She then turned to face everyone.

'It is a dangerous gamble … but one I think we must take. All in favour, raise your hands.'

In unison, all hands rose.

'Right then,' said Amiria. 'We need a plan.' As a deep rumble of thunder sounded, she added, 'And we don't have much time …'

***

The wind was not quite gale force, but the evening was still young. Simonka briefed his team at the police station.

'I want patrols out after sunset. The weather channel has issued a storm warning for our area. But stay safe and keep clear of trees and waterways, okay?'

'Yes, Sarge,' said Spurrett. 'How far away is the storm, do you think?'

Simonka looked at the distant lightning. 'Sunset is about fifteen minutes away. I think soon after that. Get yourself some wet weather gear and standby.'

'Right, Sarge.'

Simonka left the two constables and went into the cells to check on his guests. He found them all on tiptoe, staring out the barred window in the cell.

'Easy, ladies and gentleman, it's just a storm. Dinner will be in half an hour.'

The elder man came over to Simonka, the gravest of looks on his tired face. 'Sergeant, I am Vincent, the Kaumātua of our guild. That is no mere storm. Can you not feel it in the air? Something terrible is about to happen. When it does, seek us out.'

Simonka tried to scoff, but Vincent's burning eyes put paid to that. He didn't know why, but he nodded and left the cells, feeling the eyes of all the inmates on his back.

***

In the goblin lair, Meido walked with a slow march to the centre of the chamber, carrying the sacred relic. Reido followed, carrying the book of spells. All the goblins were crowded around the chamber edges, a look of awe on their faces.

'It is time, my lord.'

Harbin leapt down from his chair. 'Be quick with it. I want

to be on the march immediately.'

Meido nodded and placed the Wheel of Zulear in front of the pool of black water. Reido placed a small bowl next to the wheel.

'My lord, the blood if you please.'

Harbin reached into his leather vest and produced the bottle of Leigh's blood. Handing it to Meido, he then drew a knife and nicked his finger. Meido emptied the bottle into the bowl with Harbin letting his blood drip into it as well.

Reido came forward. His gaze swept through the assembly.

'Absolute quiet! No one is to speak until I say so.' He then opened the book and began the spell. As he did, Meido took the bowl and poured the mixed blood it into the chiselled centre of the wheel.

The very air took on a sinister feeling as the spoken spell weaved its way from the pages to caress Zulear's wheel.

'Begin the chant!' yelled Reido as he closed the book. The goblins of Mount Taranaki all chanted: 'QUEEN LEIGHANDRA, QUEEN LEIGHANDRA,' over and over and over.

Meido reached into his pocket and pulled out a small wooden box. He opened the lid to reveal a black crystal. Leigh would have recognised it as the same as on the tiara she was to wear. The goblin wizard eased the crystal out of the box and moved towards the wheel.

It began to vibrate.

The crystal hummed.

The goblins chanted louder.

Meido's fingers hovered over the centre of the wheel, feeling the power of what he held grow. His eyes met the goblin king.

Harbin nodded.

He placed the crystal in the eye.

Arcs of wispy yellow light slowly rose from the Wheel of Zulear.

Harbin's eyes radiated mad power as he watched the blood flow into the lines of the wheel. The lines of all the goblin clans were slowly filled with red.

The crystal glowed.

Meido and Reido grabbed the wheel and held it down as it vibrated violently.

The chants reached a fever pitch.

The last of the carved lines of the wheel filled.

Meido released his hands and raised his arms into the air. 'Zulear, founder of all goblins ... your power is called upon. As is ordained, as it must be ... RELEASE YOUR POWER!'

Then, the Wheel of Zulear did just that.

***

'I'd say sunset's about now,' said Bill as he stared through the window. 'Hard to tell with the storm, but I'd say we're there.'

He turned towards a screeching sound as Makoa and Beccia dragged the heavy couch to brace the pantry door. Alan stood right next to the door, holding his phone.

'Dad ... Dad it's me, Leigh! Let me out, please. I need fresh air ... please, Dad, please?'

Alan paused the recording on his phone and said, 'I'm sorry, honey, but I ... I can't.'

A snarling roar came from the pantry, and the door shook as Leighandra slammed against it. Small splinters of wood broke free from the door. 'I'll rip your frigging throat out, Dad!' she screamed as the couch was set in place.

'Ignore her, you,' said a saddened Howelia. 'She is all but

goblin life force now.'

Alan bit his lip hard to keep focused. He tapped play on the screen and Leighandra's voice repeated to his dismay.

'That should fool Harbin,' said Ari.

'Yeah,' said Makoa. 'I'll bet he'll rip the pantry door off its hinges when he hears that. I then wound him with an arrow; Alan finishes him with his sword. With a bit of luck, he won't know what hit him.'

Beccia said, 'Ari will keep Leigh well gagged upstairs. As soon as you get him, Makoa, yell out. Bill, Amiria and I will come out fast to keep the other goblins from interfering as best we can.'

Amiria said, 'Okay, let's get ready. Start barricading the windows and the back door. Howelia, we will have you outside keeping watch, please.'

'I will call my clan to watch for the foul ones,' said Howelia. 'They will send word should movement be observed.' He pulled out his flute and went to go outside when —

BOOM!

An ear-splitting sound like a bomb going off slammed against the lodge, followed by earthquake like shaking.

'What the hell is going on!' screamed Beccia.

'That wasn't thunder,' said Amiria.

'Outside! Look outside!' urged Howelia.

They darted to the windows. The forest was bathed in light.

'Oh my god,' said Bill, pointing at a massive beam of yellowish green light shooting into the night sky from the forest canopy.

'What is that?' said Alan.

'Holy crap!' said Makoa. 'Kyeua's vision … the beam of light she spoke of. It's happening! But what the heck is it?'

Ari paled. As the High Priest of the Guild, his bond with Tane's barrier was the strongest. He now felt nothing.

'Tane's barrier is gone. That's what's happening. I don't know how they did it, but the goblins have removed the barrier with that light.'

'Oh no!' an alarmed Amiria said. 'But that means …'

Howelia nodded furiously. 'They are free to roam anywhere of their choosing.'

The light continued to punch upwards towards the heavens as they tried to make sense of it. Then the light vanished.

An eerie silence descended across the mountain before the rain intensified.

After a minute, Alan whispered, 'If the barrier is gone, they can come right up to the lodge door now, right? But they can't get inside unless we let them in, right?' RIGHT?'

'Tane's barrier is gone,' said Ari. 'We didn't think that was possible. So maybe *other* rules are gone as well?'

'They could be here any minute then, but we're not fully setup yet!' cried Amiria.

'I'll buy us some time with a protection chant,' said Ari. 'Stand clear, everyone.'

But before Ari could begin the chant, the lights in the lodge went out.

***

'Sarge! Sarge!' shouted Spurrett.

Simonka came charging out of his office. 'What's going on?'

The constable threw protocol out the window and grabbed Simonka, dragging him to the window. His eyes widened at

216

the massive light show coming from Mount Taranaki. He turned to Spurrett. 'We're going up there. Grab the emergency gear!' Remembering, he added, 'Also, call the others and tell them to get back here to guard the cells asap.'

'Right, Sarge.'

Simonka hurried to the gun cabinet and began unlocking a shotgun when he heard, 'You won't need that, but you *will* need us if you want to live.'

He halted mid-unlock and turned to the cells. All ten people in the cells, glared back at him. Simonka made a quick decision and dashed over to the cell bars.

'Okay, I'm listening. Now tell me, what was that light?'

Vincent said, 'I am not sure, but it's of goblin nature and it was evil. I feel their power, you know. It has grown to frightening levels since the light appeared. Know this, sergeant, weapons like your guns will not work on them. They are spiritual creatures who can only be vanquished with Mana. If you go up there with your young lady friend, you condemn her and yourself to death. And anyone on the mountain right now is in mortal danger.'

Simonka came right up to Vincent, their eyes only inches apart. He tried to gauge any sinister intent, but only saw calmness. *And that light ...* he said to himself .... *explain that light, Mick!*

Vincent whispered, 'Please, sergeant, the time to act is now or it will be too late.'

Simonka grabbed the cell key from out of his pocket and pushed it into the lock. He looked at the Māori one last time before turning the key.

***

'Grab some torches!' urged Makoa.

They scrambled for their packs, pulling out their torches and ripping off the still attached red tape.

Beccia said, 'And the flares. We're going to—'

'Get down!' yelled Howelia.

Amiria screamed as a large boulder smashed through the lounge windows. The rain poured inside.

Bill cried, 'They're here! Arm yourselves!'

The door ripped off its hinges and flew backwards into the night. Two goblins surged into the lodge.

Makoa whipped up the crossbow and fired all four arrows. Both goblins went down, screaming. 'Well, at least we know they don't need an invitation anymore,' he said dryly as he quickly reloaded.

'Grab Leigh and get upstairs,' urged Ari.

Amiria lit a flare and threw it out through the doorframe, and raised her bow. 'Do it, Alan. Get her out of here!'

Alan heaved the couch aside. But before he could open the pantry door, it burst open. Leighandra leapt high over her father and made for the exit.

'My lord! I am coming!' she yelled.

Beccia and Bill tackled her and a three-way fight began with Leigh's powerful nails striking out at will.

From outside came the sound of many running feet.

Howelia yelled, 'They all come! Prepare for battle!'

Arcmedan flew through the broken windows and slashed at the little Natawidu. Howelia ducked in time and kicked the goblin's shin before leaping away. More goblins crashed through the back door, with Adoien and Bezenar seeing their queen under attack, and raced towards her.

'Alan! Stop them!' yelled Ari.

Alan picked up a chair and threw it at them, bringing both

down. He then drew his sword and attacked. 'I need backup!' he screamed, as Adoien and Bezenar fought back, their skill too much for Alan.

'There is none!' cried Howelia. 'For your life, fight hard!'

Window glass shattered as more goblins surged into the lodge. Lightning flashed … and then Harbin entered.

'The goblin king!' cried Ari. Makoa fired, but Harbin leapt clear with lightning reflexes.

Maorten then came crashing through a window and saw his dad under attack. He leapt forward and pushed Adoien and Bezenar aside. 'This one is mine!' he roared.

Alan paled. 'Don't do this, son. I beg of you!'

'You're no father of mine!' he yelled and swung his sword at his dad. Steel clashed as Alan defended himself, his eyes tearing up.

Harbin finally spotted his queen being restrained and leapt to free her. Bill let go of Leighandra and drew his sword.

'Now it ends, ranger,' growled Harbin. 'You die a failure.'

Bill yelled, 'Screw you, you coward!' and charged Harbin.

From under the struggling Leigh came a muffled cry from Beccia. 'I can't hold her! Invoke *Hine-nui-te-po*, Ari, it's our only chance!'

Ari raised his hands and chanted as quickly as he could,

'HINE-NUI-TE-PO, GODDESS OF THE NIGHT AND UNDERWORLD. YOUR SERVANTS WILL PERISH TO THE UN-HUMANS. THEY WILL THEN DEFILE YOUR DOMAIN. RELEASE YOUR POWER, HELP TANE. HELP ALL IN PERIL!'

A deep rumble started, shaking the lodge, followed by a

roaring wind that blew out the last of the windows, causing all inside the lodge to be tossed around like leaves. Furniture cracked and broke apart. Kitchen drawers flung open, sending pots and pans flying in all directions. Adoien and Bezenar each took a large pot into the face and were knocked unconscious.

Amiria got up first. 'Get upstairs, everyone,' she croaked. 'While we still can. Hurry now!'

Bill got up and swayed a bit. He saw Harbin trying to remove a large fallen cupboard off his back and yelled to Alan, 'Harbin is down, Alan! Kill him! You can end this!'

Alan got to his hands and knees. But as he tried to stand, he cried out. A clawed green hand dug into his calf. He looked down to see his son holding on. 'You will not harm my lord, human,' growled Maorten.

Alan looked at the green hand and something snapped inside him. He swung his other leg around and his boot connected squarely with his son's head, knocking him out.

'You're frigging grounded, Matt!' yelled Alan hysterically, and grabbed his sword. But that small amount of time was enough. Harbin wrenched the cupboard clear.

'Bill, grab Leigh. Everyone else, upstairs!' urged Amiria.

Bill hauled Leighandra up and threw her over his shoulders. As they raced towards the stairs, Alan saw Howelia unconscious against the back door, blood flowing from a nasty gash to his head. He scooped him up and raced up the stairs with the others.

'Barricade the door!' said Amiria, as they lurched into the room that had once been Matt and Leigh's, Makoa and Beccia pushed a heavy wardrobe against the door. Bill began tearing sheets to tie up Leighandra.

'That won't hold them for long,' said Ari. He bent over

Howelia. 'Alan, get me another sheet for a dressing.' As Alan grabbed a sheet and began tearing it up, the wardrobe banged and shuddered.

'What do we do, Mother?' said Beccia. 'We're trapped!'

Bill grunted as he tied Leighandra's legs. 'Great idea coming up here!' he snarled. 'Now what?'

Alan said, 'Oh shut up, Bill, it's not like there was a frigging choice.' The wardrobe began to topple. Bill jumped towards it and pressed all his weight against it. Beccia dropped her sword and joined him.

Leighandra was alone now and tore at her bonds.

'Ari, invoke *Hine-nui-te-po* again!' urged Amiria.

Ari looked up from bandaging Howelia, his eyes strained red. 'My Mana is too low, I-I can't without rest.'

The top half of the wardrobe splintered.

Alan looked around wildly, desperate for a way out. Then he had it. 'Makoa, drop the crossbow. Give me a hand to toss the mattresses out the window. We jump to them and make our way to the visitor centre. Or better yet, the cars and get the hell out of here.'

Amiria said, 'It's a long drop, we might get hurt.'

'We'll die here if we stay,' replied Alan.

Makoa put his crossbow down. 'True that. Let's do it.'

'Hurry!' urged Beccia.

Amiria strode over to the window and played her torch around outside. 'My God, there are goblins everywhere!'

Alan and Makoa stood frozen with the mattress.

The door gave a massive bang and came off its hinges. The wardrobe held, but barely. 'Help us!' yelled Bill. 'For god's sake, help us!'

Makoa and Alan ran back to lend their weight against the

wardrobe.

Bill stared intently at Alan as they strained to hold the wardrobe. 'Alan …he can't get Leigh,' he grunted. 'Do you understand what I'm saying? No matter what happens, she can't fall into his hands …'

Alan choked out, 'I know!'

Then the walls began to crack. Green fists started breaking through them. The rain came down hard on the roof, pounding in their ears.

Ari turned to Amiria, a look of hopelessness in his eyes. The sounds of tearing came from Leighandra as her bonds started to give way.

Amiria moved over to Ari and held his hand. Together they faced the wall as it and the wardrobe came apart bit by bit.

From outside came a triumphant roar.

'We gave it our best,' whispered Amiria, as a silent tear trickled down her cheek.

Ari squeezed her hand and waited for the end.

Then, from outside came a sound, a loud blaring sound that changed everything.

— Chapter Eighteen —

End of the Line

'Holey moly, Michael, it's all real. They were telling the truth!'

Simonka was dumbstruck. He stared in disbelief as the bus drove onto the grounds, its large air-horn blasting the night air. Through the driving rain, he saw the Māori were not nut jobs after all.

'Stay in the car, Melissa!' Simonka stopped the car behind the bus, grabbed his shotgun and leapt out to join the Māori.

'Get back in your car, sergeant,' yelled Vincent. 'They'll kill you! As I said before, your shotgun is useless here. Use your spotlight on them. Light hurts them.'

He tuned to face the goblins, who looked at the new arrivals with uncertainty. Vincent planted his feet and issued a Maori Haka war cry of such power that the goblins took a step backwards.

Vincent's guild came rushing out of the bus and charged towards the goblins. Simonka jumped back into the car and flicked on the patrol car spotlight, tracking the goblins. They cried out in pain and lunged at the car, but the light was too bright and they backed away, trying to dance clear of the spotlight.

Spurrett picked up the radio mic, but Simonka pulled it out of her hand. 'Are you crazy? What do we say? Goblins are attacking us and to send reinforcements?'

At the battered upstairs room of the lodge, they had heard the sound of horn, but it didn't register in their minds as they fought for their lives.

Vincent's Haka was a different story.

Ari leapt for the window and looked down

'THE OTHERS ARE HERE! HOLY COW, THEY MADE IT!'

Amiria said, 'Quickly, the mattresses!'

The fists were no longer coming through the walls, but the broken wardrobe still shook as the detached door banged against it. Makoa and Amiria grabbed the mattresses and shoved them through the window.

Ari yelled down, 'We're up here! Get the mattresses into position so we can jump.'

Simonka saw this and turned to Spurrett. 'Stay here and keep that spotlight moving. That's an order!' He grabbed his shotgun anyway, got out and ran towards the mattresses. Gregorn saw him and launched an attack. Simonka swung the shotgun like a club, collecting the goblin in the face, who went down hard.

'I'm going to wake up soon,' he muttered, slipping in the rain-soaked mud as he dragged the two mattresses close to the window.

'Ready,' he yelled. 'Jump when you can!'

Leighandra broke free from her bonds and leapt towards the wardrobe. Alan quickly grabbed her and wrapped her in a bear hug.

'Let me go, you bastard!' she wailed as she scratched at her father's arms.

Ari hurried over with more sheets to help tie her back up again. They worked fast, with Ari saying, 'Tie her up well, Alan. We need to take her outside with us, but she *cannot* get free outside, otherwise it's over.'

'Ahh, what is this? Where I am?' croaked Howelia. He stood up and swayed a bit. 'What happens, you?'

'We're under attack by the goblins!' said Beccia. 'Harbin is trying to get in. Another Māori guild has arrived and are attacking the goblins on the grounds. We're about to jump out the window and make a break for it.'

Bill gave a crazy laugh and added, 'Think that about covers it, I reckon.'

Howelia staggered over to the window, holding his bandaged head, and looked down. 'Not good is this,' he muttered, seeing the war going on around the lodge.

He turned back to the guild and said, 'We must go, but careful, be you, when landing with the queen.' Howelia then leapt out of the window.

Amiria shouted, 'Alan, you first! We'll then throw Leigh down to you. Do not let her get free.'

'Right. Can you guys hold the wardrobe?'

'Not like we have much choice,' grunted Bill, as the goblins crashed against it again. 'Get going for Christ's sake!'

Alan darted from the wardrobe and moved out onto the ledge. The scene was a nightmare. Goblins and Māori clashed with steel, the flashing police lights, the storm, the rain pelting down. He hesitated briefly before jumping, landing hard and bouncing off the mattresses, straight into Simonka.

'Oof!' groaned the sergeant. 'Get off me, mate!'

'Sorry about that,' said Alan as he got up, now covered in

mud.

'Ready, Alan?' yelled Amiria.

'Yeah, throw her down!'

A ruckus came from above, followed by some foul language. Leighandra then appeared at the window, with Ari and Amiria shoving hard. She toppled out and onto the sodden mattresses. Both men ran forward and grabbed her as she began tearing against her bonds again, screaming in anger.

'They got her,' said Amiria.

'Good,' said Makoa, 'now you, Mum.'

'I- I can't leave my children behind.'

Bill grunted, 'I won't let them get hurt, Amiria, my life on it.' The wardrobe splintered down the middle. Bill saw through it, right into the eyes of Harbin.

'Hello, ugly,' he said and spat in Harbin's face. The goblin king roared and his fist punched through to where Bill's head was a second ago.

'GO, MOTHER!'

Amiria leapt through the window and was gone.

Ari took out his last flare.

'No, Ari!' said Beccia. 'That will set fire to the lodge.'

'No choice,' said Bill. 'Do it, Ari!'

But before Ari could strike the flare, two loud sounds came from outside. The first was the sound of Howelia furiously blowing his flute.

The second came from Artex. In a loud screech, he yelled, 'The queen is out in the open. The queen is outside. Save the queen!'

The wardrobe stopped shaking, followed by the sound of fading running feet.

'Oh crap, Harbin knows Leigh's outside!' said Beccia.

'Let's go!' said Makoa, and the three ran to the window.

Ari said, 'I'll make my way down the stairs. I can't handle the jump with my injury.'

'Be careful, Ari,' urged Bill and then he jumped, followed by Beccia and Makoa. Ari began painfully removing the remains of the wardrobe.

The trio bounced off the mattresses to the scene of the Natawidu attacking the goblins in full force. Simonka came running up to Bill yelling.

'Don't start on me, Mike!' said Bill. 'If we survive this, I'll explain everything afterwards.'

'Where's Leigh?' demanded Beccia.

Simonka pointed to Alan and Amiria wrestling with a struggling Leighandra. 'I take it that's her? My god, what happened to her, Bill?'

'Save it, Mick, just help me get her into your car.'

'Right!' said Simonka. As they moved forward, Leigh broke her bonds again and swatted Alan and Amiria away like flies. She roared in triumph.

Then Harbin came tearing out of the lodge, followed by the awakened Adoien and Bezenar. The Natawidu jumped immediately onto the two goblins, beating their heads with sticks. Harbin left them behind, galloping towards Leigh.

'Oh shit!' moaned Bill and raced towards Harbin. The goblin king saw him coming and drew his sword. 'Mike, get her to the car fast!' Bill yelled before his sword and Harbin's clashed.

But Leighandra charged Simonka, her teeth bared, eyes blazing yellow.

The sergeant panicked and raised his shotgun.

Alan looked up from the ground. 'NO! DON'T DO IT!'

Simonka fired.

Artex leapt in front of his queen and took the full blast.

'I'll tear your liver out, human!' screamed Leighandra and attacked, knocking over Simonka, sending the shotgun flying.

Spurrett abandoned the car and raced to help her boss as he fought to save his eyes from being scratched out.

Amiria gingerly rose from the ground and looked around. She paled at the sight of both guilds and the Natawidu suffering many wounds. She turned to Alan and said with a trembling voice, 'We're losing. There's too many.'

Alan picked up his sword. 'I've got to finish Harbin before we all are,' he said. 'No one else can die for my mistakes.'

He staggered to where Bill and Harbin were clashing.

Adoien and Bezenar stood in his way, now free from the Natawidu.

'Come, human, time to die,' grinned Adoien.

Alan surged forward.

'Not without us you don't, Alan.' Makoa and Beccia appeared by his side, brandishing swords. The two goblins' grins faded, and they took a step back.

Bill and Harbin continued to circle each other, striking out when the opportunity arose.

'This ends now, Harbin!'

'When I kill you, Bill, I'm going to cook your body and feed it to my queen!' snarled Harbin.

Bill smiled. 'I don't think you've ever killed anyone before, Harbin. You're gutless enough to let others do your dirty work for you.'

'Is that so?' Let's see if that is true then, ranger.'

The goblin king feinted an attack, then threw his sword at Bill. The whirling piece of steel collected his legs.

Bill collapsed and Harbin was onto him in seconds, clawing at his face. His yellow eyes bored into Bill's.

'You lose, Billy boy!' he yelled in triumph.

Bill fought with all his strength, but Harbin was too strong. He gave out a scream as the goblin's nails dug in.

Amiria yelled, 'Bill's in trouble. Someone help him!'

With Adoien and Bezenar occupied by Makoa and Beccia, Alan raced towards the goblin king, but Arcmedan covered his lord from attack.

The goblin grinned and waved Alan forward.

Alan obliged.

Ari stumbled out of the lodge and saw Bill and the goblin king locked together. He also saw Alan was about to engage in a fight he could not win.

'No, Alan! Come to me, quick!'

Alan circled around Arcmedan and darted over to Ari.

Ari said in a covered voice, 'Move directly behind Harbin, but clear of the other goblin. Point your sword out in front of you and ground your feet. Face the mountain, but make sure you're in line with it and Harbin when I chant. *You must be in line!*'

'What?'

'Remember the first night you met the goblins? Remember what I did? Ground your feet hard. Do what I say!'

The lightbulb went off in Alan's head.

'My god!'

He moved quickly and positioned himself so that he was at Harbin's back, jutting his sword out and grounding his feet as hard as he could. He then leaned forward.

'READY ARI!'

'Ready for what?' sneered Arcmedan as he circled around

Harbin and Bill, making sure no one interfered with the death of the ranger. 'Ready to die? Well, after my lord kills Bill, *you* are next, so don't move now …'

Ari waited for his chance. 'Come on, Bill,' he muttered.

Alan bellowed, 'Push him up, Bill! For Christ's sake, fight, you bastard, fight!'

Bill groaned. A deep, guttural groan from where all men carry their soul and pushed against Harbin with everything he had, forcing him up. Howelia and another Natawidu jumped up at Harbin's face, causing him to stand to swat them away.

Arcmedan was clear.

Ari acted.

'For you, my dearest Kyeua,' he whispered. He looked to the heavens and raised his hands.

'HINE-NUI-TE-PO, GODDESS OF THE NIGHT AND UNDERWORLD, I PLEAD MY LIFE FORCE. TAKE ME IF YOU WILL. AID THEM! AID THEM FROM TARANAKI. I BEG YOU!'

A reddish hue lit up the rain-soaked skies once more. The ground rumbled and then a hurricane-force wind came roaring down Mount Taranaki at an incredible speed. Goblin, human and Natawidu alike were flung far apart, flying backwards from the mountain. The wind died down; the red hue faded. Only the sound of the falling rain remained.

After a minute, friend and enemy slowly rose, shaking their heads.

'What the hell was that?' moaned Simonka as he helped Spurrett up.

Bill groaned as he tried to stand. Then he saw Harbin rise

in the distance, close to Alan.

But something was off.

The goblin king did not race forward to continue the attack. He stood still, a pained expression on his foul face. Harbin turned to Alan.

Alan Dwyer looked up from the ground and smiled. With the softest of voices he said, 'Actually *you* lose, goblin king.'

Harbin looked down to see Alan's sword sticking out of his chest.

'NO!' screamed Leighandra. She flung off all who were holding her and raced to be with her king.

Harbin smiled faintly and toppled sideways.

The goblins gasped, with Arcmedan crying out in despair.

Leighandra fell to her knees and held Harbin's face in her hands, crying uncontrollably.

He looked into his queen's eyes. 'I would have worshipped you till the end of time,' he whispered. He then spotted Bill out of the corner of his eye. Hate flowed through him one last time as he cursed Bill before his head rolled back.

Harbin was dead.

The goblins roared in fury and attacked anyone in range. Arcmedan bore down on Alan.

Amiria cried, 'Tane's Barrier! It's returning!'

A blue dome of light appeared over the grounds, slowly cascading downwards.

Arcmedan looked up in panic and yelled, 'Retreat, goblins, retreat! Do not be caught inside the Māori witchcraft, it is death!'

The goblins ran, picking up their wounded as they did so.

Leighandra got up and ran as well. 'Leigh, wait!' cried Alan.

'I hate you, Dad, I—'

She suddenly stumbled and fell. She got up confused and stumbled again to fall on all fours. Then a yellow glow enveloped her. From inside the lodge, another yellow glow appeared.

Howelia smiled. 'The beginning of the end.'

Leighandra's skin changed colour, the green hair fell out, her fingernails retracted, the goblin clothes tore. The yellow glow intensified, causing Alan to shield his eyes.

'Holy heck!' shouted Bill. 'Look out, there's more!'

Everyone tore their eyes away from Leighandra to see two running goblins suddenly glow yellow and stumble to collapse on the ground.

Then the unconscious Artex disappeared as a yellow glow engulfed him as well.

Beccia turned to Amiria. 'How is that possible, Mother? Who are they?'

Amiria looked utterly confused. 'I don't have the faintest idea.'

Tane's barrier hit the ground, causing sparks of blue to fly out in all directions.

The yellow glows stopped as quickly as they had begun. Silence fell. Even the rain ceased. For that moment, nobody moved.

Then a small cry started. Alan knew that cry all so well.

'LEIGH!' He ran over to his human daughter and flung himself on her, wrapping his arms around her.

'Sssh, easy, my darling, easy now. Daddy's here.'

'D- Dad. I'm so sorry!' she sobbed.

Alan leaned back, his eyes streaming tears. He placed a gentle hand on his daughter's face and said, 'No. You have nothing to be sorry for, Leigh. That belongs entirely to me.'

Looking on, Bill said, 'I'll check on Matt.' But before he could make for the lodge, he saw two human boys walking towards him, looking around in a daze.

The ranger was stunned, not believing what he was seeing.

'Ben? Adrian?'

'Where ... where are we?' asked Ben Hellier.

Bill nearly fainted. He fell on his rump and buried his face in his hands, losing it completely. Amiria came over to the boys and held them. 'It's okay, dear boys, it's okay. Come inside and we'll get you warmed up.' She turned to her son. 'Makoa, there was another glow over past the bus. It has to be another boy. Find him.'

'Right, Mum.'

Vincent joined Makoa in the search, and soon they found a small boy.

He was in trouble.

'Makoa, find Linda and tell her we need her,' said Vincent. He then yelled, 'Sergeant! Do you have a first aid kit in your car? I think this is the one you shot. He didn't fully heal in time before he transformed back to human.'

Spurrett ran back to the patrol car to get the first aid kit.

'Ooh, my head hurts!'

'MATT!'

Alan sprinted to the lodge as Matt walked out, clutching his head, and embraced him in a hug.

'Err, that was me, I'm afraid. I'm so sorry, son.'

He then saw Ari on the ground. He was not moving.

'Oh Cripes! Amiria, Ari's hurt!'

Amiria came running over to the unconscious Ari.

'That last chant,' she cried. 'Oh my god, he wasn't strong enough.' She bent down to feel his pulse and found none.

'Oh no! No, no, no! You're not going to die on me too, Ari!' She tore open his shirt and placed her hands on his chest to perform CPR.

'Not to worry, Amiria, I've got this,' said a strong, calm voice. Amiria looked up quickly to see Linda next to her. She was the other guild's healer. Amiria stumbled out of the way.

Linda leant down and placed her hands on Ari's chest. She then softly incanted a rite. Her hands formed patterns as she continued to chant.

Ari's eyes flew open. Then came a deep inhale and his eyes blinked. 'Oh man, do I have one hell of a headache,' he finally croaked.

Amiria burst into tears. 'Don't you scare me like that!' She kneeled down and cradled Ari's head in her lap. 'Don't you ever scare me like that again!'

Ari smiled and placed a hand on Amiria's arm. 'Not likely, I hope.' he replied. 'It seems *Hine-Nui-Te-Po* still has need of my services after all.' He looked around and his eyes lit up as he saw Alan with Leigh and Matt standing over him. 'It worked. You did it, Alan.'

Alan reached down and gripped Ari's hand. 'No, you did it, Ari.'

Simonka came over with bewildered eyes. 'Someone is going to have to explain all this to me over a stiff drink or two I think,' he said.

Beccia and Bill came over with the Hellier kids.

'Mike, old son, that is a promise,' croaked Bill, whose voice was still at breaking point.

Alan said, 'So it's really over?'

'Tane's barrier is restored, Harbin is dead and the kids are no longer goblins,' replied Amiria. 'So, I bloody well hope so!'

234

'One thing I don't understand,' frowned Alan. 'We had four days, you all said. After that, the children would be goblins forever, right?'

He turned to Bill. 'So, what about them? And the other boy?'

Bill turned to Amiria. 'I don't get it either. How is it possible? It's been 5 years.'

Amiria stood up and wiped away her tears. 'It's a mystery to me, too. One that will take some time to work out. The Hellier kids should not have turned back to human. It's been much too long.' She looked over to Spurrett, who was carrying the injured boy to the patrol car. 'And we have no idea who he is.'

'We'd best get inside and treat the wounded. And I could do with a strong cuppa,' said Bill.

Simonka said, 'Mel and I will take the boy to the local hospital.' He turned to Bill and added, 'We'll come back after that. And be ready to talk, Bill, or you're going to the lockup.'

Bill laughed, more in relief than anything.

Howelia beamed as he walked over to both guilds.

'Over it is, it seems. It is time for us to go. The Natawidu thanks you for ending the goblin king. Perhaps a more peaceful time is upon us?'

Alan left the kids to kneel before Howelia. 'I don't know what words I can say, Howelia. You saved my life and my kids. I owe you a debt I cannot ever repay.' Alan held out his hand. Howelia grinned and took it.

'Yes,' said Amiria. 'We will always be in your debt. We will also keep your secret for all time, as agreed.'

Howelia smiled. 'A new beginning for us, I think.' He turned to Bill. 'We will check in from time to time. And a watchful eyes on the goblins will be kept. Should a warning be needed, a warning will be given. If you need to seek me out, the water place with the sign that reads "Wilkies" is the place to wait.'

Matt remembered. "And you like to swim there, right?'

'Oh yes,' grinned Howelia. 'The Natawidu enjoy the waters of the pools as much as we do the trees.'

'Told you it wasn't a rock,' smirked Leigh.

Matt groaned. 'Here we go again, little miss know—'

'Okay, you two …' chimed in Alan, grinning from ear to ear.

Howelia gave a warm smile and then blew his flute. His clan merged into the woods and were gone in seconds. The Natawidu leader then strolled into the waiting darkness, casually whistling.

'Well, will you look at that? He's strutting!' laughed Beccia.

Makoa grinned, 'He's damn well earned it.'

The police car's flashing lights engaged, and it turned to head out to Manaia Road. Then it braked suddenly. Simonka wound down his window and said, 'Hey, Bill! The boy's coming around. Says his name is Baxter. Do you know that name?'

Bill shook his head. 'No, it's not familiar, Mike.'

Simonka shrugged. 'Be back soon,' he said and gunned it towards the exit, heading for Stratford.

Amiria tuned to Vincent and rubbed noses with him. 'You saved our lives, dear Vincent. We would have been overrun without you. But my god, man, you cut it way too close …'

Vincent laughed. 'Well, Bill's copper mate had us in the cells for a while?'

'What!' exclaimed Bill.

'I'll explain inside,' said Vincent.

— Chapter Nineteen —

Homecoming

The four-wheel drive turned onto Burbash Road on the outskirts of Hamilton and pulled up at number thirty-six. He hoped Mel Spurrett had given him the right address.

'Who lives here, Mr. Gardiner?'

Bill turned off the ignition. 'I'm not sure. Stay in the car please, kids. This won't take long.' He got out of the car and walked up to the driveway of the small cottage. He stopped at the Indigo blue painted door and hesitated. He had thought about how to do this and concluded that this was the right way, the only way.

A lump formed in his throat as he knocked on the door. It took three times for the door to open.

A man peered out, then saw who was standing there.

'Bill? Bill Gardiner … is that you? What on earth are you doing here?'

The man staring at him had prematurely grey hair and dark lines around the corner of his eyes. He could easily pass for 50, despite being so much younger.

Bill tried to speak but suddenly found he couldn't.

'What?' said the man. 'What is it?'

Tears formed in Bill's eyes as he took a few steps back. He then turned to the car and waved a hand forward.

The car doors opened.

Ben and Adrian Hellier saw their father and ran forward. 'Dad!'

David Hellier's eyes bulged, and he staggered backwards. He fell to his knees and cried out as his long-lost kids dropped down to embrace him.

Emily Hellier heard the commotion and came running out of the bedroom. She sobbed hysterically as she saw her children and half walked, half crawled to be with them and her husband.

Bill blurted, 'I'll be in touch, folks,' before hightailing it back to his car. Once back inside his car, he let go. A cleansing, deep, gut-wrenching cry that poured out five years of built-up guilt and shame.

When he finally started the 4x4, Bill Gardiner faced a new beginning. For the man who once was, was now once again.

***

Amiria said, 'It's extraordinary the loyalty young Baxter showed Leigh when both were goblins I would think it may have something to do with them both being human once.'

Beccia frowned. 'But the Hellier kids showed none of that. According to Leigh, they showed a fair bit of disdain towards her most of the time.'

'Yes, that's true,' confirmed Leigh. 'The goblin wizards I mentioned treated me well, and Harbin, of course, was especially good to me. But only Baxter was actually kind to me.'

Both guilds, the police, Alan and the kids continued to talk and document events around the visitor centre's log fire. With the return to Australia looming, there were many loose ends to tie up. And still so many questions.

'So, what's the verdict on why they changed back as well?' said Alan.

Amiria replied, 'We have sent out this information to our contacts in Europe for further discussion. But Phil Hirons in Scotland has already suggested the influence of Māori magic may be a factor. The "forever a goblin" concept has been documented as fact … but never in New Zealand. Even now, this has generated much excitement in those who study the goblin lore.'

Ari said, 'I think it may be the will of *Hine-nui-te-po*. The goddess of the underworld helped kill Harbin, so maybe she decided she could return them as well? *All* of them.'

'The rules have changed that much we know. Why this is, will be a cause for many discussions,' said Amiria.

Makoa grinned. 'Yeah, and Mother is never one to miss having those.'

Everyone laughed, with Amiria throwing a cushion at her son.

Leigh turned to her father and asked, 'So, will we get to see Baxter before we go?'

'Bill said he would pick him up from hospital on his way back, so you'll be able to see him before we go,' said Alan, a little defensively if truth to be told. Leigh hadn't stopped talking about him since turning back to human.

'So, what now?' asked Simonka, with Spurrett sitting next to him. 'I now know that supernatural creatures exist *and* are in my area of authority. I'll have to do something about this.'

Vincent said, 'Well, Michael, I think you have no choice but to remain quiet, otherwise you may end up wearing a nice, tight white jacket for a few years.'

Spurrett chuckled.

'But I think maybe you and Melissa should receive some training from Amiria's guild on how to deal with any future goblin incursions.'

Amiria agreed. 'Makoa and Beccia will be available to provide training and I can provide all the information you'll require should you agree, sergeant.'

Spurrett grinned. 'I'm in. Fancy having "Goblin Hunter" on my resume.'

Everyone chuckled at that.

Alan turned serious as he caught Amiria's eye. 'There is one thing. The kids and I can't leave for home yet. We would like to ... to attend Kyeua's funeral.'

Amiria's smile faded. She reached over to Alan and held his hand. 'Dear Kyeua will have a traditional Māori funeral called a *Tangihanga*. She is already at her *Marae* or 'Sacred Place' if you like. She will stay there for two days for her people to mourn. Then on the third day, she will be buried. We can travel anytime now to visit her before the third day ...'

Alan said, 'The kids and I would like to go this afternoon if we are allowed.'

Ari said, 'It is permitted, Alan. And I will join you.'

'We all will,' said Amiria. 'Kyeua would like that.'

Nobody spoke for a while as sad memories flooded through.

Then, a car pulled up. Beccia stood up and went to the door. 'Bill's here,' she informed everyone.

Leigh's eyes brightened, and she started fidgeting in her chair. Alan saw this and frowned.

After a minute, Bill walked in with Baxter next to him, his

arm in a sling.

'How's the arm, little one?' asked Ari.

Baxter muttered, 'Good, thank you, sir,' keeping his eyes to the ground.

'It's going to take some time for this lad to get used to his new surroundings,' said Bill, as he put a hand on Baxter's good shoulder. 'Considering it's the 21st century and all.'

Matt said, 'Lad? He's one hundred and eighty years old!'

Leigh retorted, 'One hundred and eighty years old and still better looking than you, doofus!'

Ari and Makoa roared with laughter.

Matt gave Leigh a surprised look. So did Alan.

Baxter smiled timidly and looked up at Leigh. 'How are you feeling, Leighand — err, Leigh?'

'I'm fine. And thank you for all you did for me.' Leigh gave him the warmest smile and added, 'I won't ever forget it.'

Alan got up and grumbled, 'I'll put on some lunch for everyone.'

Bill grinned and said, 'I'll give you a hand, mate.' As he went to follow Alan outside to the lodge, Amiria got up and stopped him. She then held out her hands and Bill took them without hesitation.

'You're different, Bill. I can see it in your eyes. They are the eyes of a man who now sees clearly.'

Bill leaned forward and rubbed noses with Amiria. He whispered, with eyes suddenly glassy, 'I am not a failure anymore, dear lady.'

Amiria whispered back, 'Oh, Bill, you never were.'

***

Julie Dwyer sighed as she put the letter down on the coffee table. The first rejection letter, and so early after sending out the manuscript and cover letter. But with Alan and the kids arriving home within the hour, she put aside her sorrow and made sure the front light was on before continuing on with the meal preparations. A thought kept popping into her mind as she worked: had Alan had the talk about the pranks?

It wasn't long before she heard the car pulling into the driveway. Julie could barely hold in her happiness. She had loved the thoughtful time off alone, but had missed her family terribly.

She went to the door, but it banged heavily a few times before she could open it.

'Alright, Matt!' she laughed. 'No need to break the door down.'

She opened it, and Leigh strolled through, whistling loudly. 'High five, Mum!' she yelled, holding up her hand. A shocked Julie stood dumfounded.

'Too slow, Mummyoh. Old age catching up, eh?' she laughed and went past to the kitchen. 'I'm frigging starving. I could eat a whole goat!'

The shock compounded as Matt walked through. 'Hello, Mum,' he mumbled before embracing her in a bear hug.

'Good lord.'

Matt broke apart from their hug and said, 'You're a sight for sore eyes.'

'What happened to your face?' said Julie, noticing the faint remains of a cut on his check. She actually saw tears in his eyes as he gave her another enormous hug. He said, 'It's nothing, don't worry about it. Love you, Mum,' and went to sit down in the lounge-room.

Julie didn't know what to think. Then Alan appeared at the doorway with the bags.

'Hello, sweetheart.'

The look on his face was enough to have her rushing to embrace her husband, who gave a loud sob. 'Alan ... what on earth?'

'I missed you so very much, my darling,' said Alan, who shook a little as he held back tears. 'So very much.'

'Are you ill? What's come over the kids?' She pulled apart from Alan and gazed into his eyes. 'What the heck is going on, Alan?'

Alan replied, 'Do you still have that electronic voice recorder you use to dictate story ideas?'

'Well, yes, but —'

'I can smell you have dinner on. Thank you for that. Let's eat first and then we'll all sit down and have a long talk.'

'About what's going on, I hope?' said Julie.

Alan smiled. A rather tender smile that Julie rarely saw. He placed an arm around his wife and said, 'Yes, but also the kids and I would like to talk to you about your yet to be written next novel ...'

***

Twelve months later ...

The mailman knocked on the door of the cottage at Stratford at 10 am.

A man opened it and said, 'Hey, Glenn.'

'Hiya, Bill, how's tricks? Got a registered package here for you to sign for.'

'Wasn't expecting a package,' frowned Bill as he took the pen.

'How's the young lad you adopted doing these days?' asked Glenn.

Bill smiled as he returned the pen. 'Well, it's been a rough

12 months, but he's doing really well now. Think I've got this dad thing working right. But I tell ya, mate; it's been a steep learning curve.'

Glenn laughed. 'I'll tell you a little secret from a father of five: you never stop learning with them, from them and about them.'

Bill said, 'Amen, brother!' He looked down at the package to see where it had come from. A grin broke out on his face as he said, 'Speaking of the kid, I'd better get back to his lessons. Cheers, Glenn, have a good one.'

The mailman gave a friendly little salute and left.

Bill closed the door and walked back into the living room. He gave a wave to the boy sitting in the easy chair and said, 'So what's on the agenda today?' as he opened the package.

'Oh,' said Baxter, as he took off his headphones, 'Just researching the Cold War, especially the warships. Such a difference from the old *Springwood*.'

Bill had a hunch and darted over to the laptop for a peek.

Baxter had no time to drop the screen.

Bill smirked as he saw YouTube's latest video of cats being jerks.

'Research, huh?'

Baxter grinned sheepishly.

Bill pulled out a letter out of the package. Waving it at Baxter, he said, 'Hmmm, pink-coloured envelope ...' He gave it a sniff. 'Scented, *and* addressed to you. I wonder who it's —'

Baxter launched himself out of the chair, only to be yanked backwards by the headphones still around his neck.

Bill laughed heartily as Baxter untangled himself and took the letter, his cheeks blushing as they always did when a letter arrived from her. He left to go to his room for some privacy.

'Teenagers,' said Bill, still chuckling.

He pulled out the other item out of the package and unwrapped the brown paper covering.

It was a book.

He read the title:

The Goblin Forest
By Julie Dwyer
Illustrations by Leigh Dwyer

He noticed the small printed banner at the top of the cover stating: *"The smash new best seller by debut author Julie Dwyer."* As he opened the book, a post-it note popped out.

Bill picked it up. It read, 'Read the dedication.'

He flipped to page two.

For Bill and friends
Who risked their whole world
To save ours
Forever in our hearts till time and times are done
AJML

Bill Gardiner, ranger of Mount Taranaki and father of one, wiped away a tear that had suddenly formed before heading into the kitchen to find his reading glasses.

Epilogue

Alan pulled into the driveway, the headlights of the car lighting up Julie, waiting on the front porch.

'Uh-oh,' he muttered to himself, and turned the ignition off. He grabbed his briefcase and shut the car door. But the urge to run to his wife abated as he saw a strange sort of smile on her face.

'Hi, darling,' he said and kissed her cheek. 'Seeing as you don't normally wait for me outside, what's up?'

'Leigh was sent home with a note today,' said Julie. 'She's been suspended from school for a week.'

'What! *Our* Leigh? What the heck for?'

'You're not going to believe this … fighting.'

Alan fought to hide his grin. Putting on a frown, he said, 'I'll talk to her,' and put an arm around Julie as they walked inside.

Dinner was the now normal affair, with Matt showing manners that still had his mum in a bit of a daze. No chowing down like his life depended on it, nor any loud burps. Just a, 'Nice dinner, Mum,' followed by, 'I'll help with the dishes,' before heading into the kitchen to start the clean-up.

'Oh, lord, am I ever going to get used to this?' muttered Julie, and started clearing the table.

'Leigh, back deck for a chat, please,' said Alan.

'Sure thing, Dad,' replied Leigh and excused herself from the table. She waited for Alan to walk through the sliding door before following him, both sitting down in their favourite easy chairs.

Before Alan could speak, Leigh said, 'I know what you're going to say, but in my defence, she deserved it.'

'Who did?'

Leigh smirked. 'Hannah. She and her gang thought it would be fun to pull my school backpack off my back again and throw it in the bushes. You'd think they would try something original for a change.'

Alan frowned. 'That name's familiar. You've had trouble with her before, right?'

'Yeah,' laughed Leigh, 'but I doubt I will from now on. Oh boy, does she bleed a lot.'

'What!' cried Alan. 'What the heck did you do?'

'Relax, Dad. I just smacked her one, dead on the nose, that's all. She got a ripper of a nosebleed. Her friend Chelsea had a go next, but I picked her up and threw *her* into the bushes. Figured she could get my bag, you know?'

Alan had to hide his grin at that remark.

'She'll have some wicked scratches to show off tomorrow. The others ... well, they sort of lost interest after that.'

Alan said, 'Look, I'm not saying that *maybe* they didn't deserve it, but try to show some restraint please. You know, turn the other cheek, that sort of thing.'

Leigh turned her head slowly towards her father. 'Dad, I've done that all my life and all it did was enable people like that to act like jerks even more. Honestly, I'm through taking their crap. I won't start anything; you have my word ... but I'll sure as hell finish anything. And now they know it too.'

Alan couldn't help it anymore and chuckled. 'Okay, I get it. But promise me you'll at least try to walk away. If they follow, you can let loose. Deal?'

249

'Deal!'

Alan stood up and said, 'I'll speak with the school principal tomorrow. Especially about how we've reported Hannah and her group of trolls before, and nothing was done by them. I'll let them know *my* daughter has the right to self-defence *and* my permission to do so.'

Leigh grinned. 'Thanks for the backup, Dad.'

'A pleasure, Leigh.' Alan kissed his daughter's cheek and walked inside. He closed the sliding door, leaving Leigh on the back deck alone.

She sat for a while and watched the sunset fade. Leigh closed her eyes and smiled. Her dad was her rock now and nothing made her happier than having that. As her eyes opened, they briefly radiated a fierce yellow glow.

Leigh Dwyer, ex-goblin of Mount Taranaki, got up and went inside for a cup of tea, humming her new favourite rock tune,

'Welcome to the Jungle.'

www.ingramcontent.com/pod-product-compliance
Lightning Source LLC
Chambersburg PA
CBHW020404120726
47904CB00002B/693